ROGER KING

Roger King

SEA LEVEL

POSEIDON PRESS

NEW YORK LONDON TORONTO SYDNEY TOKYO SINGAPORE

POSEIDON PRESS

Simon & Schuster Building
Rockefeller Center
1230 Avenue of the Americas
New York, New York 10020

POSEIDON PRESS is a registered trademark
of Simon & Schuster Inc.

POSEIDON PRESS colophon is a trademark
of Simon & Schuster Inc.

Designed by Karolina Harris
Manufactured in the United States of America

10   9   8   7   6   5   4   3   2   1

Library of Congress Cataloging-in-Publication Data

King, Roger, 1947–
    Sea level / Roger King.
       p.   cm.
    ISBN 0-671-75458-0
    I. Title.
PR6061.I473S4   1992
823'.914—dc20   92-8639
                                                          CIP

ISBN: 0-671-75458-0

I would like to thank the MacDowell Colony, the Millay Center for the Arts, and the Corporation of Yaddo for the gifts of time, space, and fellowship during the writing of SEA LEVEL.

TO FRIENDS IN ENGLAND,

AND PARTICULARLY TO DOUG AND URSULA THORNTON

AND THE LETCHUMANANS' EXTENDED FAMILY

CONTENTS

MOUNTAINS

Ever since they proved the world was round it has played a cruel trick. You can travel as far as it is possible to travel—to a remote Pacific island, say; say Tonga or Ruatua—and then you decide you are still not far enough from England, so you take another step, to Indonesia, say, or New Guinea, and you find you are not farther but nearer. As you extend your flight, you return. As you put everything into your escape, you are recaptured. It makes me bad-tempered this refusal of progress by the world.

My father did not travel, so I travel. When he was a young man he twice visited Dieppe. In his fifties we took a package holiday to Austria, but soon after, he had his first heart attack and did not attempt travel again. In any case, being out there, away from England, away from his women, made him nervous and anxious to return. Distance scraped away his skin, leaving him exposed to pain. Later, when I started leaving England, he was full of admiration for my hardiness and pleased for me that I was not like him.

I've gone as far up the valley as it is possible to go. From Mastuj there is a pass going east to Gilgit, but the snows are too deep now. I could borrow the Aga Khan's helicopter, which he uses to reach the impoverished Ishmailis, but last week it landed on the fragile snow above a chasm and was wrecked. The four-wheel-drive is useless now, and although I am informed that there are yaks in the neighboring villages, no one knows how to hire them. The trail north is even higher and more difficult, though I believe it joins up with the silk route from Persia to China and the mujahedin still use it. Or I could follow the river down to Afghanistan, but this would be troublesomely dangerous, and why should I? I'll go back the way I came. There's nothing up here anyway.

Here, in Polynesia, in the mornings, I go down to the empty beach at the farthest extremity of Ruatua Island. The sand is wonderfully firm and soft. There is nothing to fear on this island, not even its people. I move from the palm trees' shade across a strip of sand which is too hot, to the water, which laps around my calves, busy and amiable. Half a mile in front of me the Pacific booms on the coral reef that divides the blue of the sea from the blue of the sky with a thin white line of surf. This, too, is pleasing, to know the lapping water is tamed ocean. Beyond the reef I could swim three thousand miles before striking land in China. Then there would be the Himalayas and the deserts of Iran, the pretty Alps of Switzerland, the farms of northern France, the Channel, white cliffs and the other green island. I wade farther into the warm sea until only my shoulders are exposed and my feet tiptoe in cooler waters. Sea level is a sly angle from which to look at England. It looks vainglorious and helpless. Tomorrow morning I will walk across the island to look at England from the other side, seeing Cornwall instead of Dover. Now I dive among the little fishes, all with kissable lips.

They're showing Kiss of the Spider Woman *on the Vava'u Ho-*
tel's back-projection video. We are a few off-season American
tourists, the crews of a couple of early yachts from New
Zealand, three British engineers from Cable and Wireless, set-
ting up a microwave TV service, and some Tongans who have
been abroad somewhere and come back; about twenty in all,
including Akira and me. In the film someone plays a homo-
sexual convict in an unnamed Latin American country. He en-
tertains his left-wing cellmate with his fantasy life drawn from
a European fascist film where beauty is ruthless. But he, him-
self, is kind to the brutalized political prisoner, who fucks him
to return the love. After his release, the homosexual gets killed
when he tries to help his lover's left-wing cause. What is this
film about? The plump Tongans are standing, stretching, and
smiling round smiles. I note it's a Brazilian film based on an
Argentinian book made in English with an American star. En-
trance was three Tongan dollars.

Vava'u is the most beautiful of the Tongan islands, with
green volcanic hills where the others are dinner-plate flat. The
economic prospects for vanilla exports are good. My clothes
hold within them the sweet smoky smell of the vanilla pod
curing sheds.

There's a need for explanations: God is like a bar of soap.

Above a pitted red-brick wall, a slow jet, too far to be heard,
makes its horizontal way across the sky, dividing with a thin
white line blue from blue.

In front of the single casement window of the Baptist church
Sunday-school room, between me and the light, he moves in
silhouette, his arms jerky with impulsive and mistimed em-
phasis. Beyond the pitted wall, I know, are the backs of shops
with their piles of refuse, and the mean yards of terrace houses.
It's curious for London that the sky is a perfect blue.

He says he was lying in his bath last night. He was thinking
about what he could say to us today. "The regulars among you

know I always do my thinking in the bath on Saturday night." He says that he knows the regulars among us know that. He stays so long in the bath, he says, that Mrs. Bender sometimes wonders if he's drowned. "But there's something about water, isn't there? Have you noticed that? I don't know what it is.

"Well, I was daydreaming last night—I'd worked overtime all week; it's a busy time for milkmen, what with Christmas coming up and everything—anyway, I wasn't really concentrating and I dropped the soap. You know, it had got wet and it slipped through my fingers, and I had to reach down into the water and fumble for it, because I couldn't see it anymore. I'd been in the bath for a while and the water was a bit dirty— young Will had taken a quick dip before me. I'd keep touching the soap with my fingertips and I'd grab it—like that!—as hard as I could. And you know what happened? It slipped out of my fingers again and the harder I tried to grab it, the farther it went."

He shows how he tried to grab it and is lost for a moment in that. "Of course," he says, "I forgot all about the Bible and my talk to you today. All I wanted to do was to get that bit of soap before it dissolved. Then I saw it. It was just below the surface and beginning to slide down again, sinking quite slowly because it wasn't a very big piece of soap, more of a sliver really. But this time I didn't make a grab for it, I didn't use all my strength to hold on to it. I just put the palm of my hand underneath it and waited until it came to rest on me. I could hardly feel it land. Then I cradled it and brought it up to the surface and put it back in the soap dish. Then, of course, I thought, what a waste of time."

But then he said, no, it struck him that after all it might not be a waste of time, that God does work in strange ways which are mysterious to us mortals. "While I was straining my poor old head to think up a lesson for you, He was showing me the way. You see, you could say that God is like that bar of soap, couldn't you? We try to grab hold of God and make Him our own and use Him for our own purposes. But He won't come to us like that. We can't grab Him. We have to be humble. We have to make ourselves ready, just like I waited there with my hand open. Then, maybe, He'll come to us, maybe the Holy Spirit will settle on us and we'll be blessed. Well, anyway, that's what I got to thinking last night."

The plane has completed its thin white line across the blue, but presumably continues.

GOVERNMENT OF PAKISTAN/DCA AIDE-MEMOIRE TO FOLLOW PENDING MIN FINANCE SIGNATURE.

ONE HUNDRED MILLION OVER SEVEN YEARS AGREED JAPANESE COFINANCE PERMITTING.

BRIEF ERIKSON OF IFC VIA UNDP LUSAKA.

AKIRA YOSHIDA CONTRACT EXTENSION REQUESTED TOKYO AGREEABLE.

AUTHORIZATION ITINERARY AND TICKETING RE PACIFIC ISLANDS SUPERVISION REQUIRED SOONEST.

KIND PERSONAL REGARDS.

Peristalsis is like this, she says. It goes squish, squish, the esophagus opens up in front and the muscles contract behind so the food moves along. It's automatic, you can't help it. Miss Khan laughs and moves across the class, her hands opening and closing like some omnivorous fish that can't help it. That's why, she says, you can swallow standing on your head. And we wonder, will she, this brown woman from Paris and Lebanon and other foreign places we can't tell apart, will she stand on her head in her tailored dress, this woman of fifty, who told us last week when we covered reproduction that she might be a miss but she'd had her fun, then laughing at us teenage boys with our silences. And so unused are we in Tottenham to animation that we are transfixed at the opening and closing of her hands, the laughing, the dangerous attraction. It's natural, she says, peristalsis, you do it without thinking. You see, squish, squish.

I'm not alone in resenting the roundness of the world. In 1898, when circumnavigation was commonplace, Joshua Slocum, the lone American sailor, visited the Transvaal in South Africa on his last stop before returning home. Its Boer president, Oom Paul Kruger, sent three experts to Slocum's boat to tell him that his voyage had not occurred. When Slocum was later introduced to Oom Paul as the American sailing alone around the world, Oom Paul rudely interrupted to say, "You mean in the world," and turned his back.

I feel ill at ease to find this common ground.

The pleasure of fascist friends is you don't have to be nice to them.

On a D.C. Greyhound bus, a generation back, she says she's on her way to her daddy's funeral, but isn't that a drag: it's too far from Georgia, and anyway, he was just a piece of shit, but if she doesn't go, she'll get none of the money until she's old, and she's only sixteen now, to my twenty-one.

She doesn't say, this girl, that her mother loved her father, her father loved her mother, and they both loved her as much as she loved them. She says her father was a shit and that he fucked her as soon as she was old enough, until Mum kicked him out, and then it was for fucking everyone else, not for fucking her. She has a flawless fair complexion and is wearing a summer dress of powder blue and I love her for her un-dressed daring.

She says, when a fat black mother and her children board, that they've got ways of dealing with them where she comes from, the Klan. She smiles and chews her gum at me. I say, I don't like that, and she says, a generation back, Oh yeah? She says, if I want, I can take her stop, she's got some time to kill, she's sort of alone, we could maybe sort of fool around, after Daddy burns. No, I say, I couldn't do that, no I couldn't do that.

In Afghanistan they play the cassettes of Paula Abdul in Kabul, on the Japanese stereos bought in Peshawar, over the border, with dollars made from selling Russian AK-47s—twice the price of the ones made in China, three times the copies from Pakistan—to their relatives in the mujahedin, who get the money from the CIA and from the heroin they are allowed to smuggle to America.

On the streets of D.C. the black from Africa, generations back, runs from the police on Adidas feet, his cache in his fist.

The girls from Kalash, Himalayan remnants, some say, of Alexander's Greeks, wear cowrie shells in their hair, old money from here to Senegal, halfway across the world, and from there to America, where the children of slaves run on Adidas feet across the sticky tar of D.C. streets with their dreams of German cars.

On the swept arcades of Belgrade, the adolescents spend their cash on the bugaboo rock of American blacks, made possible with the dollars the Yugoslavs got by selling DC-10s to Afghan Air when the Americans wouldn't.

And Paula Abdul plays on in Kabul, dancing like an infidel, on Japanese videos, to bleached rock and roll from Arabia and England and Africa and Spain, America and Cuba and so on.

I can move—let me see—from the kitchen area to the dining area to the living area to the study area without hindrance. When it's warm I slide aside the glass and screen to continue on the pinewood deck, painted rust against the rot. We've never used the circular barbecue out there, waiting like a flying saucer on legs, but I still hope to do so one day when Mireille and I are close again, one night when we'll have self-conscious fun acting out being Americans and secretly hoping it will take so we'll end up like each other. When it's cold in Reston, hot air blows up through gratings in the floor and we can walk from kitchen to bedroom to bathroom to living room in our underwear, careless of doors. We could walk naked, but

Mireille is still a modest woman, though she did once dance across the windows in a towel. Not recently though.

There's a need for explanations: a short explanation of human civilization.

First we hunt and gather and glorify the natural world, which after all has got the drop on us. Some of us still do this. When the going gets tough and there aren't enough plants and animals to go around anymore, we have to take control of things a bit and do agriculture, where we hunt and gather what we've grown and defended. We fight a little, organize a little, build towns to hold it all together. The old gods are no use in our new empires, we need something vaguer and more generally acceptable, so we come up with one God, a book and some general principles to put us in our place and show us how to act—a sort of common currency, the spiritual equivalent of money, which we also find we need now that so many of us are doing so many things that bartering's a strain. Just when we've got used to that, along comes science, interfering with the way things are done, moving peasants into cities, causing industry, generally disrupting things. It stretches the one God quite a bit, all this choice and change, and anyway, things aren't so mysterious anymore, now we've got science. Except that money begins to get strange. With all that technology, it has a way of flowing into distant hands forever and our one God isn't doing much about that. So we do something about it and set up nations that have nothing to do with God and make sure that some of the money stays with the poor, except that just as we get that sorted out, we find we sort of miss God after all and things are really getting hectic now we've replaced Him with modern art or Chevrolets or high ideals of social harmony. And then, when we weren't looking, money has got away, escaped across the borders and turned into something else, an ether of abstraction, a moneysphere above us all, a will-o'-the-wisp beyond terrestrial boundaries and beyond our control, leaving us just as helpless as when we began and even more confused.

What next?

She said when I phoned, after I'd heard from Geneva, through Shareef, she said I must know why she wanted me to call. "Is it Dad?" I asked, and left it open. "Yesterday," she said, and rattled on. "It was a mercy really. He was in a lot of pain toward the end. I expect you guessed. People have been wonderful. You never realize until something like this happens. And how are you?" From somewhere I remembered, and asked, "Was it his heart?" and, yes, she thought it was, but she was vague too, she thought it just gave up, at least that was the impression she got from Dr. Paul, though Dr. Paul was very young, and it doesn't really matter now, does it?

The funeral, she said, was in five days, Wednesday, three p.m.; she'd have the Co-op, which people said were very good. Just the crematorium, nothing fancy. "Of course," she said, "no one expects you to come. You must be very busy. Your work must be ever so important." And she could manage, I mustn't worry. People—the neighbors—they were really very good. You found out at a time like this. Of course, if I could it would be wonderful, but no one expected it, no, not really. And, "Oh," she said, "I don't even know where you are?"

"Pakistan."

"Pakistan . . . It sounds like the other side of the world. No, you mustn't come. Would they pay you if you did?"

I said, well, it was the other side of the world, but it was only a day these days, and she said I mustn't and I said I'd see.

At last I am happy and at home. Emo has found me a snorkel, mask, and flippers, and with my arms at my sides and my feet going, I head straight out for the reef like a torpedo. Then, arbitrarily, far from land, far from the reef, I stop to float calmly in the warm sea, companionably soothed by the hollow mortal sound of breathing. Below me the shoals of kissable fish meander and turn, quite tame. Handsome yellow ones trailing tails, sleek electric blues, deep reds, the occasional grumpy one in brown. I take a breath and dive to join them, passing into cooler regions. I give chase, bending around coral pillars and coming to know the landscapes of fairy-tale castles and fire-red trees. The fish run and wait, run and wait, like flirts, until I have to leave them for the air. But straightaway I want to dive again, at last free of gravity, given back the third dimension previously withheld.

• • •

When I learned of my father's death I was in an isolated Himalayan valley, staying at what was locally referred to as the PTDC, the simple inn operated by the Pakistan Tourist Development Corporation, a quasi-autonomous parastatal of the type favored by the Pakistan military government under General Zia ul-Haq. Salim, the PTDC's shabby dogsbody, who had earlier brought a pot of green tea and English chips with ketchup, came to fetch me from where I was reading on the inn's upstairs balcony. With a mixture of urgent smiles and gestures, he indicated that I should immediately follow him down the steps to the inn's small and cluttered office. There the manager was waiting, his arms bare from working in the garden and the phone held out to me at chest height. After I had taken the receiver, he apologized for his dirty hands by holding up the right one for me to examine and inclining his head with a smile that signaled a regretful powerlessness. He said, "It's the office of the provincial governor in Peshawar."

I thanked him and made a point of returning his smile. Up there, we were dependent on his inn, which was the only useful accommodation in the valley.

There could have been any number of reasons for a call from the governor's office, though reaching the mountain areas by phone was often difficult and the reason would have to be of some weight. It could have been that the governor himself had agreed to a meeting, or that our itinerary had been changed, or that the maps and statistics we had requested had been obtained, or not obtained, or had been classified for security reasons. I was ready to react to these possibilities and, if necessary, defend the agency's interests against any attempt by the provincial government to manipulate us toward a particular view of the situation. I think I was well on top of things that day.

"Dr. Bender, William. This is Shareef from the governor's office."

"Hello, Shareef! How are you?"

I sounded pleased to hear from him, and there was some sincerity in this. Shareef was probably still in his late thirties, only a few years younger than myself, and he managed to combine his responsible position with an easy informality. He was clearly going right to the top in Pakistan and he had the confidence to risk giving me the sort of information and insights that time-serving provincial officials would fearfully conceal. I sensed a sort of bond between us, a mutual recognition of useful competence in a world of older, fainter men. His education had included Yale, and his aristocratic family owned an expensive St. John's Wood home in London, leaving him with as much allegiance to the international as to the national or provincial. He had already sounded me out about possible overseas consultancy opportunities, and I had not discouraged him, although I knew that, in practice, international agencies took the view that career bureaucrats could rarely make useful contributions outside their own countries.

He replied, "I'm well. How is the weather up there?"

"Getting colder. They've had the first snow."

"Oh, I see." He sounded serious. "Look, William, we've had a message from your family. It came through Foreign Affairs in Islamabad. It says, can you call your mother? It's about your father."

"My father? I see."

In the time it took me to reply I imagined my father ill, my father dead, my mother alone in Tottenham. I considered the logistics of communication and transport, and I reminded myself that my position here was a professional one and that to Shareef my family troubles represented an organizational nuisance, not a cause for mutual concern. He might already be irritated to find himself called upon to work on a Friday. His inquiry about the weather was, of course, a concern about access to the valley through the pass and the possibility that the

PIA flights over the mountains might be canceled. "Did the message say what the problem was?"

"No; only that you should phone your mother. Look, you may have difficulty calling from up there. I'll talk to the operator and give you the governor's priority, but you know how it is. Ask the manager to help you; he's my relative. In fact, let me talk to him."

"OK. Thanks, Shareff. Sorry for the extra work."

"No problem, William. You're our guest."

I called the manager, who had returned to his fastidious tending of the inn's garden, and handed back the phone to him. Then I waited for the Urdu to stop and the manager to replace the receiver so that I could give him my parents' London number. Then, leaving him to struggle with the phone, I climbed back up the rough concrete steps to the balcony.

I moved my chair and table so as to catch the last of the day's sun and sat down to wait. The time was three-thirty, which would make it ten-thirty in the morning in London. My mother always stopped for a tea break at ten-thirty—her elevenses, she called it—or at least always had done so when I was a child. It was a word I had not used or heard in years, one that had never made it into the international. I wondered if the word's strange feel meant my recollection of it was unreliable. A calculated forgetfulness was something I had come to regard as a necessary skill for this work, but perhaps it was not a precise science. I had boasted to colleagues that I could leave behind the detail of a country at its airport and by the time I landed in a new place my mind would be clean, the danger of facts seeping from one country to another neutralized. I told them that this was the way to keep sane.

In the past I had sometimes wondered, as an only child, what I would do in the event of a family tragedy while I was on a distant mission. When I did so, I had been unable to find any equation that would reconcile the weight to be given to sentiment and family ties and that which was due to the financial affairs of third world countries. The duties seemed to be of such different orders—one large, one small, one public, one private, one affecting many slightly, the other affecting a few intensely, one present, one past, one chosen, one given—that it seemed wrong that they should need to be contained within a single mind. I had hoped, and I continued to hope while I waited on my mountainside balcony, that I would never need to address the problem.

I feared that the international organizations I worked for—on this occasion the Development Credit Agency based in Geneva—would have little sympathy with the personal life of a consultant interfering with its work. It wasn't easy for these agencies to identify consultant experts from half a dozen different countries and then to get them all to the same place at the same time, which, in the case of these rural development projects, had to be the right agricultural season as well as the right time in the host government's budgetary cycle. Even this mission, just me and two Japanese, nearly hadn't made it. November was really too late for Himalayan valleys, but if we didn't come up with a project this season, a competing international bank would step in and make the loan. With the opium farmers of North-West Frontier feeding the global heroin trade, and with the Afghani refugees and the CIA war, everyone wanted a piece of the development action up there.

If I left before the job was done, I doubted that the DCA would forgive me, whatever their published rules on compassionate leave. At least that is what I imagined. And once they regarded me as an unreliable, word would quickly spread to the other international agencies. I remembered the Belgian who had packed his suitcase in the middle of our mission to Sierra Leone. He had never again been able to make a living, and two years later I heard he had committed suicide.

Against this complex weightiness were set my responsibilities toward my retired parents in the modest London suburb of Tottenham. Of course they wouldn't understand all this; whatever lip service they might offer toward the larger world, I doubted that anything seemed real enough to compete with family obligation. I felt a brief agitation of anger at this, their false simplicity.

There should have been a norm, an accepted way of acting, but I could not think of one. When every colleague came from a different culture, there was no consistency of expectation. With some international administrators—those from India came to mind—I might get a black mark for callousness toward my family as easily as a merit point for doing my duty. The desk officer in Geneva for this job was a Japanese who liked to advertise his Western ways. What would his view be? I didn't know.

On none of the previous occasions when I had let these competing claims play in my mind had any fusion occurred or plan of action resulted. Now, with the problem pressing on me, I was no more able to form a judgment, and my mind receded from it, seeming to seek the relief of more abstract thoughts and larger understandings.

I let my attention follow my eyes toward the distance. The view from where I sat passed over the low flat roofs of the small town northward up the main valley, to where the mountains became so steep and convoluted that the course of the valley was lost in their folds and the only resting place for my eyes were the high points, the snow-covered peaks. Somewhere in this vertical landscape the snow had forced me back the previous day. I found, as I sat longer, that the local peaks would no longer hold me and I was drawn toward the great mountains of the Himalayas, whose tops were so high and pure that they shone with the sun's light long after we, among the lower peaks, had fallen into shadow. Up there, I reflected, the whole world met, its great disputes and wars coincided and were frozen into inactivity by the forbidding cold and airlessness: Afghanistan met Pakistan, met Russia, met China, met India; Hinduism met Islam, met communism, met the West. Instead of considering my response to the possible bad news in my life, I found myself lingering on the great high wastes of frozen impulses.

It was six-thirty when the slavish Salim returned with his

urgent mixture of grins and gestures. My preoccupation had become so complete that I had overlooked how quickly and sharply the mountain chill invaded at dusk, and I had become stiff with cold. When I climbed down the concrete steps to the manager's office, I was forced to hold on to the iron railings and hobble like an old man.

After the call to my mother I returned to my room and sat on the bed. I asked myself what I felt, then I asked myself what I should feel. Then I paced up and down, agitated that I could not settle on an answer to either question. Nor was there anyone I could talk to. Yamada, the older of my two Japanese colleagues and supposedly the mission leader, was once again locked in his room, as he had been for most of the five days since we first met in Islamabad. Since our arrival in the mountains he had not appeared at all. He was too old for this; he shouldn't be here. In any case, a personal conversation was unthinkable. From the beige Land Cruiser standing in the yard, I could tell that Yamada's subordinate, Akira, who was about my age, had returned from his field trip, but his English was poor and in the few days we had worked together there had been nothing to suggest any relationship beyond the professional. If anything, there was a slight antagonism between us. In the morning I had tried to dissuade him from spending his scarce time visiting the valley of the Kalash, an obscure pagan tribe with an unrepresentative agriculture, but he had been deliberately obtuse. I suspected, but did not say, that he favored the pagans because they were the only unveiled women in the district.

I tried to force memories of my father into my imagination, but although pictures came readily enough, some devilment in me made them mocking. A picture of him in scoutmaster's uniform slipped its focus to his knock-knees. Shockingly, an attempt to picture him with his arm around my mother turned into something else, even though he was the most modest of men. Indeed, I'm not sure I ever saw him put his arm around my mother.

I pushed aside the attempt to artificially heighten my emotions and sensibly settled on an interim decision that would allow for unpredictable later emotional developments. I would attempt to fly to the provincial capital, Peshawar, as soon as possible. Communications from there were good, and I would be able to call my mother again, send telexes to Geneva, and if necessary, book international flights. I could go to Peshawar, and also on to the national capital, Islamabad, without making a final decision about whether or not I would abandon the mission to return home for my father's funeral. Peshawar and Islamabad were respectively the venues for roundup meetings with the government of North-West Frontier Province and the federal government of Pakistan, and I reasoned that I could make use of the journey to bring negotiations forward. The agency would be satisfied that the work was progressing and I would remain en route for connecting flights to London. I could see a further advantage in that the pretext for travel would allow me to brief government officials in the absence of my Japanese colleagues, whose interests, as representatives of Japanese aid as well as DCA finance, might prove to have a different emphasis from my own. The postponement of any decision about my father came to seem reasonable, even inspired.

...

Sitting here under the palm umbrella, writing pad on my knees, feet up on the white wood lounger with its paint all but gone, I do try to be rigorous. I try to trace the short, simple downhill path from there to here—only some weeks—not judging too much, keeping to the facts, not letting myself be carried away. Most days I take an early swim alone, leaving Emo to her undemanding tasks, then I sit here next to the sea until the fleshy edge of my hand on the paper becomes wet with perspiration so that the ballpoint soon after reaches a damp place on the page where it can no longer roll out its ink. Then I throw down Pakistan and go back to the lucid blue of the coral sea, as easy a thing as slipping into Emo in the night—her body always relaxed, a child nestling close by—the temperature of the water in the shallows at body heat by afternoon.

I do try to remember how I was, the way things were. Against the practiced habit of forgetting I set a carefulness of record, a guardedness of tone, trying to steer clear of false versions and hoping that if I get the circumstances right, the setting for them in my mind, the rest will follow and I will remember exactly how the recollection of Mireille struck me on the steps, how the news of my father worked on me, the way Akira spoke, and the precise location of Yamada's scars, where he placed on me the little healing bonfire of herbs. For although it has only been months since, and at the time these were the people I loved best, I have to strain to separate all this from the years of things lost, denatured, altered, discarded. I am trying to be honest.

Ruatua is not sympathetic to my dryness. Instead of the sterility of mountain peaks and the arid denials of martial, Muslim Pakistan, I have the sound of sea to my left and the smell of a Large White pig being roasted to my right. Beyond the pig are the ragged thatches of Coconut Beach Holiday Village with its succulent plants and entwined frangipani. And beyond that, the coconut palms mat Ruatua's single central hill, which mocks the promise of a dark hinterland by delivering at its summit the sight of another beach, the same glittering sea, and the coral reef again. You can walk across the island in half a day and never outdistance the casual forest cultivation of the coastal villages. Still, I'll tear my eyes from this and push myself back into the chill airlessness of the morning Himalayas, now wishing I had done a better job of repairing this palm umbrella, woven the palm leaves tighter. I was cool toward my father, calculating in my work.

The pig really needs my attention. The comic rigor of my task is increasingly distracted by the temptations of these small chores, which spring up like the green shoots of a new disorder. I've made a botched repair of the outrigger for one of the little dugouts that were made for tourists to play with, and I have somehow acquired responsibility for cooking the barbecue pigs. Yesterday I solved a problem Emo had with her desktop computer. I'm not good at cooking pigs and this one will probably be ready hours late, though nobody here will mind. One of Emo's brothers is sauntering down to the beach now to turn it and baste it, saving me the trouble. He hitches his lavalava and smiles over at me. Perhaps I'll just go back to the sea.

...

That night was the coldest of the three we had spent in the mountains. There was a stone fireplace in my room but it was not yet late enough in the year for fires. The blankets were too few and my suitcase had been packed for Zambia, where I was completing an assignment for the World Bank when the request came to help out the DCA in Pakistan for the sake of interagency goodwill. I was, in fact, packed as I always was, since the poor who were the subject of my work normally lived in the world's hot places. I had one thin sweater and a single lightweight suit, which I wore only for formal meetings or for reporting writing in the capitals of the more temperate countries, where the international agencies are generally headquartered. My overcoats were currently distributed in Geneva, Rome, and Washington.

Frustrated by my inability to get warm, I felt that there had always been something wrong about this mission to a cold place. The mountain people looked very much like myself, with fair skins and European features, and instead of papaws and pineapples, the local fruits were apples and apricots. It was hard not to feel that the poverty here was just willful perversity. There was even a minority of the population with blond hair and blue eyes and at one point I had embarrassed myself by warmly greeting a junior Pakistani official as a potential colleague, in the mistaken belief that he was a young Scandinavian aid expert.

I tried to keep the cold—and the agitation caused by my bad temper, this feeling that something was incorrect—at bay with chains of reasoning. From the idea of firewood I went on to consider its role in the local economy, where winter survival depended on the wood that could be stored before the snows set in. Over time the result had been deforestation and the erosion of soils. A Dutch doctor working for Unicef had pressed on me the information that fuel was used so sparingly that smoke was retained in the houses, with the consequence of widespread blindness. I expressed the view that under the circumstances a proportion of blindness was acceptable, even optimal, which had made the man indignant. I had felt at the time that the doctor's warmth of feeling was self-indulgent, and now its implied reproach further fueled my irritation. In the real grown-up world it was not always possible to enjoy the comfort of doing good. I knew, for example, that there would be no point in recommending to the DCA a project to reforest the mountains. No matter how worthy this might be, such a long-term undertaking would never satisfy the banking requirement of an adequate return on investment. I wondered, too, whether Yamada and Akira understood this or whether, if I left for London, they would make rash decisions, perhaps approving the tunnel through the mountains, with its shadow objective of consolidating political control over Pakistan's marginal montane people. Shareef was certainly clever enough to pull the wool over their eyes. And perhaps it made no difference whether I went to London now or in two weeks or in two months—my father was dead, and I would be, in any case, too late to help with the funeral. It might well be that my mother would prefer a visit months later, when the neighbors would have forgotten her bereavement and she would be more alone.

I think, though it's always hard to tell, that at the time this was the view I honestly held.

When I slept, I overslept. The sun had already reached my window, and according to my alarm clock, which I had forgotten to set, it was eight o'clock, an hour and a half later than I had intended. There had been a knocking at my door and I tried to call out, "Who is it?" but my throat was thick and it came out just as a noise.

"William! Transport here!" Akira's delivery had an explosive quality.

"All right. Thanks. I'm coming."

"You want breakfast?"

"I'll just have coffee."

"No coffee here!"

"Yes, of course. Tea. Green tea. No, nothing."

"OK."

I was tired in spite of the sleep. My body felt too heavy to push upright and I wondered if I was sick. Though it was already warmer, the cold of the night was still deeply in me, and it seemed to radiate from me, resisting the heat. A pain had lodged itself in my stomach—a nuisance but a commonplace nuisance, one that it seemed right, at the time, to ignore.

I reminded myself that it was the nature of the work that you sometimes had to push yourself against the grain of your inclinations. Of course there were the times when you found yourself, in the course of the work, in a luxury hotel by a tropical beach that the rich paid thousands to visit, but equally often you might find yourself forced to spend grueling days in poverty-stricken places with few amenities and, as often as not, untrustworthy food. So it was with the familiar feeling of a soldier going against nature that I put papers into my briefcase, shook dizziness from my head and splashed water on my face. Between the bathroom and the door I jerked myself upright and prepared a smile for whichever officials were waiting with the vehicles for the day's field trip. I was ready to apologize for keeping them waiting.

Halfway down the steps, a "Morning!" already on my lips, I remembered that when I was woken I had been in the midst of a memory of Mireille. I had a wife. Although I had spent little time with her in the two years since my affair with Han, and we were more formal these days, she was still my wife. On the way down the last few steps to shake hands with the deputy commissioner, I wondered if it was the thing to do—the correct etiquette—to tell Mireille that her father-in-law was dead.

Mireille had always said she liked my parents and that it was good of them to welcome her with open hearts. She even said how much better they were than her parents, especially her father, the baron, with his cold, inflexible ways. Yet as time went on, especially since the business with Han, I think she came to depend more on her visits to France to find a sense of balance in the world. And I did not know, the morning after I heard of my father's death, whether she would be at our house in the Washington suburb of Reston or at one of her family's homes in France. I had no clear idea of the extent to which she still thought of my life as part of hers, or whether her fondness for my father was real or feigned, or whether the rules of family she had internalized long ago would lead her to attend the funeral or stay away. But she was, however ridiculous and unsatisfactory the relationship, the closest person in the world to me. This in itself was shocking, and as I completed my last steps toward the smiling DC, I felt a moment of dizziness at finding myself eight thousand feet above sea level and hardly attached to anything.

I was told, when I inquired, before I agreed to be led toward the vehicles, that all flights by the PIA Fokker 27 propeller plane that served the valley had been canceled until further notice due to the threat of snow. According to the deputy commissioner, an educated young man who claimed leadership of the group by virtue of his responsibility for law and order in the valley, no one could tell when the next plane would arrive. He added that the road which connected the valley to what he called the "down areas" via a pass at ten thousand feet was, according to his army scouts, blocked by drifts.

"Then how do you suggest I leave?"

"You can't leave yet. You have to stay with us." He closed the reply with a quick smile flashed from under his mustache, the sort of no-nonsense briskness adopted by members of military regimes worldwide, no matter how inefficient and corrupt the regime's nature.

"What about helicopters, military transport?" It was my experience that there was always a way for the sufficiently important.

"When the plane comes, I promise I'll get you a seat on it. But I can't make it come." He evaded my demands, and I was grateful to him.

The other officials—the chief engineer of the Public Works Department, the ones from Agriculture, Irrigation, and Planning, the political representatives of the district and the province, and many whom I could not place—drifted closer to the deputy commissioner, wondering at the delay and placing me at the point of a chevron of Pakistanis. I felt it was for the benefit of these, some of whom might dispute the DC's leadership, that he continued our conversation by asserting that if only the DCA was willing to finance the construction of a tunnel through the mountains, travel problems like mine would no longer exist.

The timing of his remark, making use of my father's death to promote a pet project, struck me as opportunistic and in bad taste, improper. Perhaps it was because I had conceded in the matter of military transport that I felt obliged to give a sharp reply: "We've already had this discussion. A tunnel is a hundred-million-dollar loan. With only a quarter of a million people at one end of it, there's no way the return can be economic. If you need it for security reasons," I added, "I suggest you talk to the Americans." I was deliberately high-handed, and as I turned to go to the vehicles, I further asserted the dominion of international money over local authority by adding that I would hold him responsible for informing my counterparts in the governor's office—his superiors—of my travel plans.

The moment I saw the line of four-wheel-drive vehicles pulled up for our field trip, I had known, without needing to reflect on it, that I would learn little about the local situation that day. With over a dozen officials—including the DC and the chief of police—only the official version of events could be available to us. If I was able to ask villagers questions at all, they would be a carefully selected sample, and their replies would be constrained by the presence of men with arbitrary power over their lives. If we were shown any projects for the development of the valley, they would be the government's best projects, revealing little about the competence of the government or the difficulties of developing the region.

I regretted all this but saw no way to avoid it without offending the officials who were taking the trouble to accompany us. At least, on that morning, the effort to take control of events seemed beyond me and I saw that Yamada and Akira had already established themselves comfortably in the lead vehicle. In any case, I was no longer as concerned as I once had been to break through official versions to a more honest and more complex sense of things. I had learned that on a mission such as this, any attempt to understand the local situation could not hope to be successful and mainly served to antagonize local officials and politicians. The intricacies of a foreign culture, economy, and history were such that even social scientists devoting their lives to a single place were rarely able to predict events with accuracy, and every expert explanation had contending explanations held by other experts. I had, when younger, taken it upon myself to investigate foreign places more vigorously and made attempts to solicit the views of the poor, but I had found that the evidence of misrepresentation, dishonesty, exploitation, and political intrigue that I inevitably uncovered was unwelcome everywhere. Financial agreements, after all, were between governments and banks, not between banks and the poor. Questions about the probity of borrowers only served to interrupt the flow of money, on which so much depended. Han, who had always been more clear-eyed than myself, put it bluntly once when she felt I was indulging in a pointless and time-wasting sentimentality. "Forget it," she said. "You can't work for the world's poor. They can't pay your fees." Though perhaps I underestimated her sentiment.

And it was hard to see this group of polite Muslim officials as dishonorable. Their pay was small compared to mine, and unlike me, they no doubt had families to support. With a large development project moving in to transform their region, creating jobs and opportunities, disrupting the existing organization of government and patronage, demanding alien technical standards of employees, they would be understandably nervous and defensive, each wishing to show himself and his department to the best advantage. What might seem a conspiracy to conceal the truth beneath official misrepresentation might equally well be interpreted as the expression of human goodness, each individual guarding the welfare of the family that depended on him. And the official version—however fantastic—did at least have the virtue of public definition; it was a basis for doing business.

All the same, I would normally have paid a more skeptical attention to our route than I did that morning. Instead I took my place next to the driver of the second vehicle and let myself fall into reverie while we outdistanced the brief stretch of tarred road and started to grind our way up a track blasted out of the granite mountainside. The Land Cruiser rocked from side to side as the driver made his painstaking way over the bouldered surface and I held on to the grab handle above me, resting my head on my arm and letting myself go with the motion.

Mireille had got on well with my father. Perhaps it was because they were both flirts, or maybe it was that Mireille loved me then and, loving me, loved him. I saw in my father at their first meeting the sort of animation that I remembered from when, as a child, I had accompanied him on his milk round, where he became lively among the fleeting contacts with his housewife customers.

The visit to my parents' house in Mafeking Road came just after we had completed our first visit to Mireille's family in France and I was acutely conscious of the difference between a terrace house in Tottenham and the homes she had lived in as a child. To the great displeasure of her family we had married in America without consulting them, and I felt they hated me. I was nevertheless shown the country house with its vineyards, and the château, which Mireille's mother passed off as an eyesore, saying what when she thought of the château she thought only of its plumbing. The apartment in the septième in Paris, which was kept vacant for visits by family members to the capital, was itself greater than anything I had yet hoped to achieve in my life.

At the time I thought I was doing as well as a young man could: my doctorate was completed; I had landed a job with the World Bank in Washington; I traveled widely; we had rented a spacious modern house overlooking woods in the planned suburb of Reston. All this had been brushed aside by Mireille's family. The baron looked at me as he might have regarded a disease caught by his child, with which he would now have to coexist, and asked about my family. I had not said that my father was a milkman; he worked for a food corporation, I said. Mireille's mother concealed her feelings under a lively charm, which chilled me in its similarity to Mireille's.

We sat in the small front room, the windows net-curtained against the neighbors, the door closed against the drafts. Uneven heat—too hot in front of us, insufficient behind—came, in this room kept for Sundays, from a two-bar electric fire with badly simulated coals flickering at its base. In recollection, the sun now heating the Land Cruiser, its windows closed against the dust, I could feel again the oppressive intimacy of it. Mireille had chosen the hard chair, in the same way that I had since learned to win the cooperation of peasants by choosing an ordinary seat over the place of honor. She sat on the edge of it, a cup and saucer balanced in her lap, and while I was driven to silence by conflicting loyalties, she came to run the conversation. She questioned my mother about her job as a part-time nurse, and my mother, in turn, asked Mireille about her studies in America. When Mireille said she had failed to complete her degree, my mother sympathized, not understanding that for Mireille, degrees were neither here nor there; she had no ladder to climb.

Only when my mother left to fetch cakes from the kitchenette did my father become enlivened, getting up to turn on the second bar and asking, as he passed, "Is that the latest fashion, then?" raising an eyebrow toward the slit in Mireille's skirt.

"Oh, yes. It's the fashion. Do you like it?"

"Gay Paree!"

"No, it's not so immodest. Look." She stood up and pulled out the lacy slip beneath the skirt. "You see?"

"Careful, son," he said to me. "I might run off with this one."

We all laughed at the Sunday-school teacher being risqué.

To her, he said, "Voulez-vous coucher avec moi?—it's the only French I know." And Mireille was taken aback for a moment before collapsing into the laughter that always saved her. She put her hand lightly on his shoulder.

"You know what it means?"

"No idea. It's what the soldiers were told to say to French girls."

"Well"—still laughing—"only say it to very special French girls. It means, will you go to bed with me."

"It doesn't, does it? Too bad I never got to France."

When we left to go back to the room we'd taken for the night at Heathrow's Post House Hotel, Dad had whispered to me, "She's a cracker," and he gave Mireille a strong hug with his clumsy arms, while she had encircled him with her light ones.

Somehow I forgot, while Mireille was leading me back to my father, to keep hold of the Land Cruiser's grab handle, and a particularly violent lurch threw my head hard against the side window, hard enough that I was not sure whether or not I had been momentarily concussed. My instinct was to conceal the incident from the officials in the seat behind, and I made a point of turning to the scenery. Far below the sheer drop from the road, a white river carrying snowmelt water from the high mountains made its way through a plunging landscape of vertical rock faces. Occasionally I was able to spot a horizontal corner where a patch of soil had been caught, and there—seemingly unconnected with anything—families had constructed a few irrigated plots and built a house or two. We were so far above these settlements that a single cow could barely be distinguished, and I could not make out any people. The scale of it pressed against me and it suddenly seemed overwhelming that it should be my job to set about changing all this, the lives of those tiny families and thousands like them. I turned away from it. I told myself that I had seen a rare and spectacular thing but that it would be best if I put it aside for later consideration.

I turned to the officials. "What's the cost of a road like this? How much a mile?"

They disputed among themselves, then told me it depended on the terrain, the amount of blasting.

"Of course. But on average. An approximate figure."

They hazarded something and I pressed them further, took the upper hand. "And what sort of surplus does the average farm have? How much do they sell in a year? And what would be the cost of transport on a road like this from here to town? What if we improved it so trucks could come?"

I rattled them with my questions and made them think in ways they had never thought, let them know that in the company of international money they were moving onto new ground where things shifted underfoot. I raised the temperature in the car, but maybe it was that I wanted to shake up myself more than them, chasing out the scenery and thought.

The remainder of the journey to the mountain village was tumultuous. The sheer drop beside the road was dizzying and the curious insistence of my memories of Mireille, and the way they brushed my father as they circled, mixed awkwardly with my grim attempt to force the grandeur of the scenery into an analytical framework. I still was unsure whether or not I had been concussed by the blow to my head. If I had been unconscious for a while, it was likely that the officials behind me would only think that, like them, I was able to doze in a lurching vehicle. I was therefore both relieved and unprepared when we emerged into an area of rounded hills and irrigated fields surrounding a village of flat-roofed houses set into the hillside. I could see a cluster of waiting villagers, uniformly mustached and wearing the thick waistcoats and rolled wool caps of the region, but I insisted on a briefing from the officials before we greeted them. It had suddenly become a matter of urgency for me to know where I was, and the answers I had so far received were so vague as to be useless.

"Who has the map?" I demanded of the dozen officials surrounding me. No one replied and, exasperated, I looked around for support from Yamada and Akira, but they were sitting quietly in their vehicle, their backs to us.

At last the chief of police stepped forward amid the awkwardness to tell me, in a gentle manner, that because of the war just across the border, and because the nearby Afghan refugee camps were a matter of military, not civil, authority, the maps had been classified for security reasons.

I knew how to handle this. I checked myself, then said: "Of course we understand the security considerations, but I'm sure you also understand that it is difficult for us to respond to your government's request that we plan the development of the region if we don't have a map."

While the group receded to discuss this in a mixture of Urdu and the local language, I leaned back against the car. There was something relaxing in the situation, the knowledge that I would certainly get my way. I was confident that international money would outbid local secrecy if put to the test. From where I rested, I could see that my colleagues had not stirred; the back of Yamada's well-groomed head was silhouetted next to the lower, bristly one of Akira, both of them facing the whiteness of distant mountains.

An engineer's map with strikingly few lines on it was eventually found and unrolled on the hood. "We are ... there!" A finger indicated a place with no marked road or settlement.

"We've been going south?"

"Yes, south."

"But I thought we were going north. This is the prosperous part, isn't it? The part we already know about." I had not even noticed the direction of the sun.

"Not so prosperous. There's poverty everywhere."

"But we specifically told you north."

"Yes, but there is nothing to see there."

"That's why we have to go. To see what needs doing."

An embarrassed silence settled over the group, as with help-less onlookers surrounding the scene of a tragic accident. There was a sort of petulance in me; it did not really matter what I saw. I continued: "We'll just have to go back."

"Please, Dr. Bender, the villagers have been waiting." The chief engineer made a graceful Muslim gesture toward them.

Another said, "There is no time to go north now. It is not possible to travel after dark."

It must have been a wish to reclaim some sense of authority from the confusion of the journey that made me press further, even though I knew there was nothing I could gain and that the officials were in an impossible position. They would have been charged by their superiors to both win our goodwill and ensure that we saw only the things we were supposed to see. There was therefore a cruelty in my demands, a tearing at the smooth surface of things, which was unprofessional but which I let persist while quiet disputes broke out between local and provincial officials and between representatives of technical and administrative divisions. Some of the drivers began the laborious task of turning their vehicles on the narrow road.

Yet, in the end, I did draw back before the crisis went too far, allowing into play the old, practiced skill of putting aside emotion, capturing it and holding it for later consideration, arguably the most important qualification for an international expert. All too often an initial—emotional—reaction was sim-ply a cultural prejudice presenting itself as instinct, or equally damaging, it represented a narrow, short-term perspective that disregarded how immediately repellent people or events might contribute to a desirable long-term outcome. I took pride in this understanding, and as I moved to rescue the situation before it went too far, there was a pleasure in my sense of worldliness to compensate for the self-indulgence I was denied. I smiled.

"Gentlemen, we'll make a compromise. Since we are already here, we'll make use of the opportunity to look at the south today. But we must have an understanding that on the next mission you will arrange for us to see the north of the valley."

Voices competed to assure me that next time it would be different, though we all knew that if there was a next time, it would be with other experts and all this would be forgotten.

The meeting was in one of the village houses and I had hardly got past the formalities when Akira came to me. I had shaken hands and taken tea; I had declined the only chair in favor of squatting on a rug with the officials; I had made an apology for needing an interpreter and I had made a joke about how the villagers and I looked much the same, though they had been mystified by this. I had easily established that it was the wealthiest village in the region, that it was the only one with a government clinic and a government drinking water project, and that it was the home village of the valley's Member of Parliament, who was also the region's princely ruler and its richest man. They had asked whether I could promise them money for an irrigation scheme and I had said I would have to ask some questions first and it wasn't only up to me. It was all familiar and useless and I was doing it because it was what I did.

Akira said in my ear: "Mr. Yamada sick," then stepped back as if this was enough.

"What's wrong with him?"

"He say we must go back."

"But we've only just arrived."

Akira did not react and I felt again the difficulty of making contact with him, a problem compounded by my difficulty in deciding which of his divergent eyes focused his attention.

"Is he seriously ill?" I claimed the right to evaluate the situation.

"Let's go."

"Why don't you suggest to him that I stay on awhile?"

"No. He say you must come with us."

I took a breath. "OK, I'll be right with you. Perhaps you could go and get the vehicles organized while I explain to the villagers."

I told them I regretted our early departure, but it could not be helped in the circumstances. An official translated back to me that the village's invisible women had prepared food for us. I added further regrets and I saw once again the familiar air of puzzlement among the villagers, that such strange people should come so far with such a flourish of vehicles and importance, yet should do so little on their arrival. I lied to them that although our meeting had been short, its value had been great.

Yamada was as I had left him, sitting upright in the front seat of the lead vehicle. His eyes were closed and his face had the fineness and stillness of a sculpture.

"Mr. Yamada."

"Ah, William. Can we leave now?"

He did not open his eyes and I recognized the demeanor of a man intent on conserving each particle of energy.

"Yes, we can leave. Do you need a doctor?"

"No. No problem. . . . Should not be here. Too high."

On the road back down, my thoughts ran more freely. My work was over for the day, and the vehicles were going downhill. My stomach still hurt, as it had when I first woke, but my ability to overcome the pain only served to remind me of my robustness compared to, say, Yamada. I enjoyed the renewed sense that I was good at all this. The day had been unproductive, but I'd taken charge when my colleagues had failed to perform. I'd asserted the agency's authority to local officials, and it had taken me only fifteen minutes to figure out exactly which sort of wool was being pulled over our eyes today. And it had been done with some diplomacy: I had agreed to accept the version they offered me and they had understood that I wasn't really fooled. It was, I thought, a lot like personal relationships, this ability to get along in a foreign place, to get enough of what you want without breaking the bonds. You had to know when not to press too hard for truth. There had to be things on which you agreed to agree, even if they did not bear close examination. A tender dishonesty. It might even be called love. It was what had held Mireille and me together—this false shared version—even after the time when we stopped making love. It was what had made us a family in Tottenham. My father was over seventy, I reflected; his life had run a full enough course. It was a good enough life.

She had been a delight when I first met her, and now I noted, in passing, that I had been like my father in noticing her skirt. This observation did not, I think, lead me, as it might have done, to memories of him and our similarities, but to memories of Mireille. And then it was not the later, difficult years I remembered, when I strained away from her, determined not to be enslaved as he had been by duty and goodness, but the early days of pleasure and victory, long unconsidered, which ran easily with my oddly elated state of mind and the downhill road to town.

She was balanced on her haunches, the first time I saw her, pretending to play with my divorcée lover's three-year-old. I noticed she could do this in a skirt with perfect modesty, her knees tight. I noticed, too, the short hair, the cashmere sweater, the single row of pearls, the trimness of her, and that she was the only woman—girl really, at twenty—at the afternoon party in Massachusetts to wear a skirt. The total effect was to make her seem valuable, and like all fine craftsmanship, it invited touch. I was too untraveled then to recognize the commonplace artfulness of French gentility.

Neither did it seem to me anything but irrepressible natural charm when she burst out, "Look at this stupid toy. 'Ow can he play with it?" She dropped the wooden toy at the feet of the crestfallen toddler and broke into a bubbling laughter, adding, "I 'ate children. I don't know what I'm doing 'ere."

I like the dropped *h*'s and I liked her treachery toward our host, my divorcée lover—older than me—who taught psychology, and who had lectured me on the superiority of unwarlike toys, and of whom I was tired.

Mireille stood, brushed the creases from her lap, brushed her hair from her forehead, looked up at me—she was not tall—and continued by saying she also did not like parties of this sort, ones where everyone was left to himself and no one was introduced. "I know it's supposed to be informal, but I think it's just laziness, don't you? It's huninteresting."

Sometimes she added *h*'s, and I liked that too. I was charmed by her confidence and gaiety and unprotected air, and I said—though I had not long before said the opposite to my lover—that I agreed with her, that this American informality went too far, and that perhaps it seemed so to us because we were both European. I said this although in my three years in America I had been consistently delighted to lose the formalities of England.

The child tugged at my knee. "Play with me, Bill," and I shook him free, something I had not done before.

I drove her home to her rich girls' college, the skirt, the pearls, her tender naked nape, thrillingly enclosed, and I don't believe she once turned to notice me while she told of the tedious scheme that exchanged rich girls from Grenoble with rich girls from Massachusetts, and I told of my worthy studies for a Ph.D. in economics. She did not notice my caught breath when I laughed with her laughter at her stories of the rich Americans who had tried to impress her with their wealth. There was, for example, the couple who took her to Florida in their private plane, who amused her because the man was like a child with a toy and the wife had thrown up somewhere over the Carolinas, giving rise to a vulgar midair argument that dashed the pretense of their cultured wealth. She bent double in her seat in remembering the comedy of this and she did not have the guile to notice that in joining her, I stepped out onto a daring new elevation where I laughed at rich people instead of resenting them. I wanted to capture Mireille and capture all this.

Three months later I had her eating pizza with her hands, drinking beer, charming rough types in bars with her bubbly laughter, and I had her telling me, after we'd walked through the snowy Berkshire hills, that she hadn't known there was all this. She had not known there were simple, cheap pleasures, or that conversation could be earnest, that people could have ideals, or that you could meet strangers in strange places just like that, and wear old clothes, and drive a beat-up American car like mine, have crazy fun. "I was so stupid," she said, "so narrow."

I watched her across the booth from me, the hand with the pizza caught in a Gallic gesture, and I saw she had fallen in love, and I felt that I had somehow tricked her.

In a year, when my doctorate was done and I had landed the World Bank job in Washington, it seemed to me that I was as successful as a young man could hope to be and that I was the right size and weight to marry Mireille, who—bless her even now—was at heart a modest girl who doubted herself, who never learned the habit of calculation, and was so used to altitude that she never guessed how heady it was for me and how daring was my offer.

I relived the romance in a happy reverie on the bumpy downhill road: the beautiful French girl, the working-class boy winning her love, the young couple full of promise and ambition, the impressed reaction of my parents, how my father loved her. By the time we reached the PTDC at dusk, something felt settled.

He said, he said . . . He said so little across the years.

About shoes he said you should never forget to polish the backs; you could tell a man by that. And you should do it every day and the shoes should be black. Some men, flashier types, just polished the toecaps and left it at that, but even if no one noticed, it still mattered. And the heels too, underneath the backs, they should be polished. Even if the boss never noticed all your life, it still mattered. He said it was what his father said to him.

Expert explanations:

Development: Any change we like.

Developing country: A place we like to change.

Basket case: A country that can repay its debts to us only by borrowing from us (abusive).

The soft and warm: Welfare considerations, health, education, women, children (abusive).

In the mountains of the Austrian Tyrol he joins the other men as our holiday group spreads out across the flowery summer meadow. We lengthen our strides to descend the mountain into a pine forest, then to a village where the Cosmos Tours representative has organized sweet white wine and chocolate cake. The women walk with the women and the men with the men. At fifteen, I walk with my new fourteen-year-old girl-friend. The men, strangers to each other, talk of their parts in the Second World War, still fresh enough in 1960. One says he stabbed a German to death in France. Another has been in a landing where more died than survived. The third hints that his role was so horrible and secret that even now it can't be talked about, his present job as an accountant's clerk in Gloucester merely a salve for the horrors that went before.

My father spent the war in the Home Guard in London and, going last, lacking guile, he makes too much of it. He says, it was the worst place to be, London in the blitz, and that, though he wanted to, they wouldn't take him, too valuable as he was where he was, delivering milk, and anyway, there were some people, and he was one of them, who did not care for war, to whom the sight of blood was abhorrent, who could faint at the sight of it, and he was one of those men, actually, he fainted at the sight of it. And that's all there was to it.

So we cross the silent meadow, the men with the men, all silent now, me with my teenage girlfriend, and I wonder why, why this rush to confession that no one wanted, and why, when he never flinched at my childhood wounds, or even when he put the garden fork through his foot on the allotment, and when he was absolutely the bravest of fathers when it came to climbing on the roof, why he should shame himself this way and claim the lowest place, this cowardice. I want to protect him, the son protecting the father, and I do not want to be like him.

Peristalsis is like this.

On Sundays the loneliness in Nuku'alofa is terrible. Recently I have occupied myself with attempts to swallow. I have three hamburgers, which I bought yesterday from the Little America Café and which I have lined up on International Dateline Hotel stationery. When they are least expecting it, I take a bite from one and go to swallow as if this was normal. I'm pleased to say that so far I've had no success. Peristalsis has not been achieved. On two occasions the food has sneaked past my epiglottis only to be detained further down my throat, achieving a sort of oscillation where the impulse to swallow is exactly balanced by the tendency to throw up. On these occasions I have nearly suffocated. I have begun to talk to my father about this.

They decide the world is round. They mend the roads in Tottenham, or don't. They raise taxes. They impose, then re-move, food rationing and discover penicillin. They invent washing machines and goodness-knows-what-next. They get the weather forecasts wrong, change the numbers of the bus routes for no good reason, and declare war on the Egyptians. They give us free medicine and public libraries, spectacles on the National Health, close the school we like and put tuppence on the price of cigarettes just when we've got ahead for once. They do all right for themselves at our expense, take care of the things that aren't our business, decree the Ger-mans are OK after all—and the Italians, and the Japanese—replace the horses and milk carts with electric floats, decide it's best now not to have colonies after all and that it's good now to spend when it wasn't before and that we're doing well now in Tottenham, having it good. They are our weather and our God and the limits of ourselves. A certain slavishness persists.

So I'm in my fine blue linen shirt and the dark-blue tie with the little red spots and the summer-weight gray suit, jacket over the back of the chair, and I'm raising World Bank paperwork for the next trip, which is Colombia—which the men at the Bank here link with Thailand as the two countries with the prettiest women—just filling in the forms, working through the low stack of in-tray files. Outside, D.C. stinks with tar and summer heat and the quick tempers of American blacks crazed by the invisibility of the border between them and money, and I don't think I'm thinking now of the girl on the D.C. bus twenty years back. Louise has gone home to whatever life it is that secretaries have, and I'm finding a special virtue in this after hour when I'm here but I don't have to be. The corridor is quiet and I've closed the blinds against the street. The cleaner has been in and called me Sir, emptied my wastebasket and mumbled that he'll leave the cleaning until later, and I've said, fine, because although I know he wants to do it now, I don't have to let him. And the files are clean and the paper crisp and I'm good at all this, and I can't help admiring my pressed shirt cuffs and the cleanliness of my underwear, and how tidy and effective I'm being, and virtuous, and probably scoring promotion points too, and how fine it is to be well paid, to travel the world, to be seen to do right, and how it isn't bad to make Mireille wait for me, the dinner waiting, when I've got an excuse she can't argue with. And I'm in all this when Han walks in.

Here they tap you on the shoulder. I don't know why. I'm sitting on my steps, and one of the girls who weave the frangipani around the roof posts in the mornings passes behind me and taps me on the shoulder. She extends a dancer's arm toward me—long fingers—then, tap, a little flick of the fingertips to tap me just above the shoulder blade. I don't know why. There's the smile as she moves away and, of course, the flower behind the ear, but the tap is perfect and mysterious, not the sticky clasp of a hug, nor the false sexual import of a squeeze or stroke, but a pert, brisk tap, seeming to say, hello from me to you, and also, I've chosen you to tap, and also, nothing serious, just passing, and also, isn't life fun, isn't it light. Emo tapped me first, now they all tap me. I don't know why.

Yesterday, in the trading store across the island—mainly dealing in imported cans of pilchards, beef, and beer—I was caught by the display of *Time* magazines while I waited for Emo to buy the Foster's. Some old instinct in me scanned the faces set out on a trestle table, trying to spot the most recent issue, even though the mere presence of *Time* on Ruatua rattled me with its dissonance. The task was difficult because recent issues and issues years old were similarly priced and displayed in no particular order, so that customers could choose according to the attractiveness of the cover rather than the currency of the news. The idea of reading *Time* magazine shrank in me as quickly as it appeared and I turned away, but I was pleased to keep the thought of Ruatuans selecting world news according to their mood. Today, though, back to my own factual reporting, I am finding this unhelpful; it's hard to relive the dawning understanding that Mireille might have had a breakdown and I might have caused it, when no one—not me, nor Mireille, and certainly not Mireille's family—would want to hear it. Once again I'm inclined to stay lingeringly with the early romance, and I have no doubt the Ruatuans would also select it over later episodes. Can anything be more absurd than a truth with no takers? I have considered trying out my efforts on Emo, who quietly reads the paperbacks left behind by guests, but she shows no interest. Sometimes, when I get under her feet, she tells me to "go and write," in exactly the same indulgent tone with which she tells the children to "go and play."

Compared to my last visit, when I was supervising the Ruatua Pig Development Project (Rua 001), Coconut Beach Holiday Village now has few guests. The young Australians and New Zealanders who sometimes find their way here on the basis of oral information must be willing to accept that they might need to prepare their own meals, or eat with us, but in return they can stay in a beach cabin and wake each morning to the sound of sea on a deserted shore. Emo is flexible in the rates she charges, and nowadays there's a good chance we will throw a barbecue, a feast really, a fiafia, on which occasions friends and relatives from Emo's home village come down to play music and dance. It might be that since Emo's Australian husband left, the hotel is evolving in its nature from a commercial undertaking toward that of a Ruatuan village. The thatches are becoming more tousled and the buildings seem more settled under the palms at the edge of the beach, sand hugging up against them, little gardens of shells and succulent plants joining them to the rest of Ruatua. Each morning, regardless of whether or not we have guests, women come to weave fresh flowers everywhere possible, or, where there is nothing to hold them, they plant thin sticks and attach an extravagance of blooms to them, so that everything inert is made to seem to blossom.

I have decided that my fastidiousness has nothing to do with telling the truth after all. It's really an attempt to rehabilitate my memory, an abused and damaged faculty. My hope is that a diet of pure fact will detoxify it in the same way that a victim of junk food might begin his rehabilitation with an exclusive diet of brown rice. I try not to ask too much of it. In a recent reverie I found myself trying to recall my first visit to Ruatua, four years ago. I was fairly sure I never left the hotel across the island, next to the airstrip, and I must have cooked up Project Rua 001 with government officials. Probably I stayed only one or two nights, and I seemed to remember a drinking session in my hotel room with the director of agriculture and the secretary of the treasury. But that attempt at memory quickly maddened me with my inability to be sure whether it happened, was simply likely to have happened, or happened on some other island, very much like Ruatua. Now I'll restrict myself to the weeks since Pakistan.

I do try to avoid distraction, but recently I have accepted three invitations to become a mateii, a sort of honorary village head. This is my own fault and arises from my association with pigs. Ruatuan pigs have an almost religious role in village life and are roasted at every festival and rite of passage. Now that I've come to know them better, I have come to respect these pigs. They are small, brown, and hairy and lie around the villages' green spaces like pets, occasionally scampering in mock fright but generally affecting an independent air. They keep the place clean and ask for nothing more than tossed-out household scraps. Though every pig is somehow attached to a household, ownership is incomplete, so that the village can demand a feast-day pig at any time, and having cost nothing to raise, they can be freely given. Their comfortable, snuffly lives end with their being the life and soul of the party.

The reason for my apparent popularity is that I am helping the Ruatuans rid the island of the foreign pigs, which have been causing so much trouble. These pigs, the Large White variety imported from Germany, were brought here under my own Rua 001. Although I heard rumors through Emo of the trouble these pigs caused, this information passed me by until I witnessed a violent argument in Emo's home village. Even then it did not occur to me that there might be something I could do to remove the cause of the disputes. It was not possible, for example, to buy up the pigs, because Ruatuan pigs, being free, could not be bought; the very idea was offensive. Only after Emo's village courteously made me a mateii did I see the way ahead. I noticed that during the two days of my initiation ceremony, village pigs were roasted in large quantities and also, at frequent junctures in the proceedings, I was expected to give money to the village. At some point during the two days of ritual, perhaps helped by the reputedly narcotic effect of kava, I had my idea for undoing Ruatua's pig problem. I believe this was the first time since my arrival here that my mind had truly turned toward the future. I let it be known that I would be happy to be a mateii in other villages and that I would be a most generous mateii, but only on condition that during the celebrations all the village's Large White pigs should be eaten. It still distracts me from my writing to think of the fun of this, my project being eaten up in cheerful celebration. I try not to get carried away.

...

In the evening, Akira and I were left to eat alone in the PTDC dining room. Salim hurried in with rice, lamb, and water, then backed away grinning, as if he was getting away with something. I looked toward Akira, but Akira was already busying himself with the food.

Akira ate noisily, leaning close to the plate and chewing the meat more times than seemed necessary. When he stopped to drink, he drank a complete glass, then immediately refilled it from the jug. Everything about him was crude and abrasive. When he slept, which was little but at odd times, he immediately fell to snoring, with a grating resonance that could be heard several rooms away. In the silence of the dining room his food habits disgusted me and twice I tried to divert his absorption by starting conversations about our work. Each time he had looked up as if startled to find he was not alone and grunted, "Ha!" then made noises of agreement without formulating a reply. I started again.

"Oh, Akira, I should tell you, I had a call from Shareef in Peshawar last night. I got some bad personal news. My father has died."

Akira extracted a piece of tough lamb from his mouth and put it on the side of his plate. "Ha?"

"I thought you ought to know since there's a chance, though only a small one, that I will have to go back to London."

"Ha? Your father? Your father die?" He had stopped eating and his attention was on me, so that I thought I knew at last which eye—the right one—was the one that counted.

"Yes. He died two days ago. The funeral is on Wednesday, but I probably will not need to go."

"You know last night? You don't say anything today?" He was openly aghast.

"There was nothing anyone could do."

"Ha? Oh, William-san, sorry. Your father! Very sorry."

Akira leaned back in his chair and looked so grave that I felt a pang of sadness. It did not seem quite my own and was accompanied by annoyance. I looked down at the dirty table-cloth.

"Well . . . it happens."

"Why you not tell us? You should not work today. When your father die you do not work. No!"

I shrugged and I believe I started out on an unconsidered sentence—I can't remember what—before I steered myself back and said, "It's best to keep busy. And I didn't want to leave you and Mr. Yamada with all the work."

Akira remained looking at me as if trying, and failing, to recognize my state of mind. I continued, "By the way, how is Mr. Yamada now?"

He ignored this question and, still looking at me, stood up. "Wait!"

In a minute Akira had returned with a full bottle of Red Label Scotch. He cracked the top open with a practiced twist and the next sound was of my water glass being filled with whisky. Both of the Japanese traveled with enormous, heavy cases and perhaps the whisky was the reason for Akira's. After he had filled my glass he filled his own, but instead of drinking from it, he held it aside and studied mine, like a doctor concerned to see that a patient took the full dose.

I said, "Please, join me," but he did not react. Even after I had emptied the glass he continued to study me, as if expecting a transformation, an improvement. I was warmed and upset by all this and when he went to fill the glass again I put my hand over it. "We have to work tomorrow."

He leaned back now and drank his own drink.

I said, "I think I'll go to my room."

"Take the bottle."

"No, it's yours."

"Take it! I have other bottles." He had so far never asserted himself in this way. His manner so far had been to show a stubborn deference—it was impossible to make him go through a door first—and to affect a lack of understanding when it suited him, only insisting when he relayed a request from Yamada, his superior.

I conceded. "Thank you, Akira. I'll return what I don't use."

He made a vigorous dismissive gesture with his arm.

I had been lying on my bed for half an hour, unaware of the fact or of my thoughts, when Akira knocked. "William!" My immediate reaction was to feel guilty about not drinking more of the whisky he had given me, but I quickly dismissed this as foolish.

"William, come and see Mr. Yamada."

"Is he ill?"

"Ill? No, no. He want to see you."

"Ah, William. Come in."

Yamada had chosen not to make use of the single light bulb suspended from the center of the ceiling, depending instead on candles placed on a chair, giving the room a sickbed twilight. Next to the candles was a small city of medicine containers, so much like the arrangement I had last seen on my father's bedside table that for a moment I was shocked by the compression of time and space between the Himalayan PTDC and a terrace house in London. When my attention went to Yamada I was relieved to see he was smiling and jaunty.

Since we had met at the Islamabad Holiday Inn, I had not had a personal conversation with Yamada, and I did not want one now. And there was something trying about his apparent good spirits after his days of idleness and the disruption he had caused on the field trip.

"Akira said I should come by."

"Yes, yes. Please sit down, William."

I sat on the edge of a hard chair and kept hold of the notebook I had brought with me in case the meeting should prove to be substantial. My posture was intended to inform him that I was receptive to what he might say but not short of other things to do. He sat cross-legged—more flexible than me in spite of his age—and I could see beneath his pajamas the elasticized cuffs of thermal underwear. A herbal cigarette was poised in his hand, but he made no move to draw on it; he was smiling and composed. On the rug next to his bed a camping stove was set up beside a neat pile of food containers labeled in Japanese.

"Special diet," he said, following my look, and smiled more broadly, as if this were a shared joke.

Yamada was unmistakably aristocratic, just as Akira was clearly stamped a commoner. It was in the calculated raffishness of the way his gray hair fell across his forehead and in the elegantly careless gestures. So far he had used his charm to eliminate himself from labor, and our brief talks had followed a pattern in which I would point out some element of our work that he had overlooked and he would flatter my astuteness, suggesting that my competence made me the logical person to take the matter in hand. But now I could not perceive the immediate purpose of his charm.

"Please, William, take a drink. There's Japanese beer and there's whisky. I can't, but you should."

"No, thanks. I've already had a drink with Akira. I wanted to so some reading tonight, and if I drink any more I won't be able to work."

"You work hard, William. I've already told Geneva how hard you work. But it's too late for work now." He poured me a whisky. "Here."

"OK. Thanks."

He fell silent again, still smiling, composed, neatly folded. I sipped and matched his silence.

"I had a friend named William. Dead now. He was British ambassador in Cairo. He made me call him Bill. Is that right? Is Bill the same as William?"

"Yes; it's a nickname."

"A nickname. English is strange. It's difficult for us Japanese."

"Your English is excellent."

He waved away the compliment with his cigarette. "Should I call you Bill?"

"Will."

"Will. You see how complicated it is for us. Why Will, not Bill?"

"It's a family name. My father's uncle was Uncle Will. My grandfather's brother. I was given his name."

"And that's the custom, to continue family names like that?"

There was no such custom. The very idea of tradition in our family was ridiculous, a conceit out of line with our limited sense of importance. Yet I found myself offering Yamada a version of the family story and the way my name had changed with time.

I told him that my father's uncle, Uncle Will, had been a war hero and was therefore respected in the family. He had no children of his own, and to honor him—I think it was my mother's idea—I was given his name.

"Ah." Yamada settled back on his pillows as if ready to receive intelligence of great interest and reassurance.

"It was the Boer War." I waited for his expression of fascination to shift toward recognition or inquiry but it remained unchanged. "You might not have heard of that one. It was between the British and the Boers in South Africa. Toward the end of the last century."

Yamada's face continued to register interest and I found myself wanting to rush on into the space he had made for me. I also found, though, that I could remember very little of Uncle Will, except that he lived with Auntie Beth in a house as small as ours and even dowdier, and that he could not properly speak. He sat rooted in an armchair, a big untidy man, and uttered long-drawn-out barks which only Auntie Beth could interpret. To a child he seemed scarcely human and it had never occurred to me until now that I should feel any affinity with him.

I explained to Yamada that Uncle Will had lost the powers of speech and hearing during the trauma of battle and as a consequence had been decorated and given a disability pension. This did not seem untrue, but I was troubled that the only detail I could recall was that he had been run over by a train while lying between the rails. I tried to make sense of this while presenting the simpler version to Yamada. The train could have been in South Africa and might have involved a heroic deed, but I also had the vague sense that Uncle Will had worked on the railways in England. In fact, the only specific praise of him that stood out was my mother's forcefully pointing out to my father that Uncle Will had achieved two pensions, one from the army and one from the railways, while his brother, my grandfather, had failed to achieve one. It was a side issue of the ongoing tussle over whether my father should take from us to give to his mother, itself a side issue of the struggle between mother and wife for his unresolved allegiance.

To Yamada I left Uncle Will a hero, left his rank—private, probably—unstated, and did not hint that I was named to honor the achievement of a small pension. I moved on to the way my name had shifted from time to time with fashion and geography, between Will and Bill and William, a little lecture on the mores of English-speakers, but part of me remained snagged on the puzzle of why I had not been given my grandfather's name, or my father's, why they should have been passed over.

I was disconcerted to discover that I had no idea of the first names of either of my grandfathers. I tried to resurrect my father's father, a hatmaker to the gentry, I thought, an artisan in a dying trade—which would help explain the absence of a pension. On our dutiful Sunday visits he had sat silently at the tea table, while Grandmother talked for them both and gave my father all the attention. He was gentle, patient, henpecked, and the only steel I could find in him was his determination that no one should ever read the evening newspaper before he did and that it was forbidden to help him with the crossword. His was no name to carry on: he was too faint for it, too faint for a new mother who hoped her baby would be more successful than its father, who she still hoped then would be more successful than his father.

I concealed the faintness of our men while I explained to

Yamada the way my family had worked to keep my name Will against the popular tendency to Bill. The women in particular called me by name more often than was necessary. I let him think that this was from family pride and skirted the English truth that it was because Bill was seen as lower-class and common, and I was being set up for other things. They took up William when the cute, middle-class "Just William" stories appeared on TV and made it seem acceptable, though my schoolmates mocked the pretentiousness of it. I was complicit, eager to move up myself, migrate, and as I told Yamada, William was my accepted name through English university. In America voices louder than mine would not indulge anything as fancy as William, proclaiming, "Bill! Bill Bender!" as if the name were an achievement. I took it on, feeling more robust, more honest too, a real migrant now. "Americans," I pointed out to Yamada, "like to be more casual."

Mireille had called me Bill. Though, early on, on the pillow, she had breathed "William," a French "William," fine and light and distinguished, a secret, noble European identity she gave me, something extra that the Americans couldn't know. And in recent years, since Han, there seemed to be no one left to call me Bill, and Will had been all but forgotten. Foreign officials got William from telexes warning of my arrival, or from my résumé, faxed ahead for approval by ministries of foreign affairs, which must have been where Shareef got it. There had not been anyone close enough for me to say, "Look, don't call me William; call me Bill." Instead I'd said to myself, "OK, I'll settle for importance now. I'm getting too old for friendship."

I had surprised myself by offering "Will" to Yamada, and although my explanation of the name had tried to be objective, it had dipped more than once into the personal, each time eliciting an encouraging animation on the old man's handsome face.

"And what was your father's name?" he asked at last, when he saw that I had finished.

I was flustered by this directness and had to look away to find my answer, which even then was garbled. "Ben. Well, not really. Everyone called him Ben. From Bender, you see. His name was Jack, but I don't think anyone ever called him that, not even his wife." I collected myself and laughed. "Well, that's the story of Bill and Will. I didn't mean to go on so long. I'd better leave you to get some rest."

"No, don't go. I am enjoying this. I don't need to rest now. It was just the altitude earlier. Please, give me your glass. And I don't want you to work so hard. It would not do for both of us to be sick. I've been worried about you. You've lost your pink cheeks."

I said I was a little tired, nothing I could not handle. He nodded in reply. If Akira had told him of my father's death, he did not want to be the first to mention it. I tried to leave again but he affected not to notice, instead offering me a cigarette— not one of his herbal ones—which I refused.

"I wish I had given them up at your age. There were some things I could never resist: cigarettes, whisky, a pretty girl." He gave a surprising dirty laugh. "But now look at me." He gestured at his medicines. "Soon I will have taken a pill for every cigarette I ever smoked. And I can't stop. I have to smoke these fake cigarettes. I've tried a dozen types and these are the least bad. Here, try one."

I said, "No," and he said, "No?" as if pained by the refusal of one of those pretty girls.

There was a determined liveliness about him, and I gave up my attempts to leave. I took another drink. He said, "I've always liked working with the English. I think it's because we're both island nations. And we both lost empires. Americans are always telling the Japanese that we don't show our emotions enough, and I think they say the same about you. Isn't that so?"

"They usually say we're reserved."

"That's right. They call it reserved. But they don't like it. They make it sound dishonest, but I think it's just a different custom. If you live on crowded islands like we do, you have to be reserved to get along. The English and the Japanese both understand that."

"Well, I'm not sure I like it either. I feel more American now."

"Yes, I can see that. But you never really stop being what you first were, do you?"

He paused, so that the suspicion grew in me that he knew of my father's death and all this was to lead me to talk of it. I decided to remain silent and let him do the work.

When he spoke again it was to tell me of his own upbringing and the route that had taken him away from the comfort of being simply Japanese. His childhood before the war had been pampered. His family was related to the emperor and as he got older this gave him privileges with the girls. He said he could put his hand up the skirt of a girl, even in public, even on a bus, and she would not dare to complain. He laughed and looked to me for a response, which I denied him by only smiling faintly. "It was different then. Women saw themselves differently. You can't do that with Japanese girls now." He was regretful.

At the outbreak of the Second World War he had been in Washington, where his father was a diplomat. That's where he got his English. The war had left him with a deep sadness about his own people, he said.

He seemed to have forgotten me now, and to have forgotten charm, so that he spoke with greater hesitation. "It was a mistake—our racial pride, the sense of being separate. I saw this early on when no one else saw it. That's been my life story—to try and bring us out from isolation, even when everyone hated us. I think I've achieved something. I've almost done enough. I think I've done enough. Only this is stopping me."

He slowly pulled up his pajama jacket and undershirt and drew his finger along the welts of scars that crossed his thin chest. "Bypass surgery here. Removal of lung here." The scars looked fresh.

For the first time I was led to speak without circumspection. "What are you doing here? Surely you shouldn't be up here in the mountains with only one lung. There's not even a hospital up here. Maybe not a doctor."

"You sound like my wife. She doesn't want to lose me. It's understandable. But it doesn't matter, William—Will. What's life for?"

He took time to pull his clothes back into place, before continuing. "For me, this isn't just another development project. It's a little part of something I've been building all my life. A final brick. I want to bring Japan into these international projects. I want us to take international responsibility. I want us to see other people's problems as our own. Since the war we have been too shy to lead. This project is maybe my last brick—no, seed is better: the last seed I will sow. When you're an old man you have to be specific."

He told me how his life had led to this and how there were stages in a life and how these only became clear with age. While you were living a life, he said, you could miss the completeness of its journey, the full pattern. There now seemed to be a purposefulness in his talk, and I wondered if he was searching for the chord that would comfort me for my father's death. He said that in the earlier years a man needed an older, more powerful person to help him make his way. That was the nature of things. Later, when you had position, you could do the helping. For example, during his early years at the Asian Bank, when he was the only Japanese and the Japanese were still distrusted, he had won the respect and affection of one of the Americans who ran things then. The man had smoothed his way and Yamada said he had understood only later what he now knew to be true, that old men need young men to press their ambitions as much as the young need the protection of the old.

"I wasn't much younger than you. You're still comparatively young. It's the cycle of life, like having children, watching them grow up, setting them free. I have a daughter about your age, married of course, with four children. No son. My life is nearly complete and I'm not unhappy. My work is nearly done."

He could not have known how uneasily my father sat within this conversation and how the invitation implied in it caused within me a vague agitation of betrayal. He would not have known that my father had worked for thirty years on the same milkman's round, which ended not in fulfillment but in redundancy. The talk of great works completed in the cycle of a life was so far from this that I had more of a sense of mockery than comfort. Although I did not flinch from Yamada's flattering suggestion that he and I were fellow actors in a single play on a global stage, there was something in all this that made my jaw ache with sadness and left me tired, too tired even to leave. The pain that had nagged me earlier seeped back into consciousness, more toward the side this time, so that it no longer seemed like indigestion. My thoughts went toward it, wondering if the jarring travel over rocky roads had aggravated it. Wasn't there something called a bruised kidney?

Yamada spoke again. "Now, Will, will you help me do this? Akira usually helps me, but if you could . . . ? Just hold the paper there." He uncovered his arm and gave me a fragment of tissue paper to hold against the inside of his elbow.

"Japanese medicine. For my lungs . . . Good!"

I could feel the faint warmth of him, and there was in me the flicker of an impulse to hold him more strongly.

He made a little pile of herbs on the paper and handed me some matches. "Now light it."

"Light it?"

"Yes, go on. They have to burn. It will not hurt me."

The herbs smoldered briefly and consumed themselves.

"Good. You don't know Japanese medicine?"

"Not this."

"Oh, it's very good. Do you have any pains? I saw you make a face earlier."

"Only a twinge."

"A twinge? Where? Show me."

"Here."

"Ah, maybe the kidney. Give me your foot. Pull up your pant leg. This is the kidney point, here. You've got European legs, Will. Hairy."

He parted the hair and set the tiny bonfire, lit it. "You see. It doesn't hurt."

I laughed to see the little fire on my ankle and he laughed back at me with a greater gaiety, finding all the lines that his more serious face concealed. "Good! Good!"

The evening had been completed in a way that perhaps he had designed and I had not understood. Now it was possible for me to leave. I carried with me through the door a confusing mixture of happiness and sadness, which seemed inappropriate for a meeting with a mission leader. I don't think I recognized then the extent of his kindness.

When I had learned of my father's redundancy, I was outraged. Mireille had been puzzled by my vehemence. I told her that I would write to the chairman of Kendel-Peat in London or, better still, to the CEO of the parent company, NBT Foods in New Jersey. My intention—which, now that I thought on it, seemed youthfully naive—was to use the most impressive World Bank notepaper and let them know that although they might think they could push small people around, some of those small people might have sons in Washington, D.C., on just as high a level as themselves.

Mireille had said, "Bill, do you really think they will listen to you? What can they do anyway? They can't give him back a job that doesn't exist."

"They could if they wanted. There are other milk rounds."

"My dear, you are being ridiculous. Do you have that sort of power? NBT Foods don't take loans from the World Bank, do they?" She laughed affectionately at the folly of me, my mistakes in the world, the frailty of my learning against her inherited wisdom, an assumption that I later grew to hate.

"No, of course not. But he always trusted them." I was petulant.

"You know, sometimes you overestimate your position. Either you overestimate yourself or underestimate, never the balance. I don't understand it. You 'ardly write to your parents. You don't invite them . . ."

"They wouldn't like it here."

"Well, never mind. In any case, my dear, you don't think of

them from one year to the next, then you get a letter to say your father has lost his job and you want to turn the world upside down to put things right. It's not reasonable!"

I said nothing and Mireille calmed to become tender; it was still the early days. She came to where I was standing backed against the kitchen counter and placed her hand on my chest.

"It happens all the time, doesn't it? It's just a fact of life. And what if you did persuade them to give his job back? How would that be? Wouldn't it be an 'umiliation for him to be given a job just because his son bullied someone into being charitable?"

"He might not know."

"Pouf! Bill, leave it alone. Just write him a nice letter."

I had immediately recognized my mother's hand on the air letter, and as usual, I had torn it open on my way to the shower, skimming it for disasters and intending to throw it down somewhere for a later reading. Instead I was caught by the news and read it standing in the kitchen, my anger growing.

She had written, after the "We're fine" and the "Hope you are well," that Dad was a bit "down in the dumps these days" because Kendels had given him his cards. "Not even a golden handshake, after all these years, thirty-seven in November." She thought it was a "poor show," but I was to "never mind" because they would manage; she still had her part-time nursing job and there would be a bit of a pension from that in time. And the mortgage was all but paid for. And he had the church, of course, thank goodness—they'd been marvelous. Still, it was a shame, to see a man like him signing on at the dole, and who's going to take him on at fifty-nine? "Still, mustn't grumble."

I postponed writing to Kendel-Peat, and to NBT Foods, with the argument to myself that I first needed to be better informed. During the following month I demanded copies of official records from corporate registration offices on both sides of the Atlantic and had the staff of the Documentation Division track down detailed references from forty years of food and milk industry trade journals. I assembled a dossier of my father's economic life, utilizing resources he would never have imagined to exist. There was an obsessiveness about me; it seemed vital that I should not miss anything.

I already had one version of his working life, the one composed of his own sparse comments during my childhood. He had spoken with pride and pleasure of the visits to the Tottenham plant, of Old Man Kendel. He had said: "I'll say one thing for the Old Man—there's not a year goes past that he doesn't come by to say hello, and he always remembers my name." He seemed to feel there was a bond between himself and the owner of the dairy. "He always says, 'Hello, Ben. Glad to see you're still with us.'" It never occurred to my father that there was an undermanager outside the door briefing the boss on the employees inside, in the same way that I asked clerks around the world to refresh my memory while I waited in the anterooms of government officials. His job stayed the same for thirty years, the boss stayed the same; it was like a marriage, something to hold on to in an unreliable world.

There had been an occasion when some younger milkmen tried to unionize the firm, but my father, who was poorly paid, would have none of it. At the time, I was in my early teens, just claiming my first intellectual confidence, so I challenged him on this, but he was not one for arguing. He became uncomfortable and left his seat at the kitchen table to go to the stove, where he was cooking a stew.

"The Old Man's always treated me fairly . . . ," he began, his back to me, and did not finish.

While I marshaled my clever arguments to say that his lack of self-interest was misplaced, he became agitated and clumsy, banging pots together as if there was a terror in my words. Then, uncharacteristically sharp, after spilling something hot, he said, "Look what you've made me do!" Then, in the silence that followed my surprise, he added, almost muffled, "Unions —they're the devil's work!" The intensity of it, and its darkness, stopped me short and scared me, so I went quiet and after some moments he was able to move things along by asking,

"Get me the flour from the pantry, will you, son? Reckon we could do with some dumplings in this."

During his early years at Kendels, wartime rationing of food was in effect. My mother had said more than once that the only good thing about the dead-end job of getting up to deliver milk while other men still slept was that he could occasionally come home with something extra. According to the records I accumulated on my Washington desk, Kendels was a small independent dairy in those days. There was a photo of Old Man Kendel in a late-forties issue of *The Milk Industry*—a round-faced man with shrewd eyes—on the occasion of his taking over from his father, Grandad Kendel. In the background was a Kendels horse and cart, and I fancied I could remember my father's horse and cart too. The horse had a name, just beyond memory—Ginger?—which, first at my desk in D.C. and then, fifteen years later, lying on a bed at the PTDC, I badly wanted to remember. Nor was I sure how old I was— four, five, six—when they took the horse away and gave him instead a jerky electric handcart, which could not follow him up the street on its own.

I spent an increasing amount of my work time poring over the Kendels dossier, with the unconsidered feeling that I was constructing a formidable weapon for joining my father in the defense of his life. It was clear that the younger Kendel—not yet the Old Man—had immediately set out to improve on his father's business. In 1950 he bought out the competing dairy of H. J. Peat and consolidated their delivery routes, renaming the firm Kendel-Peat. This would not have affected my father, I thought, except that he would have had more milk to deliver.

According to a later editorial in *The Milk Industry*, the next decade was a period of amalgamation, when fierce competition forced dairies to grow in order to gain the economies of scale made possible through automated processing and bottling. Although the name Kendel-Peat remained the same, the Old Man acquired half a dozen additional dairies in north London in an attempt to meet the competition from the larger United Dairies and Express Dairies. There was an occasion when I heard my father boasting of this expansion to a man we met on a family holiday at a boardinghouse in Clacton-on-Sea, as if the success of Kendel-Peat was progress and he was going places with it. The man had looked puzzled.

Probably, the workers at the Tottenham depot were not aware of subsequent developments, or, if they were, the developments meant nothing to them. In '57 Kendel was persuaded that his best course of action was to finance new investment by going public and raising capital on the stock exchange. Although this achieved its short-term objective, Kendel-Peat was now exposed to the larger economic forces of the world. I traced with an odd fascination the widening extent of my father's innocence, as the events that shaped his life shaded into the elusive rationalities of international finance, which were becoming as comfortable to me as they remained alien to him.

The next decade was a bad time for small food retailers. With rising labor costs and the change in shopping patterns as more wives went out to work, supermarkets started to push aside the local shops and home deliveries. These newly powerful retail chains were often larger than the food manufacturers that supplied them, so that food companies sought countervailing power through integration. It was explained in the financial press that Kendel-Peat was both attractive and vulnerable to predators and that its purchaser, Bartel House Ltd., a company that had previously concentrated on baked goods, was attracted by the potential of milk rounds as an additional, premium-price retail opportunity. At this time there was a picture of Old Man Kendel in *Dairy World,* which showed a fit, silver-haired man in his sixties shaking hands with the managing director of Bartel House. Kendel was reportedly made a millionaire by the deal and was given a seat on the Bartel board.

My father would not have known that the Old Man no longer had any power in Kendel-Peat. The annual visits continued; my father's name was remembered each time, though the visits were probably now organized by Bartel's Personnel Division.

It must have been around then that my father confided to me that the Old Man had a Rolls these days, his voice quiet, as if anxious that the pride he took in it might rise up and over-whelm the lessons of his Sunday talks. His version of things held.

During the late sixties the economic weather changed again for Kendels, storms so far above my father's head that I doubt he even heard them. The realization of postwar economic dominance by the United States, with all its complex origins, led to a positive trade balance that sent American companies on a spree of overseas acquisition. Bartel House was bought by NBT Foods of Trenton, New Jersey. The main motive was be-lieved to be acquisition of Bartel's Devonshire baked goods brand name, and Kendels was only mentioned in passing by the item in the *Wall Street Journal*.

Under NBT, it seemed, Kendel-Peat performed poorly. Prob-ably, the American owners saw home milk deliveries as a doomed enterprise and therefore starved it of investment. The system had all but died out in the United States, and the En-glish industry was subject to the same pressures. Easy credit and affluence were leading to increased refrigerator owner-ship, which made daily deliveries unnecessary, and shopping by car removed much of the burden. But the new owners appeared to have missed the significance of the British dairy farmer lobby, which persuaded the government to subsidize home deliveries as a means of maintaining milk consumption.

Through all this my father's job remained unchanged. Each day he joked with Mrs. Evans, Mrs. Burnage, and Mrs. Hyatt, he got their orders right, he checked on the welfare of the solitary old ladies on his round, and he believed, I think, that it was the simple usefulness of this that made his job exist.

I finally discovered that it was not, after all, the Americans who made him redundant, though by then it hardly mattered who. By then American financial dominance was being lost to the Japanese, and NBT Foods was itself subject to a highly geared takeover by the international conglomerate Carroll Holdings, registered in the Cayman Islands and administered mainly from the City of London. The takeover was financed by a credit line from a Japanese bank and by high-interest bonds sold on the New York market. Following its standard practice, Carroll Holdings refinanced its bonds by selling off marginal subsidiaries. Kendel-Peat was bought by a management buy-out. It had been young English executives in Kendel's local Ilford headquarters who had eliminated the less profitable milk routes, my father's among them. The rationale was suggested in a *Milk Industry* article. The Tottenham neighborhood was among those that had undergone a demographic shift from family homes to flats for young professionals, people who went away so often that regular milk deliveries were a nuisance. They favored shops, and route volumes had fallen below the critical level.

By the time I had all this, I found my righteous anger was gone and I was unable to write any letter of complaint. I could not focus blame; the international forces that had borne down on him implicated me and I could not separate myself from them to take his side. I understood that the new owners of Kendel's would not have inherited a pension fund or cash for redundancy payments. Their actions were unavoidable. And there was something immensely tiring about all this, its size and weight and elusiveness. I believe the file stayed on my desk for a couple of months, after which I put it in a drawer, which gradually filled up with other things. I never told my father of my concern or challenged his version of his working life with mine.

Thinking of this, I came back to Yamada and his grand design for making Japan a responsible economic power, and the way he assumed me to be part of such grandeur. And I felt an impatience with my father for his helplessness, for not taking on the world, for settling for the easy comfort of delusion, for leaving things up to me. I had to admit it was true; I was not like him. All the research had not brought me closer.

We left the mountains by road the following day. In the morning the deputy commissioner sent a messenger to the PTDC with the news that his scouts now judged that four-wheel-drive vehicles could make it over the pass but we should leave immediately. I took the unevenly typed sheet of paper from the messenger and went to Yamada's room. Akira tried to make me wait, saying Yamada was resting, but I had already argued with Akira that morning, and I was in no mood to pay attention to him.

Yamada was still in bed, copies of loan agreements splayed out across the blanket. He was lying flat, looking at the ceiling.

"Mr. Yamada, I'm sorry to disturb you."

"Will. Come in."

I held out the note. "The DC advises us to leave by road today. I think we should go."

"Go where?"

"Peshawar."

"Peshawar?"

"Well, we'd stay tonight at a rest house somewhere the other side of the pass. We'd reach Peshawar tomorrow."

"What do you think?"

"What do I think? I think we should go."

"Good. Good. You're very good. I've told them that." Yamada had not attempted to raise himself and there was none of the previous night's liveliness.

"How are you this morning?"

"I'm well. Tired." He turned his head and smiled.

"But you can travel?"

"Yes."

"And you want to go?"

"You decide, Will. You take over."

"I'll ask Akira to come and help you pack."

"Good, good."

As I turned to go, he called me back. "How's your pain, Will?"

I was in mid-movement, so that I had to stop to consider. "Worse," I decided, and I closed the door behind me.

There was a lot to do and I welcomed the relief from self-reflection. Yamada appeared to be sick again and Akira had chosen today to show himself as dangerously incompetent. It was all in my hands and any pains in my abdomen would have to wait. I liked the self-importance and the urgency of it.

I had woken early but rested. The whisky had somehow washed out my head without leaving a hangover and in the morning light the previous night's conversation with Yamada already seemed distant, a bizarre distortion of normality. It was sometimes the case when working among strangers in a remote place that intimacies and antipathies grew which would have no place in normal life. It was a matter of character as well as judgment to avoid mistaking these circumstantial emotions for authentic friendships or justified grievances. A good consultant learned to hold his feelings to himself and not to expect to find warmth or commitment in professional and transitory relationships; he took a detached view.

I had seen many examples of the harm resulting from the loss of this detachment. In Bhutan a mission had been disrupted by a German who formed a loathing for the noisy eating habits of a vain Bangladeshi. A major mission to Brazil had to be restaged when a Frenchman used friendships with other team members to build a dissenting subgroup. And on the occasions when women consultants were present there was the danger of sexual competition.

When I woke feeling refreshed and well-balanced, I sensed immediately that there had been in the previous evening's conversations something of the falsely heightened emotion of a mission and I was eager to lose myself in work. Akira had come to my room at six-thirty—his eyes repulsively bloodshot, as usual in the morning—while I was already busy organizing my documents. He waited silently until I stopped. I saw there was a sheaf of loose papers in his hand, all covered with tiny handwritten figures.

"Morning, Akira."

"Something not right, William." He looked troubled and preoccupied. "These figures . . . no good."

He immediately set about explaining his problem with the figures, as if their importance was a matter of agreed concern between us. His solicitousness of the previous evening had disappeared and I could see that he was caught up in some sort of obsessive concern. I tried to counterbalance his intensity with my coolness.

"Why don't we look at these together sometime later?" I walked around my room, putting things in order. Akira followed me, trying to explain each of his calculations. I closed my ears to the specifics of his explanations, only understanding that it was all too detailed, too scrupulous, inappropriately fastidious. There was always a danger of becoming lost in statistics and forgetting that figures were for supporting decisions, not making them.

There was whisky on his breath. While he spoke in his halting English he looked only at his tables, not at me. When I made my way to the door he stood against it, bristle-headed and stocky, still talking, still insisting. If I was to leave I would have to move him forcibly, which was impossible to contemplate and perhaps difficult to achieve.

"Akira, hold it. Akira!" I put my hand over the table he was quoting so that at last he had to look at me. "Stop. Please. I have no idea what you are talking about. We haven't even had breakfast yet."

"I work on this all night! No sleep!"

"All right, all right. Just tell me, very simply, what's the problem. In a sentence."

He looked up at me as if the idea of simplicity was madness. "Lies. All their statistics, lies."

Overnight Akira had taken it upon himself to compare official statistics from numerous government departments, census results, economic studies by Pakistani universities, reports by the World Bank and other international agencies, and to combine them into a single quantitative portrait of the region. He was shocked that none of the published figures agreed.

"Farmers grow this much, how the people consume so little? . . . If this their average income, where it from? . . . Look, the population divided by land area"—he pulled out his calculator—"it must equal population density, yes? But not the same—completely not the same. This figure for grain production is half this one. We can't use these. They lie to us."

I looked out the window toward the cool mountains in the morning sun, and it seemed the coolness might be lost forever.

I took a breath. "Akira. Akira-san. Listen. We live in an imperfect world. Our information is never complete. It's never perfect. It doesn't matter."

"It matters! It must not be like this. We must have big meeting. We must make departments agree which figures are right. You tell me, will I take the Department of Trade figure for grain balance or the Department of Agriculture? Which? Tell me. We can't do anything with this. Nothing useful. We know nothing."

I touched his shoulder and smiled. I felt him tense and pull away. He said, "You say no problem. You are irresponsible. You don't do job!"

"Akira. Don't say that." I lowered my voice to draw attention to his loudness. "There is a problem. But it's your problem. It's up to you to come up with the version you think best. It's your judgment. That's what you're paid for. There's no truth, just judgment. So don't bother me with your problems. Make a guesstimate."

"Ha?"

"Guesstimate. Your best guess."

While Akira stood dumbfounded, I was able to reach the door and pull it open. It was clear—and in a way I think I welcomed the responsibility it gave me—that I would have to add Akira to my problems. He might know about agriculture, but he knew nothing about the world. Although we were similar in age, I had long ago put aside the luxury of certainty and I was angry that Akira wished to burden me with his childish scruples. These official figures were like most official figures; they varied according to who wrote them. When a department wanted more money, the figures made the situation look bad. At another time the figures showed how well the same department had done. We all knew—except Akira, it seemed—that the official figures omitted the money from the CIA and the opium trade. And even an honest statistician would need to guess his figures; the place was hardly known. I remembered Han, who I thought had cured me of all resistance to this, but there was, perhaps, in my anger a proof that the cure was incomplete.

Akira called me back. "So tell me what to do. You my boss."

"Yamada's your boss."

"No! Yamada sick. You take over. He told me."

"OK, I'll tell you what to do. I want figures on each crop: production on irrigated and unirrigated land, first and second harvest, by agricultural zone. I want salable surplus at international prices and imports to the valley, shadow-priced to account for real transport costs and foreign exchange. I want milk and livestock production and fodder yields. I want the quantities and prices for the inputs you propose and the projected impact on production and exports for the next twenty years. And I want that to fit land use and population figures. I want everything to fit. And I want to know how much it will cost, and I want it all done in such a way that no government department will raise an objection and I want the internal rate of return on investment to come out at fifteen percent per annum when discounted back to the present day. Give or take a percent. And I want a sensitivity analysis that shows the outcome isn't sensitive to anything. OK? And I don't want to know how you did it."

He looked at me, then away, then started to push past me. "You not professional."

"No, you're not professional. Ask Mr. Yamada. If your figures don't help get this loan through, you'll never be hired again. Forget what's true. We'll never know the truth. We're going to leave. Make a version that works. You'll get paid for that."

He took two steps, then stopped again. "I thought you were OK," he said, then carried on.

I tidied my papers, then said, "Shit!" for the trouble of him, then calmed myself and emptied my head of everything but the things that needed to be done.

...

He did say that HB pencils were best, a sensible compromise between hardness and softness. They leave a good line but don't blunt too quickly. And the way to overcome knock-knees is to sleep, as he had in childhood, with books tied between them, although it didn't seem to have worked for him. And if you treat people well they will treat you well in return, although there was no evidence for this.

There's a need for explanations: a revision of the earlier explanation of human civilization.

The earlier explanation of human civilization is, of course, laughably wrong. Its propositions are in essence emotional, depending as they do on our sentimental attachment to reason. Such material determinism now has few serious adherents.

    Though it can be conceded that human civilization is responsive to material reality, the specific responses draw on the possibilities for life that preexist in man. Rather than being inevitable, civilization is an expression of our innate human potential, so that a true understanding of our world lies not in natural laws but in the depths of the human mind, which are, of course, as impossible for us to know as it is for an eel to swallow itself.

    Seen this way it might well be argued that the intricate, complex, and unknowable workings of the supranational financial stratosphere represent the highest extant expression of man's deepest potential. That is, by revering its combination of abstraction, unity, practicality, and myth, we can come closest to knowing the God that is in us all.

A pink sea anemone vagina fills the screen. Then another. We are lost in faceless, bodiless moist womanhood. Seaweed cocks wave upright in the current and we're taken in, lost for a time to the too difficult world. Akira grunts, and there's a sort of mewing from the old man in front of us, who is suffering the perfection of his longing. Then it's lost, and a man with brute features drives a Rolls-Royce through the streets of Paris. We're beached while two gangsters acting as actors pretend to be executives in an ersatz office. They're speaking French dubbed into German, though we're in neither place. "Let's go," Akira says, though it's only ten minutes since he brought me here. "I want live sex show," he says. "With fucking."

We leave into the Bangkok street, but I'm sorry to lose the coral sea of timeless cunts groomed by seaweed cocks in international waters.

There's a need for explanations. God is like a pane of glass.

For some reason—I don't know why—when the builders built our house they decided to put the bathroom in the front: you know, above the porch, not above the kitchen at the back, like most houses. It doesn't make sense to have it at the front because all the pipes have to go farther. Ours freeze in winter if we don't keep the boiler on, which we don't want to, because of the cost. Usually we just light it Friday and Saturday, and then we lose a lot of heat between the hot water tank and the bathroom in the front.

Anyway, you don't want to hear about my plumbing. The point is, because the bathroom's in the front, they had to put frosted glass in the bathroom window so people couldn't see in from the street. Well, it's not exactly frosted—I'm not sure what they call it—it's that glass that distorts everything into pieces. The light comes through and you can see a bit of leaf here, a bit of roof there, a bit of sky, but none of it in exactly the right place, so you just get a general impression of what's outside. The bit that's greener is probably a tree, the whitish bit means a cloud, and so on. It can be very annoying when you're trying to see if the milkman's coming up the road or something—because you think you should be able to see, but you can't. If you press your nose right up against the glass, it just makes it worse.

So I thought last night when I was sitting in the bath—you know, the way I do—looking out the window, I thought, it's a bit like trying to see God. I mean, we look up and strain our eyes. We see a bit of Him here, a bit of Him there, but we never see the whole picture. And some bits don't seem to fit in at all. Sometimes terrible things happen—a plane crash or a famine somewhere—and we can't believe God had anything to do with it. We move our heads this way and that and it still doesn't make any sense, whichever way you look at it. Well, I reckon the only thing to do then is to lie back and enjoy the colors. You know that out there beyond the frosted glass it all makes sense. Because it's all part of God's design. Part of His picture. We can't see it because we're not God. We're only humans. It's not for us to make sense of everything, is it? If we could do that we wouldn't need God, would we?

So that's what I did. I just lay back in my bath and watched the colors playing through the glass and let my mind wander. I just let the light shine on me. And maybe that's all we can do—let His light shine on us and hope that other people can see it. Of course I usually don't get my bath until after dark, after Will and Mrs. Bender have had theirs. But there's one of those bright orange sodium lamps in the street outside our house now, which makes it nearly as bright as day.

Emo's brought my baby to me, and at last I've cried. She looks at me and asks, what do I think of her son, and I look and see that he looks like the picture of me at one year, though darker of course, and more calm in the warmth of Ruatua than I ever was in Tottenham. I touch the soft part of his head, where there is no bone between my fingers and his mind. I stroke the fine angel-thread hair, entering into him then, so I sleep in his

---

sleep, and blink open in silent amazement when he does, seeing the astonishing brightness of the world, the endless complexity of it, its shapes and colors, its warmths and smells and sounds, none of these explained.

I turn to Emo and say, "He's my child. I can feel myself living inside him." She smiles and says, "Is he?" as if she does not know but is happy to accept that I might know, or as if it does not matter, or as if by saying so I make it true. Then I weep, passing the baby back to her, weep silently staring at the sea, and Emo lets me for a while, untroubled by my tears, until with a smile she reaches out her hand and taps me lightly on the shoulder.

I'm a master of forgetting, virtuoso of not seeing:

In Pakistan I don't see the opium fields I'm not meant to see, or the mujahedin among the refugees, who officially aren't there.

In the Philippines it's not up to me to know the way the money goes to those who support the status quo.

I'm unconcerned, in India, that accidentally, by the way, the poor go under once again because of what we say.

Or that in Brazil the ones who officially did not exist, no longer exist.

In Beijing I can't see the blood on the square, no longer there, now that our credit program has been resumed.

In Liberia it doesn't help to know that half the money we gave for the roads is in the pocket of Minister Cole.

I turn blind eyes to genocide—I can see through starving men—and I can't tell the sound of lies from the whisper of a friend.

The pleasure of fascist friends is you don't have to be nice to them.

She's so neat in Zanzibar, so clean—the cut of her black hair, the skin without lines, the definition of her limbs, the sweet tidy Chinese eyes. She says it doesn't matter what we do in Zanzibar; they'll mess up the project anyway. In Zanzibar, where tourists no longer come, we are on the sand, making love within the scent of cloves and the sound of chattering women making coir just out of sight. In Zanzibar the penalty for adultery—for women—is death, but Han says they can't touch us; if they did, they'd never get their World Bank loan. She says, don't worry, don't worry. She says that when she walks through the offices of the agricultural ministry in the heat, in a skirt without underwear, she goes squish, and all the Muslim men there know there's something, but they can't do anything. She knows what to say. She says she'll fix the figures so the rate of return is just right, fifteen percent; that way we'll win an extra day and have time for a stopover in Mauritius.

You can't buy toothpaste on Zanzibar. Not anywhere.

Expert explanations: The poetry of economics.

The shadow price is what it really costs you, not what you pay.

The analysis of sensitivity shows how much it matters if you get it wrong.

The opportunity cost is what you could have done while you were doing something else.

The internal rate of return is what you get back for what you did.

I reluctantly explain my work to the bony American missionary in the airplane seat next to me. I don't like anything about this man. He is tall and shifts around, trying to fit himself in. He is thin and I take this to result from a needless and self-righteous deprivation. His knuckles are red and raw, as if he farms with his bare hands. His hair is badly cut and his glasses are damaged and aggressively plain. We are both on our way to Africa. I explain that I visit poor countries and design projects for which we lend them money at concessionary rates. The projects are for the benefit of the poor. He calms his fidgeting and turns his coarsened face toward me, looking at me in a new and hungry way. "You are doing a great work," he says, and folds his hands as if this were a prayer.

I can't sleep on this flight, for the fury he put in me.

He says, in his book Sailing Alone Around the World—Captain Joshua Slocum says—that the waves rose high but he had a good ship. Still in the dismal fog he felt himself drifting into loneliness, an insect on a straw in the midst of the elements. He lashed the helm and his vessel held her course while he slept.

I've slept with Han but I've woken with Mireille, my own young wife. I can no longer hear the grinding of Han's teeth, like machinery in the night, and I've woken instead to the cool light touch of Mireille's slim remembered limbs, a hand laid across my heart, a face caught between my shoulder and my cheek. I lie quietly here because I don't want to wake her. Most of all I don't want her eyes to open and I don't want to see that slow, wide smile of trust and pleasure grow upon her face. Still, I steal a moment lying here—the blankets above me too thin for the mountain cold—to feel the touch and remember the warmth of love.

He loved Mireille, who, loving me, loved him. He trailed teasing jokes to her across his shoulder as he stumped into the kitchen to make a cup of tea. She laughed her light, reckless laughter, which belonged to no one. He hugged her strongly with old, clumsy arms; she hugged him strongly with slim, graceful ones.

There were times in the morning light when her smile was an absolute blessing, so that I had to leave her. Only Han was strong enough for the night, only Mireille light enough for dawn.

During those days a feeling of awe crept over Slocum. The ominous, the insignificant, the great, the small, the commonplace—all appeared before his mental vision in magical succession. Pages of his history were recalled which were so long forgotten that they seemed to belong to a previous existence. He heard all the voices of the past laughing, crying, telling what he had heard them tell in many corners of the earth.

There are so many doors in Tottenham, more doors than rooms, so I move—let me see—so I move with difficulty. Each door leads into the cold of the hall, each door with a patent draft-excluder which Dad buys each year from Woolworth's, each year different, once strips of felt with tacks, once soft rubber piping, once foam strips backed with adhesive. None of them effective, so that the edges of doors and windows are scarred with holes and stains, evidence of making do, of being certain of defeat. And each triumphant draft must be defended against again by high-backed chairs facing the fire, the fire glowing with the patent coke that we judge burns longest for the money. We camp here close to warmth in winter. The hallway is an arctic waste. We run to the kitchen. The best room is locked in cold till Sunday. The bathroom threatens your life. The bedroom should only be approached with a hot-water bottle.

But the mother loves the father and the father the mother as much as they love me and I love each of them. We are grubby and beleaguered, short of breath in the smoke, not too clear of vision.

From the cooler waters I let myself slide upward toward the burn of the sun, surprising the little fishes with my speed in ascent.

All the Japanese I know are inefficient. Morita, in Geneva, with his wavy hair and European ways and cowboy boots, is so excited by his life he's unable to deal with the paperwork. Yamada is too sick to be useful and has forgotten that form is supposed to have content. Akira hardly touches the world, hardly sleeps or dreams, only grabs at it. It's curious that all these Japanese are inefficient, not what is expected.

He said, he said . . . He said about swallowing that he gobbled like a turkey, the food wouldn't go down or up. He said my mother hit him on the back but it did no good. He said he was like a centipede which stops to consider which foot to put forward next and is forever immobilized. There's no reason why he should tell me this, that the life of duty done was inability, not choice or modesty. The untamed white hairs left on his head dance gaily in the last of the light.

And Slocum said that he never knew loneliness again while he sailed alone around the world, or through it. He said, "The acute pain of solitude experienced at first never returned. I had penetrated a mystery and by the way sailed through a fog." His ship's log read: "Fine weather, wind south-southwest. Porpoises gamboling all about."

. . .

It's hard to read here, hard to write, though I am well used to dashing off reports in uncomfortable locations. Slocum's book, which is now worn and is becoming bloated with the sea damp, is propped against the lounger's foot as talisman, and I've been trying to push my pen through Pakistan to no effect. My thoughts go to babies, my unexpected child, and then to pigs via the pinkness of them and some half-remembered nursery book of mine which pictured a piglet in a woman's arms, wrapped in an infant's blanket. The story escapes me. It is luxuriously hot and my muscles are luxuriously used. And I did not sleep well last night, kept awake, though not unhappily, by the jagged cough of the funny old man now staying in the cabin next to ours. I kept him company in a way.

I am wondering what the Large White pigs, imprisoned in their pens, think when they gaze out from their little satiated eyes at their miniature Ruatuan cousins. Do they recognize them as the same animal? I would guess so, since an attempt to cross-breed the two did not fail from lack of interest among the pigs but only because the local boars were not tall enough to reach. I imagine the big white sows to be envious of the little Ruatuans, who lie in the sun snuffling at dreams and who briefly scamper like cats when disturbed, free to go in the village where they please, owning the place, dapper in their hairy coats where the Large Whites are pinkly, fatly vulnerable. I imagine it to be tragic to be so large that you can't keep the insects off and so numbed with fat that you can't help, when you fall off the high heels of your trotters, to inadvertently squash to death your children, whom you were unable to perceive. I am being fanciful. A new thing.

Yesterday I was once again made a mateii. I am becoming more used now to sitting for hours on a mat with no support for my back. The old bunched stiffness of my spine has nearly gone, cured by the hours spent swimming. I have ceased, too, to be preoccupied with peering down the scooped and careless necklines of the maidens—are they really virgins, these girls, as tradition demands; how can the elders be sure?—when at each stage of the ceremony they come to kneel in front of me and offer rich smiles, food and cups of kava. Those smiles were strange to me at first since I could not identify their purpose; they contained neither fear nor calculation, neither invitation nor rejection. Now they have come to seem to exist just for themselves, a sort of confidence.

I have also become used to taking the gray strained extract of the kava root, as unappealing as the water wrung from washrags, to give a little to the earth, that is, to the wooden platform floors of the open-sided houses where we sit—there being no walls in these houses, no doors—and to drink the rest in a single draft. The taste is muddy but with that underlying bitterness common to caffeine and kola nuts, which lets you know a tougher magic is at work. Even so, its reputed narcotic effect does not seem to affect me in any way, at least if it does, it also fools that part of me which could notice it.

The speeches go on through the day, while food and drink are brought to me and money taken from me. Sometimes it is a young man who serves instead—I don't know why—and he performs his task with the essence of young manliness, just as the girl is perfect maidenhood. Where she moves gracefully, kneels slowly, and offers the kava with both hands, smiling up, he is all briskness, his bare torso taut and flat, advertising a favorable comparison with the surrounding circle of sitting elders with their piled bellies and breasts. He bends from the waist and offers the cup with one hand, the other held stiffly behind his back.

They are built, the people here, on a larger scale than other peoples; even the smaller ones have a largeness in them, an extra rise in the muscles of their calves, a completed roundness at the shoulders, as if God had said, there's space and plenty here in Polynesia, I'll put a little extra into man to match it. Perhaps it was the last place he filled, when he'd got the hang of things, when he found he'd been too economical and had ingredients to spare. Even Emo, who I love to see walk about her business as I lie here, and who is unusually slim for Ruatua, holds an extravagance in her: eyes larger than the norm, hair more abundant, cheeks higher and rounder, an athlete's profile to her thighs and buttocks, though she makes no effort.

The young men at the ceremony smile too, but unlike the maidens, there is some challenge in it or, if not challenge, then irony, or at least complicit mischief. It might be to say, welcome, but if you want the maidens you must account to us. It might be that or many things, because although yesterday was the seventh time I've been made a mateii on Ruatua, I still have no clear idea of the meaning of the two days of ritual. I have learned when to throw my kava stick into the middle of the floor with the rest of the men, and I have learned at which points I must make long responses in praise of Ruatua, the village, the hospitality, the gifts—someone usually translates, sometimes my message is only in the length and spirit of the speech; I have not yet learned the language, except for a few accidental words, preferring not to set myself against the tide of things with too much understanding.

Becoming a mateii in so many places is expensive, but I have the money. I realize, of course, that my popularity as mateii is partly due to this, and it is this that has allowed me to be given the position in seven villages when, I suspect, tradition dictates that a mateii should only represent the interests of one. I asked Emo if it was just for the money that they liked me, and she reproached me—though reproach is too strong a word, for Ruatuans do not easily fall to the abrasion of reproach. Emo only let me see a frowned dismay, a sadness for me that I was not quite with them. She said, "I suppose it could be seen that way . . . ," and turned away from me in calm preoccupation.

I am becoming suspicious of Slocum. He also visited the South Seas and in Samoa took kava with the village men, though he called it "ava." I now think he dwells too long on the charm of the maidens who served the drink, on the daughter of the chief, on the girls who visited his boat, or the ones who swam up to his dinghy and flirted with him by taking him in tow, or the ones who teased him with flattery of his manliness. Then he labors it by saying that it would be wrong to "mistake for overfamiliarity that which is intended to honor a guest." And he adds, with uncalled-for pomposity, "I was fortunate in my travels in the islands and saw nothing to shake one's faith in native virtue." I think it must be the gratuitousness of this that makes me suspicious.

While we lay in bed I read to Emo Slocum's appreciation of the girls and his prim disclaimers, inviting her opinion. "He's a guilty one," she said, then laughed and added, "Those girls were up to no good. I hope he did not disappoint them."

So I wonder now whether old Slocum was really as alone as he reports during his thousand days and nights of sailing alone around the world, or if there might not have been a woman here and there. The comfort I have taken in his manly independence and his certainty is a little undermined by this, though my suspicions might have to do with my own overfamiliarity with meretricious versions of the truth. But perhaps there could have been another book written by Yankee Joshua of other adventures that he had and the other preoccupations of his mind. Perhaps the hallucinations he suffered off the Azores had more in them than the pirate mariner he imagines piloting his boat and also contained lightly clad maidens, memories of women he had lost or those he had abandoned, tragedies of early loves or a mother's loveless hand, the whole clotted curse and blessing of it all, which set him out around the world alone, all Yankee crustiness, leaving only to return and then cursed to leave again until he was finally lost to a mid-Atlantic grave for no reason anyone has ever learned.

All the same, I have no evidence to set against him. Emo is not a simple island girl and her intuitions might not be sound. Indeed, I am now convinced, though at first I was not sure, that the girls who serve me kava with such open smiles are not meant for me.

Today I cannot find in me the right pinched tone to pick at

memory and keep it honest. I feel a suspect primness, kin to Slocum's, making me avoid a record of Han, though she still laced and mocked my thoughts in Pakistan. It leads my pen from the rigor of simplicity to the sin of omission and causes me instead to puzzle on my marriage to Mireille, which for reasons of neatness, for reasons of reestablishing for myself a place in things, I sometimes imagine reviving, resisting the knowledge that the easiness of those memories is due to their completion.

Also, the turbulence will not die down in me today, so that the sea calls me back and the distant boom of the Pacific on the reef is a promise of belonging. I think today I would rather swim than write, though I have not long returned to this chair. I am drawn each time to go farther and stay a little longer, so that I recently went out to the reef's most distant point, perhaps a mile from land. I was drawn on by the expanding beauty and sinister complexity of the deeper underwater landscapes, by the company of the larger fish that live there, by the mesmeric rhythms of my breathing and my kicking feet, the songs that sang in me. I knew I was going beyond prudence, beyond any physical capability for which there was evidence. No one knew where I swam, and I anyway doubted that a rescue might be effected in the little outrigger dugouts we keep pulled up on the beach. But I discovered, after I had let this knowledge into conscious thought and turned to look at Ruatua's smallness, that my growing fitness had outdistanced any tendency to death, so that I could not avoid my ability to swim the mile back to shore.

When I dragged myself out of the water, my limbs suddenly leaden without its buoyancy, Emo was there on the edge, wrapped in a red-flowered lavalava, letting the water lap over her, rolling slowly in it the way the Ruatuans do, holding our laughing child under his armpits, keeping his head clear.

"I thought you were swimming to England," she said. She told me to turn around, then told me, scolding, that it was as she suspected; I had swum too long and the sun had burned my back anew.

While I was out there, at the farthest point, I could feel a tug in the deepest, coldest water, out toward the reef, and I've been told today of the underwater break in it, a great, ornate coral archway connecting the lagoon with the ocean. There is great beauty there, they say, but the water sometimes rushes out with such force that everything living is carried with it, and outside the opening, sharks line up in tiers, keeping stationary against the current, waiting for food to be delivered to their mouths. I wish I had not been told this, since I cannot keep it from my mind. It calls out to the turbulence that remains in me, asks me questions about my courage, and informs me that there is somewhere farther that I might yet go.

LOWLANDS

It was a curious thing but I do not believe that there was one occasion in the next three days, during which we traveled to the city of Peshawar and then settled ourselves at the Pearl Continental Hotel, when I considered going to the PIA office to make a reservation for a flight to London that would take me to my father's funeral. The first day—occupied by the journey over the pass to the government rest house—was given a distracting energy by my argument with Akira. My bullying, the crude use of an authority I had acquired only shortly before, surprised even me. Usually I was more circumspect. This time I seemed to be determined to nail everything into place. I would allow no questions about the right way to do things. There would be no consideration of the aspects of the project that were hidden from us—the war, the opium, the corruption, the imaginative accounting, the unspoken objectives, the extra push we'd give a tottering ecology too complicated for us to comprehend. I absolutely would not let Akira raise awkward questions. I think there must have been a terror in me at this unsuspected innocence erupting from Akira's roughness—as inappropriate as human love expressed in the midst of battle—that led me to be so firm. My reaction was excessive, and it seems equally significant, in retrospect, that the disturbance of anger once begun could not be subdued even after it had prevailed. Inside I railed at the easiness of Akira's dangerous innocence, disregarding the way he had labored all night to find a consistent truth.

I did not show all this to Akira; instead I concealed my feelings. When the cars came, I made a point of sitting with him, although, with my new responsibility, it would have been more appropriate to join Yamada in the DC's jeep, which would stay with us to the limit of the administrative district. But I judged it important that the mission should not fly apart because of personal differences.

I said to Akira, "If you have any problems with what to do, let me know. We can work together."

He replied fiercely, "I'll do it!" but did not turn his head toward me.

"Thanks. I'm sorry for the wasted work." I touched his shoulder briefly but firmly. There was no reaction. His muscles felt very hard beneath the jacket.

It might have been during the convoy's long, slow haul up the pass, or perhaps it was later—I can't be absolutely sure—that this fury at Akira's ingenuousness conjured up in me an occasion when I had also sided with robust worldliness against those concerned with a more fragile understanding. The words I remembered saying I had said more than once, but the time I best remembered saying them was a dinner party in Reston. I recalled everything about the occasion—the names, the conversation—though I had not thought of it for years. Later it came to seem that it had marked the time our marriage began to end. It was an occasion of loss and during the next days, while I did not directly face the decision of whether or not to visit the PIA booking office, it was this unconsidered loss of Mireille rather than thoughts of my father which turned in my mind and prevented me from thinking further. Like Akira's ingenuous insistence on a simple truth, it irritated me, a nag that said, look at this, look at it straight.

I remembered saying at the dinner party that for people like me, people with ordinary backgrounds—did they know, by the way, that my father was a milkman in London?—all this psychiatry, this digging around in childhoods, was so much nonsense. In a family like ours you simply had to get along. There was no way out; you just had to get on with it. The husband had to be a husband, the wife a wife, and so on. No doubt my parents had their problems like everyone else but you'd never hear them talk about them. Especially not to a child; that would be a selfish thing to do, the giving of a burden. And to people like us, no-nonsense, modest people, divorce was something that wasn't even considered, just another indulgence of the wealthy. I had enjoyed being a barbarian at the dinner table.

There was an edge that night. Mireille had just told the company, without first telling me, that she was visiting a psychotherapist. I think it was the first night that we were both at home in Reston and did not sleep together.

We had discovered through trial and error that it was not good practice to invite my friends from the World Bank or Mireille's friends from the French Embassy to the same dinner parties as ordinary Americans who were not concerned with international affairs. Inevitably conversation would turn toward inside knowledge of events in obscure countries or the politics of international finance, and guests unfamiliar with these subjects would either recklessly forward their own uninformed opinions or would be reduced to an audience.

Because of this policy of separation we had neglected for too long to return the invitations of our neighbors and had begun to sense their reproaches. There was the suggestion built into Reston, with its community club, strategically distributed tennis courts and carefully arranged housing clusters, that neighbors should be neighborly. Mireille had never liked this suburban obligation but the neighbors had been pleasant enough, and since our house was one of a small secluded group of Reston's more expensive home types, the pressure was hard to ignore. And Mireille's lively manner had misled them; both Fred Barkin on one side and Dan Sondergaard on the other had separately complimented me on her Gallic charm.

We decided to clear the slate by inviting the Barkins and the Sondergaards at the same time, even though they already knew each other well. Dan was a doctor in his late thirties whose wife, Amy, stayed at home with their three children, though I believe she had a Ph.D. in literature. She was younger and had the youthful habit, I had noticed, of spending her days at home dressed only in a T-shirt and socks. Fred and Irene were older and childless, and there was a hint in Fred's face that he must have done something more bruising before arriving at his present job of systems analyst with a defense contractor. Irene was working up her own real estate agency and always volunteered too quickly that it was doing well. We had little in common with either couple and friendships never developed. The evening was a curiosity, and it remains curious that my memory should leapfrog years of forgetting to keep its names and detail.

During dinner, between compliments on Mireille's cooking and an almost awed discussion which followed the discovery that the wine came from Mireille's family vineyard and that the picture on the label was her family château, we cast around for subjects. Mireille made a light comment about a recent faux pas of Ronald Reagan, only to discover that Dan was an unexpectedly pious conservative. A skirmish on the heartlessness of American health care was abandoned for the same reason. I shifted the conversation on to Irene's real estate and then on to computers, which Fred deflected in favor of the instinctive skills displayed in John McEnroe's tennis game, which was currently in the news. Amy remained detached, perhaps sulky, giving my inquiry about the children the shortest of answers: "They're fine." There was a tension between her and Dan and I wondered if this was responsible for his dogmatic manner. I remembered Amy drifting past their living room window in socks and underwear.

Mireille said, apropos of John McEnroe, "But Fred, don't

you think there's something wrong with him? I mean his behavior—he seems mentally unstable. I don't like to watch him. I keep hoping someone will lead him away for psychiatric treatment."

Fred shook his head and started to say something about the special conditions at the cutting edge of ability, when Amy broke in. "I go to a psychiatrist."

Dan gave her a fierce and exasperated look, so that Irene moved in to say, "Doesn't everyone? I've been going to a psychotherapist for years. I practically support her single-handed."

The conversation missed a beat while several of us hesitated. Then Irene said, "Fred has a psychotherapist too, don't you, darling. Of course, being a man, he doesn't like to admit it."

"No, I'm not ashamed of it. I've found it helpful. Are you a new convert, Amy?"

"I'm a traitor. Dan doesn't believe in them."

"It's not that I don't believe in them. It's just that I don't think you need one."

"Well, that's the problem, isn't it? You decide what I need and don't need."

"There! That's exactly my objection. The psychiatric profession panders to its clients and lets them blame everyone else for their problems. Amy hasn't stopped being angry at me since she started."

"I go to one too," said Mireille, talking toward her wineglass, then glancing up at me. I leaned back, masking my shock. "I've discovered things about myself I never would have guessed. The way my father treated me as a child. My goodness! He was a monster. So unfeeling. I did not realize how I hated him. And you repeat the same pattern all your life if you're not careful. I think that's why therapy is helpful—it helps you stop repeating your mistakes."

I don't know if I understood then the sting in this, its implied accusation of cruelty, but there was enough defiance in her words to lead me to side with Dan. That's when I said psychiatry was for the useless rich, as was divorce, and that it wasn't for the useful down-to-earth like me, like my mum and dad.

I took my eyes off Mireille, who had tightened her lips and was reaching for Irene's plate, and passed them over Amy, who for no good reason I imagined might be impressed by my assertiveness, and arrived at Dan. "Don't you agree, Dan?"

He looked at me oddly. "Well, I'd certainly go some of the way with you."

"And another thing—it's difficult to put your finger on it—but it saps your energy. Maybe it's all that buried stuff from childhood, all those neuroses, that give you energy. When you're poor you need all the energy you can get just to work your way up. If you're rich, of course, you can afford to sit around thinking about the meaning of things."

I was willfully crude. It was not the first time I had boasted of my modest family background in company, but it was the first time I had used it against Mireille. Irene saw the danger and again took things in hand, to say lightly that the only thing that bothered her was the number of therapists who ended up in bed with their clients. And did we know that this was how the Delaneys had met? Did we know the Delaneys? Down by the nursery school?

For the remainder of the evening, which ended early, Mireille made a competent contribution to the conversation—those generations of good breeding—but addressed none of it to me.

Later, after the guests had left—Amy refusing to catch my eye for a goodbye—after she had changed into her nightdress, Mireille came and stood over me in the bedroom, looking down on where I was stretched out, still in my clothes. She said, "I don't want to be next to you tonight. You were 'orrible." I could see tears.

"Come on, I didn't mean anything."

"I don't know 'ow to live in this hawful place."

"Hawful?"

"Don't make fun of me. It's because of you I need a psychiatrist."

"Therapist."

"And this place. It 'as no 'heart! All I do is wait. I thought we would travel together. Help people."

"It doesn't work like that. What could you do?"

"Nothing. I can't do anything."

She walked out. Probably we had all drunk too much, because I did not bother to follow her.

While all this went on in me, puzzling me and unaccountably asking for my attention, weaving itself in with my subsiding anger at Akira, we slowly made our way up toward the summit of the pass. The town in the valley was easily made to disappear by the folds in the landscape and by the accidental camouflage of soil worked into its flat roofs for winter insulation. We went through a band of government forest and emerged into the baldness of high mountains and newly fallen snow. There was a comforting steadiness in the grind of our first-gear progress around the hairpins. Akira's head, which had been facing straight ahead in its determination to avoid my eyes, fell forward onto his chest, and he immediately began to snore. I remembered that our statistics recorded an incidence of yaks in the high villages, and I looked around for them, or habitation, but found neither.

The vehicles from the next administrative district were waiting at the summit of the pass, proof that the journey could be completed. After we had hurried through the cold from one group of vehicles to the other, the DC came over—underdressed for the weather: that false military bravado again—to shake hands. I waited for him to mention the tunnel, which must have been on his mind, and I was gratified that he did not. He said, smiling, "Tell Peshawar how we managed to get you out, in spite . . ." He gestured at the snow-laden peaks still above us.

I said, "I'll mention the support you gave us." I was formal.

This time I chose a vehicle on my own, leaving Akira to go

with Yamada, and although I had some slight anxiety about the two Japanese conspiring against me, I welcomed the solitude. The government driver was fortunately not one of those determined to assert his equal worth by making conversation, and the downhill road flowed past like film. After the snow ended, the slope flattened out and the road picked up other traffic. The driver turned off the heater and, not long after, turned on the air conditioner. Forest turned to green pasture and then to sandy flatlands, with noisy market towns pressed up against the highway. Once we had to stop for a camel train to slope its way across the road on a route more ancient than our own. The laden camels looked at us out of the corners of their eyes but could not hurry. I stepped outside my thoughts of Mireille for long enough to note that in three hours, going from the mountains to the down areas, we had gone from yaks to camels. It was just one of those things that had to be accepted.

The inquiry that was assembling itself in me asked whether it had been as I had asserted in Reston: that in Tottenham we had been so simply solid, so good-sense, no-nonsense in our stability, so much wiser than those who held up the thinness of their lives to the testing flame of authentic love. This simple old idea of my father's life did not sit well with the summing up of death, but I could not see the irritant then or recognize how it kept me from return.

He had loved Mireille, and I had always imagined he would not like Han, though I had never put it to the test. He was a prudish man, attentive to his duties, and the story I made for myself of my estrangement from Mireille was, by contrast, one of triumphant self-assertion. This official story—the one I gave the people I knew and, before the pressure of memory was in me, had also done for me—was that I had encountered a sexy younger woman; my head was turned; at forty I'd gone off the rails. It was an age-old story, one everyone could buy.

"Chinese," I had said significantly to a curious mission colleague who had once met Mireille and liked her, as if this would explain everything. I cultivated the habit of looking rueful, like an old fool who should have known better but who you had to admire for being such a dog, being so susceptible to special Oriental skills, taking such risks with his life.

For women I shaded it differently, suggesting a helplessness in the face of feminine wiles. I mentioned to one listener that the woman I had become involved with had, it turned out, once been a high-class tart and I was satisfied with the response: "Sounds like a real homebreaker."

Now I was made to see I had been ready. Perhaps the most blame I could give to Han was that she had perfect timing. By the time Han introduced herself, Mireille had long set out on her irresolute steps to make her own life in Reston, achieving a distance without any sign of an arrival. First she had taken a job in a dress shop, coarsely offered to her by a local woman, "Because you're French and you've got class." But it distressed her to serve, not so much because she was unwilling as because the distance from her origins was too long a stretch for her self-confidence. Later she joined a women's group suggested by her therapist and tried to feel she shared the concerns of the American wives. She offered French lessons at home, but the students who answered her advertisement were all air force officers who leered at her and annoyed her because: "They have to tell me their childish ideas about the world. As if they think they have God's wisdom and it is up to them to tell the rest of us. My father was an officer in Vietnam when they were babies!"

At some point during those years she stopped meeting me at Dulles Airport on my returns from missions, which for reasons inaccessible to me was the withdrawal that hurt most. It is possible she started to drink more—I was not at home much. Certainly she became less careful of her dress. She was less tender to me, and I told myself not to be surprised; I could never please her parents, why should I hope for more from her? She spent more and more of her time with smart French friends in the city, and soon after I met Han and traveled more, she made a prolonged visit to France. It was supposed to be because of her mother's health, but now I wonder if it might not have been for her own. Her mother is, I believe, still alive. They were discreet, her family; it's just the way they would have handled failure. This was the thought that nagged at me: that I had extracted Mireille from the life for which she was prepared, and then I'd driven her to despair. But at the time I had hardly noticed, and on the day when Han came uninvited into my office, I had once again spent the night separate from Mireille following a bad-tempered evening.

This time it was a dinner at the Georgetown house of Mireille's cousin Philippe, where everything that had come to trouble me was present. During that evening I had become more than usually irritated by the superior manner of Philippe's embassy guests and Mireille's vocal admiration for the house with its old furniture, venerable Persian rugs, and dark paintings. I had talked too much, and I suspected that Mireille had seen before me, from the small smiles of the Frenchmen, that I was being used. While they pressed for indiscretions about World Bank policy toward Francophone West Africa, their smiles suggested that they thought: This man's only an employee with useful information; we represent a country. They thought, while their wives tried out on me the tired stimulation of their décolletages: This man is overreaching himself trying to impress us; he does not have the position for these opinions; he's passing off corridor gossip as knowledge; he's a salaryman; we must check later with someone on our level.

After more than ten years of Mireille's family, I was confident in my reading of their thoughts. They had not wanted me in the beginning and it had gradually set in as a permanent thorn that whatever I achieved they would never want me. In the beginning, when they saw the danger of me, they had gone so far as to hastily arrange an alternative marriage for Mireille. The baron had conferred with another man of position, and a son had been interviewed. On a visit home, Mireille was brought together with the young man at a garden party, and when she did not immediately take the bait, the offer became increasingly overt, with talk of the money and the life Mireille would have compared to the misery she would find with me should she displease her family. She returned to Massachusetts in distress, and I felt barely succeeded in returning.

Her family's wish for coherence had been stronger than its wish to punish Mireille, and I had been tolerated. On our visits to the family homes, Mireille had been conspicuously loyal to me, just as she was energetically affectionate when we visited Mafeking Road. All the same, she could not conceal from me that even though I was more educated than her brothers and cousins, cleverer, I could never be considered equal. Education was, to her family, a ticket the ordinary could buy, which qualified them to travel but only on certain lines and for a limited distance. And a job was a sort of submission, something shameful. I could never win the right, whatever my achievements, to sit as Mireille's parents did under an umbrella at grape harvest and set the price for grapes and grape pickers and have everyone accept without dispute because it had always been so. Even if I turned to business, became a millionaire, and bought a château to outshine theirs, I would never, in their eyes, own a château. Nor could I own land, at least not in Europe, though they had a silly innocence about America, as if they found in it a flattering equality, as a hunter might flatter the strength and cunning of a wild boar—something crude equal to their cunning.

Though Mireille had been loyal, I increasingly tried out in my mind the idea of us as separate beings with separate fates. I had expected her to raise me up, lift me with her into the ruling classes that had so awed my parents. Instead, as the years passed and my professional confidence increased, I found Mireille's family to be a reminder of inferiority, which worked against the satisfactions of success. A mood of defiant self-assertiveness had grown in me, and it had been the unexpected expression of this mood that led me to humiliate Mireille at the dinner party where she first revealed her need for psychotherapy.

The breach had never closed. In the months that followed, she began to use on me the quick, bright smile—too much part of her to be called false—that she used to secure goodwill from waiters and shop assistants. I think she meant well. The smile effortlessly informed the serving classes that she was congenial and charming and that her anxiety was that they might try too hard to please her, not too little. I never told her, though I became increasingly conscious of it, how it irritated me that no matter how expensively I was suited, or how authoritative I had been in the meeting I'd just left, no matter how many millions had been my concern, the waiters always sought her eyes, not mine, and always checked for her concurrence in my decisions.

There had been a time when a passing touch was enough to close the distance between us, or she would do it with her laughter, which was everything in her that had not been tamed. But now she relied on the quick bright smile, and I refused to see that it was only because she no longer had the confidence that she had my love.

We no longer made love. I had quite suddenly lost interest, and when I tried, for reasons of policy, to overcome my indifference, the results were unsatisfactory. I could not explain it. Mireille was as pretty now as she had been when we met. Perhaps she was now more handsome than pretty, more of a madame, but she was still shapely and chic. She could still hold a good conversation.

I wondered whether there had been a time, when she was on the edge of womanhood, when her mother—a woman who knew exactly how to act—had taken her aside and instructed her on how to remain fascinating to a man. In over ten years of marriage, I had not seen her on a toilet seat. She kept the details of our contraception—we had postponed decisions about children—from me. She undressed in the bathroom and had a stock of hand-sewn nightdresses which were in themselves beautiful things, intriguing to touch and watch. These she always wore to bed, where we made love in the dark, or with only a low light, the nightdresses rucked up but never removed. In all the years, she had never spread her legs wide. She held me tenderly, and if I became too vigorous, she whispered, *"Doucement, doucement."* At first I had loved the slow delicacy, preferring it to the thoroughness of my American divorcée lover and the clumsiness of English girls. It suggested something fragile and secret. Then it was suddenly lost. I suddenly doubted whether there was any secret worth the repeated effort. I became bored.

I believe it must have hurt her that we made love less, but she had no words to speak of it. Instead the frequency of her phone calls to relatives at the French Embassy increased, as did the bright smiles, which nevertheless had insufficient wattage to cross the distance between us. We attended more dinners with diplomats. I was asked about Chile and China, and Mireille started subsidiary conversations in French, from which her old bubbling laughter sometimes escaped like a memory.

In the car on the drive home from the Georgetown dinner, I was at first silent and I don't think Mireille noticed the silence or the black mood it represented, this insensitivity itself further justification for my mood. When she spoke she said the wrong things: first that I was driving too fast after the drink I'd taken, then didn't I think the Georgetown house was beautiful?

"Not really. I'm not impressed by that sort of thing."

"Oh, Bill, come on. It's lovely. Did you see the Persian carpets? You have to be blind not to see they are beautiful. And the furniture."

"It's not to my taste, this worshiping of the past. It's just something rich people buy to give themselves a substance they don't personally possess."

"Don't be stupid. It doesn't matter who owns them; these things are beautiful. It's wonderful just to have them around you."

"I prefer our home."

Now Mireille did laugh. "Our wooden box? Please, Bill. It's a nice house, but that's all. In fifty years it will be gone. Sometimes you are ridiculous."

It was not said without affection but I was in no mood for

condescension. I did like our house. I liked the fitted carpets which let me walk barefoot everywhere. I liked the light coming through the windows overlooking the deck. I liked the absence of doors and the large spaces; our living area alone was the size of my parents' house in Tottenham. Where my parents had six tiny rooms and more doors, countless fussy walls, we had only space. I even liked our bamboo-framed couch, which Mireille despised. She praised the house for its plumbing and its heating, but her feet had hardly touched it. She smiled at neighbors but took nothing from them. Only the few things from her parents' homes—an old print, a sewing box, heavy hand-painted china—provided a gravity for her.

I made an argument of it. If she did not like our home, we were not together. I would sleep alone. To hell with her. I left her, and above the sadness of it, the sight of Mireille's tears, I was happy. I liked the way I could spend the night on the couch in my clothes without feeling the cold. It was all right. I liked the way I would wake up with the morning light to look down on trees. At seven next morning I slid open the glass door to the October air and heard the birds at our feeder.

I loved the shower too, turning it up to high pressure—no more soapy European baths. There was nothing musty, old-regime, old-blood, about it. I was getting up, getting on. I let Mireille sleep, forgot her. I made strong coffee and filled a mug, which I put inside a foam insulator with a crass University of Virginia logo on it. I took a clean shirt, clean underwear, dressed, picked up my briefcase, took the coffee to the car. I was moving along. Uncharacteristically, I turned the radio to a rock station. It wasn't so bad to have a desk to go to, on a high floor, to have smart Louise in the outer office, not so bad to know what you're doing in the world, to have a big world to do it in. Not so bad to be here from being a milkman's son. I was ready to be impressive, tired of trying to impress.

And this did lead to Han. I still had in me by the end of the day something of the vigor and energy of the morning's new start. I worked late, postponing my return home, hanging on to the mood, though there was nowhere else to go but back.

Louise had said good night, the cleaner had looked in and left. My suit jacket was over the back of the chair, my tie, I remember, was silk, blue with red dots, purchased on Thai Air. I was coming to terms with the wretched inevitability of return. I had gone as far as I could go. My desk was clean except for a short stack of files. I was only just all right.

"Scuse me."

"Yes?"

She was Chinese, bespectacled, trim. She was not, I guessed, a secretary, because of the gray business suit and the cream silk blouse. Not general admin either, since the suit was too well tailored and that hair fell across her face in the casual way of an expensive cat. Not professional staff, I thought, because there had been a tentative knock at my open door as she walked in, and now she did feel the need to give a winning smile. She was, I correctly guessed, one of those women who inhabit the insecure no-man's-land between support staff and professionals: statistical assistants, report editors, technical translators—women neurotic with their uncertain status and short-term contracts.

"All right if I interrupt you for a minute?"

"Sure. What can I do for you?"

"You're Dr. Bender, right?"

"Bill Bender."

"I'm Han. I work for Coburn. Off and on."

As she talked, she approached the desk with a purposefulness that contradicted the impression of hesitancy in her speech. She kept her smile, but it shifted a little sideways to seem ironic, as if to say: We both know this is bullshit, right? I leaned back, ready to enjoy both her nervousness and her determination, aware of an energy in her, an availability.

"You're . . . on his professional staff?"

"Not exactly. I'm a statistical assistant right now. I'm over-qualified, though."

"Yes. I see. And how can I help you, Han. Han?"

"Yeah, Han. Well, they call me Hannah sometimes. Used to call me Honey, but that's a different story."

"But you prefer Han."

"Whatever you like. It doesn't matter." There was a wonderful carelessness in that, like giving herself away.

She had reached my desk, and the real nervousness was gone, or changed, so that it was more like a show of nervousness, a playful submissiveness combined with confidence.

"Why don't you sit down."

"No, it's OK. I like to fidget. Look, I'm looking for some help. I'm stuck in catch-22. I know I'm good, but they won't let me move up to professional staff until I have third world experience. Like I wasn't born there. But because I'm only a statistical assistant, I can't get overseas assignments to get the experience. At least I can't with Coburn. Crazy, right?"

"You want to get yourself promoted."

"You got it. I've always had to fight to get anywhere. Little Oriental girl, right? You can help me if you want."

"How do you see that?"

"You can take a statistical assistant on overseas trips with you if you want."

"I never have."

"Well, you can. I checked your grade and the rulebook."

"And you want me to take you?"

"Why not?" A shrug. "I'm good. Ask Coburn. I'm no trouble."

I looked at her and bet she was good. She was pretty, sharp, looked about twenty, was older. I thought I deserved her.

"Well, it's an idea. I could use some help. But I'll have to look into it."

"Colombia. That's your next trip. You're going on your own. Project supervision."

"You're well informed. We've never met before, have we?"

"I've seen you. I told you, I'm efficient."

"And why me? Why not Folger, say."

She looked up at the ceiling, looked down at me. That ironic smile again. "Folger's fat."

And she was right for me, I thought, after I had reorganized my work so that we could go everywhere together. She was a fighter too; she had come from the bottom against the odds. We could be a team. She had no family she still spoke to for me to please. For the posh who so impressed my parents she had, when she wasn't using them, a rude gesture. She was intelligent, knew the work, went straight to the point. Unlike genteel Mireille, she was most at ease naked, her knees fallen apart; she liked it in the light, in dangerous places. She had an energy, a hunger; we were formidable. My father, I felt sure, would sense the wantonness in her, the absence of niceness, and be appalled. I liked that too, the break of it, the shedding of all that slavish fear, respect for betters, all that settling for half a loaf. She didn't ask me to be dutiful, didn't claim my obedience with hers; she only invited me to take her on. Or so it seemed to me.

I had said in my office that night, playing to her script, "And what will you do for me?" She had played it mock Chinese, pulling her schoolgirl glasses down her nose with a calculated winsomeness: "Suk yor kok?" She had me then. I was lost then.

The government rest house was set in a softer, hilly landscape and I found in its arrangement and atmosphere a sense of England, and also the familiar, awkward sense that I ought to feel at home but did not. With an eye to coziness and comfort, the bungalow was built on the grassy banks of a wide, shallow river at a point where round hills protected it from the weather. I could imagine a young colonial officer wading in the water, casting and recasting his line, one of those confident types who combined personal gentleness with a firm hand toward the natives. The two old servants had been there since those days and the food they served that night was the old colonial food: dry roast meat, stewed vegetables, potatoes. Yamada and Akira made ineffectual passes at their plates and muttered in Japanese. I ate so as not to offend the servants.

Akira was characteristically quiet during dinner and I also was not in the mood for conversation. There was still tension between us and I could see Yamada taking in this situation and marshaling his energy to take responsibility for it. I wished he would not; the livelier he made his talk, the more I was aware of the cost to him, so that I tried, in spite of my distracted state of mind and the nagging pain in my abdomen, to respond to his forced animation. I wanted to tell him that it was all right, better for all of us, if he relaxed his instinct for diplomacy and let things go, but a Japanese silence at the dinner table offended his cosmopolitan pride.

He chose to talk of home. He said that once he had finished with the responsibilities of the mission, there were equally pressing responsibilities waiting for him in Japan.

"When you are old and you have position, there are some things which you have to do. As soon as I return, my wife will have a long line of couples ready for matchmaking. You know what this is?"

"You arrange marriages?"

"Yes. I know you Europeans don't. It is not exactly arranged. It is more like a negotiation between the interested parties. Not so different from international negotiations."

"Some Europeans still do it. The upper classes. They tried to arrange my wife's. She's French."

"I didn't know that. That's interesting."

I made an effort to involve Akira—"Was your marriage arranged?"—but he only looked down and made the familiar abrupt, effacing, dismissive gesture.

"Well, it's a bit the same in Japan. It is because I am related to the emperor that we have to do it. And because of my associations. My wife loves it, and I must give her that."

He described the delicacy of the process. Young men and young women were invited separately to his home without the true purpose of their visits ever being stated. Everything was deniable. Without directly questioning them, he learned of their qualities and prospects. He put them at their ease so that they forgot the unspoken purpose of their visits. It was the same skill, I noted, that he had used to charm me so that I would not notice that I was doing his work. Then there was the entertainment of the couple's parents and the subtle exploration of the material conditions for the marriage. Finally the young people were introduced and were made to feel that none of this had happened, that everything could be for love.

"I don't like it, of course. It takes too much time, and I would rather be working. But my wife will have my schedule for me when I step off the plane, and I have to play my part. And a powerful man cannot refuse to listen to me when I have arranged his daughter's marriage, or his son's career. Family is as important as work in its way. You should remember that, Will. You need a family and a professional institution behind you. Maybe you can do without both now, but when you are older you need position to have a role. You have to take responsibility, Will."

I did think then of my father and his old age. He had a family, but neither his wife nor his son had asked his opinion or permission. He had no influence. His employer had shed him and it seemed he had finally shed the church. Yet it struck me in passing, as a completely novel thought, that there had been something wise about him toward the end, which I had not acknowledged. Perhaps there had even been, in his odd confidences, an unspoken invitation to confide, which I had refused to recognize.

Yamada, watching me in thought, took my silence to be consideration of his words, an acceptance of their force. "Will, you should not be traveling around like this. One day this organization, the next another. Why did you leave the World Bank? I want you to give me your résumé. I can find you a serious position. In the Asian Development Bank maybe. A man can have a wonderful life in Manila."

"Thanks. That's very flattering." But the offer made me uncomfortable, a patronage that put me at a disadvantage. And I recognized my own ploy of collecting obligations by offering future rewards that need never be honored. Or perhaps it was that the offer was too much like adoption and my distaste was a rush of loyalty toward my powerless father.

A great tiredness swept over me at the dinner table, like a sea that could no longer be resisted by coastal defenses. The world was too large, too complicated, and my attachment to any place too slight. As I struggled to respond to Yamada I lost my way in midsentence, my eyelids fell and the muscles holding me upright in the chair withdrew their support, so that it was only with the greatest effort that I prevented myself from falling to the floor. The act of falling itself seemed suddenly attractive, and I visualized myself falling indefinitely, comfortably curled, with no danger of impact.

"Will, what is the matter? You have gone white." I heard the alarm in Yamada's voice and saw him signal to Akira from far away across the table. Akira stood and came to support me with a firm hold on my arm, which I leaned into.

"It's OK. I just felt tired all of a sudden. I think I'll go to bed."

I heaved myself dizzily upright, Akira still supporting me with his farmer's hands. I was enjoying the touch, but I said, "It's OK, Akira. I can walk. Thanks, though."

Whatever it was that had been breached over dinner in the colonial rest house continued to insist on sleep, not consciousness. I slept on the next day's drive south to Peshawar and arrived at the Pearl Continental Hotel in the same dozy state, only concerned to find a room and a bed.

Peshawar, we learned, was being subjected to a terrorist bombing campaign connected with the Afghan war, and the hotel, the best in the city, had few guests. An instinct for separation led the three of us to take rooms in three different parts of the hotel, mine on the top floor, overlooking the swimming pool. My tiredness was greater than could be explained by work and travel, and it occurred to me that it might be connected with the aching pain that now spread around my waist from the right side. I imagined an infected organ, the poison seeping into my body cavity and my immune defenses draining my energy in their attempts to combat it. At the reception desk I asked one of the slim, smart young men about a doctor, and he told me with an enthusiasm I found suspicious that a doctor could be arranged, there was one he knew who was much favored by Europeans.

I hesitated, then said, "OK, will you ask him to come sometime tomorrow? I'll be in my room."

I was bound to pay his bill myself. Though I was entitled to claim medical expenses, I knew it would be better not to do so. Consultants who fell sick were considered troublesome, and it was preferable to maintain an impression of invulnerability. There was a general feeling that sickness proved an incapacity to deal with the stress of international work, or at least an unprofessionalism in coping with the health hazards of third world places. I went to my room to rest, grateful that there was not yet a schedule of meetings.

Inside, I went quickly to the window and closed the curtains, although it was still afternoon. There was a glimpse of the shining blue of the swimming pool and a few white bodies lying in the shade. The water was undisturbed; no one swam. A comic-opera guard with a fierce mustache and a long old rifle stood watch. The white bodies struck me as dead, obscene, after all the trouble the local women took to cover everything. Later I learned that the guard had been introduced recently after a Muslim radical had shot to death a British volunteer nurse sunbathing there. In any case, the view was all too light and open; I wanted to be enclosed.

After I had excluded the last chink of sunlight, I hung the Do Not Disturb sign on my door, double-locked it, and prowled to check that I had everything I needed—a clean bathroom, soft drinks in the minibar, a properly functioning air conditioner. Then I turned on the in-house video without consulting the movie listings, removed my shoes, loosened my clothing, and lay back on the wide bed's pile of pillows, with the relief of making safety. The colors of the movie flickered around the room like a fire in the hearth and I was grateful for that, the way the color and motion drained away the pressure from my mind.

With that I could at last attend the nagging pain in me. I wondered how I would describe it to the doctor, or to Yamada, and there may have been in this rehearsal a suspicion that the pain could not be easily justified. It was always there but it moved and changed. Once sharp and concentrated in my right side just below the waist, it had extended itself leftward, but in expanding, it had been diminished in intensity. Now it seemed to have burrowed deeper, to the center of me, consolidating itself, yet I fancied that the slightest pressure on the surface of my stomach would be unbearable. On one occasion I had bent down too quickly and a sharp thrust of pain had curved its way up from my abdomen and along the inside of my spine. It would be difficult for a doctor to make sense of all this.

I believe that among the hotel's movies there was a *Rocky* film, perhaps more than one. There were also a number of American romantic dramas. Of course there would have been no sex left in; not even touching. I watched whole films and then, immediately afterward, I found myself unable to recall anything I had seen. My mind was active too, but as with the films, there were long periods when the events in it were lost to me, never captured by the part of me that ordered things. Among the inner nag of pain, the outer stimulation of American films, and the rush of unconsidered memory, the quiet closed room was wildly busy.

Maybe he would have liked her. There was one of those puzzling memories of him from his last years. It was so separate from the idea I held of the man who was being cremated in Tottenham that the thought of it did not lead me to thoughts of going home. The idea was of a timid, prudish, churchgoing man, but this late memory was full of vulgarity. My mother had said the medication changed him, and at the time I had left it at that.

He asked as soon as I entered his cramped bedroom, "Hey, have you heard this, son?" and he extracted his hand from underneath the blanket to show me the tiny radio he held there, its volume set so low that at first I had not heard it. The program was a commercial radio phone-in and I had to bend near to him to make out what was being said.

"No; what is it?" I had not heard British commercial radio in years.

"Listen."

An inarticulate young man was earnestly describing the problem he had with dates, when the excitement of a girl's proximity led him to ejaculate even before the foreplay was completed. Dad laughed, and I looked up at him, surprised at both him and England.

I went to speak, but he stopped me with a confiding smile and a finger, while the program's host replied: "Lots of men have this problem. Some people find it best to masturbate before they go out. Takes the pressure off, if you see what I mean."

The caller hesitated, then said, "You mean have a wank?"

"Precisely. In the vernacular."

"What?"

"Never mind. Have a wank and take the pressure off. Problem solved. Next caller."

My father switched off the radio with a small, practiced movement of his index finger. "You wouldn't believe the things they say here, son. Things we never even said to our best friends in my day. Well, maybe you'd believe it. With your life."

Again there was a hint that we were disconnected, our lives so different that I was exempt from his limitations. Or was it that he guessed at Han and sensed the sort of trouble I was in?

He continued, "There was one bloke the other day who thought you had to do it in the tummy button to get a girl pregnant. Where do they find these people? And there was a girl who said her boyfriend had never done it properly, only, you know, up the bottom."

Again he laughed at the wonder of it. I was unable to find a reply—I was embarrassed—but he did not seem to need a reply, so delighted was he at his discovery of a new wacky world out there, one so outside his old rules. It was as if illness had exempted him from responsibility and given him a freedom. I was shocked, and even resentful, to find, after all I'd risked, that the cramp of disapproval was in me, not him.

"Here, son, have you read this?"

I took the library book but did not recognize the author's name. I looked at the back of the dust jacket and saw that the reviews were respectful and came from the quality press. I did not remember him reading books, and I felt myself surprised again and reluctant to know more.

"Damn good, he is. Only a young chap. Colored fellow. Just won a big book prize."

There were too many questions raised by this: the wide interests, the liberality on race, the intellectual level—all unexpected. I did not want to pursue it. I suspected a spuriousness in this appreciation of things beyond me. It did not fit with the timid, uneducated, local man; there was no context for it and I pushed it aside.

I had put the book back on the crowded bedside table. "I don't get much chance to read books. Too many reports. Anyway, Dad, how are you?"

Oddly, for a sick man, he had to consider this question. "I'm all right, son. Not bad for an old'un. Still life in the old dog yet." He glanced at the array of medicine containers. "Course, if I move about, I rattle."

We talked for another ten minutes and I told him the bare bones of my news: my resignation from the Bank to be an independent consultant—no mention of Han—the countries I'd gone to, the ones I was going to. His spirits dampened as he listened, so that he lost his sparkle and looked at me in what might have been a disappointed way. I told myself I had brought him down to a balanced normality from a drugged intoxication, but perhaps he had only been happy.

Maybe he had guessed about Han. Maybe this had been his way of saying he was more broad-minded than I thought. Maybe he had wanted to draw me closer and for us to talk of women.

Once I had asked my mother whether the marriage was a happy one. It was the only one I knew, and at seventeen, with my first serious girlfriend, I felt a sudden urgency to know. She was caught by surprise and stepped back from me and away, as if I had threatened her with a blow. Her eyes on her work, she replied, "Of course," and it came out sharp. After a silence, she added, "In our day you had to settle for what you could get. You had to make the best of it."

It was less than a declaration of love, but it was more than I had learned from my father. I could not have asked him the question. There had been a privacy about him, something hidden or protected, perhaps vulnerable, which signaled that curiosity would be assault. We kept to the safe areas, as narrow as cliff paths, which included football, the garden, boy scouts, the maintenance of the fabric of the house. He was a quiet man. Personal life, politics, his working life, even religion, were marked as dangerous. His Sunday talks were kept harmless by their vagueness, so that divination of the man from them was difficult. I could not say whether or not his marriage could be called happy, or his life. Or whether he would have been able to understand the lonely, stretched confusion of mine. He had never offered advice, so that it might have been that he felt he'd got it wrong himself, or it might have been that he regarded us as so different that his advice would not carry, span the gap. He had tried to do what was right, he'd said, and this meant duty, mainly duty to women, his mother and his wife, and to his boss: dues paid to those who might protect him. It was difficult to believe he could have approved of Han, or me with Han. Han was never intended for approval.

Among the films there was one curiosity that registered, the black-and-white *All Quiet on the Western Front,* which did show the possibility of love between enemies in battle. It seemed wildly out of place among the hotel's repertoire of colorful movies, and it must have caught me then for me to remember it now. Otherwise it was only the sentimental tale of old people in *On Golden Pond* that engaged my imagination. They were wealthy, they were spoiled, they were bad-tempered; we were asked to admire them for their courage. Something in this undeserved approval disturbed me, and my fragmented and distant thoughts coalesced around it, leading me to the dangerous consideration of age and death and courage. As soon as I recognized what was happening, I dived·for the TV switch on the bedside and console and turned it off, only turning it back on hours later, when I felt I would be safe.

There had been one occasion when my father did not sleep with my mother. A smooth surface existed before and a smooth surface after, and I had not thought of it since. Now it presented itself as another puzzle. When I was eleven or twelve, my father had spent a night away from home, and I never discovered where. I did not ask; it was something we agreed not to know, to forget. On the following morning, a Saturday, my mother said, without looking at me, "Why don't you go down to Kendels and meet your father from work."

I sensed from the tone and circumstances that I was being offered a serious responsibility. The journey to Kendels involved a bike ride across the Great Cambridge Arterial Road, feared by all neighborhood mothers as a place where speeding strangers on their way into or out of London mowed down local children. Though I had made the crossing many times, I had never done so with my mother's encouragement or knowledge, and the seriousness of her request was measured by her willingness to risk my life.

For explanation of my father's absence the previous night, my mother murmured something about an emergency down at the depot, and again I knew I must not press. I went to leave the kitchenette to fetch my bike from the shed, and some opportunistic part of me made use of my advantage.

"Can I go to the flicks this afternoon?"

"Yes. If you want." That she did not exact a chore or emphasize her generosity in exchange for this permission was unprecedented.

When I arrived at the plant the men had already returned from their rounds. It was nearly midday, and the depot was closing. I encountered one of the last to leave at the gate, someone I had met once or twice before.

"Hello, son. Looking for yer dad, are you? He's in the canteen. Still making the mistake of supporting Spurs like yer dad, are you?"

"Good team."

"Couldn't beat a bunch of blind cripples in a month of Sundays."

"Beat Arsenal."

"We let you win. Felt sorry for you. Go on, you cheeky devil. Yer dad's waiting."

He was sitting alone in the canteen, which had finished serving for the day. His white milkman's coat with *K-P* on the breast pocket was draped over the next chair, and he had his milkman's order book open on the refectory table in front of him. There was an indelible pencil lying next to it, but instead of writing, he plucked idly at the thick rubber band that kept the book's pages from fluttering on doorsteps. I suppose he was handsome—dark wavy hair and large regular features—but because he was my father and because he wore plain National Health spectacles, I could not see it. I instinctively knew it was my job to lure him home with suggestions of normality, like a torch shone down a familiar path.

"Hello, Dad. I've come to meet you."

He allowed himself a little smile but did not push himself up to say, Right, let's see what sort of cyclist you are, or, This is a nice surprise! He said, "Hello, son," and remained sitting at the canteen table.

"Mum says, can you pick up some crusty rolls on the way home?"

"Did she? Well, you'd better go home for your dinner, son. You tell her I've got one or two things to do this afternoon."

I sat down next to him, full of the sense that I was responsible for a crucial and delicate task, which I would never be able to admit had existed.

"Are you going to the scout hut? Can I come?"

I almost never agreed to go to the scout hut with my father, preferring to play down my family relationship with the shy assistant scoutmaster and Sunday-school teacher. For the same reason I refused to win scout badges.

He shook his head. "Not today."

"There's steak and kidney pie for dinner."

"You go along ahead."

"Shall I tell Mum to keep yours hot?"

He sighed. "Tell her I'll be along later. You go ahead, son."

I jumped up. I'd done it. Now he had to come. "I'll tell her to save some for you."

I went quickly to the door before anything could change, in high spirits now. Perhaps because he saw this excitement, he called after me.

"Go slow on that bike of yours. Mind how you cross the arterial!"

He had arrived home only five or ten minutes behind me—cutting losses—and I did the chattering through dinner, while they said little. For months after, he gradually lost weight, though it was never talked about to me. Then he regained his weight with the same steadiness.

When the doctor knocked at the door I felt my heart jump up with shock at the violation of my intense and personal world. I discovered that, along with my thoughts, I was watching a science fiction film—*Battleship Galactica,* I think—and that my absorption in a space battle, which I would otherwise have immediately forgotten, was equal to my absorption in my thoughts.

As soon as I saw him I understood, from his perfect suit and smile, that I was to be fleeced and I believe I found a comfort in this. My customary reaction would have been a determination not to let the doctor get the financial or moral better of me and it was perhaps a measure of my need to have my illness validated that I welcomed his unctuous sycophancy. Each hair of his dark mustache had, I noticed, the appearance of being separately groomed and polished. I sensed that whatever version of my illness I offered this doctor, I would not receive in return any suggestion that I was malingering or succumbing to stress or imagination, or that my symptoms were the result of my belonging to a weaker race or being where I didn't belong. He was simply after my money. I experienced this understanding as an inexplicable relief.

The doctor placed his unscuffed bag by the bed and lowered himself into the easy chair opposite mine.

"It's nothing much," I began. "One of these nagging pains that won't go away. I thought it best to have it checked."

"Of course. You're very wise. Too often patients delay too long before calling us. Where is the pain?"

"My side—an ache really. Sometimes a shooting pain. Here."

"Ah, I see. And it no doubt causes you considerable discomfort. Perhaps there are some other symptoms? However slight."

"Some nausea. Not to the point of vomiting."

"No. And how long have you had the pain and nausea?"

"Oh, not very long. Three days."

"Quite long enough. Now, Dr. Bender, perhaps you have some idea of what might be the problem."

"You know I'm not a medical doctor?"

"Of course. But perhaps you have given it some thought. I am not the sort of doctor who discounts the insights of an intelligent patient."

"Kidney perhaps?"

"Yes, I think it might very well be your kidney." He sat thoughtfully for a moment, then stood, smoothing his suit. "I think we should do some tests. To be on the safe side. Now first, how long do you plan to be in Peshawar?"

"About three more days."

"And in Pakistan?"

"A week."

He calculated, then nodded and refreshed his smile. "Good. Now may I just ask you to raise your shirt, Dr. Bender."

After he had pushed my flesh with manicured fingers, had tested blood pressure, balance, eyes, and reflexes, had collected blood and urine samples, he straightened himself and his suit and said, "Good, good. I'll take these samples for testing. It will not take long. Please don't worry, Dr. Bender. You were right to call me but I'm sure we can treat this problem. In the meantime, I counsel relaxation. No, please don't get up; I'll see myself out. It has been a great pleasure."

The smooth doctor returned on the evening of the same day— surely not long enough for laboratory tests. I did not question it. Again he detached himself from his doctor's bag and settled in an armchair.

"I'm pleased to say we caught it in time. Your suspicions were quite correct. It is an infection which has also affected your kidney. It's not serious in the early stages and we can cure it completely."

I don't think I believed him even then, but instead of considering my illness, I only imagined presenting the diagnosis to Yamada as proof of the reality of my symptoms—although he had never questioned them.

"Take these three times a day and these once a day. For ten days. I'm sure you will be fine, but you can always visit your doctor at home if you want to be completely sure." He gave a tight, confirming smile.

"Thank you." I took the bottles and looked at them without seeing.

"Oh, I'm sorry, but there is this. Laboratory tests are a little expensive in Pakistan, I'm afraid."

He took a crisp, unmarked envelope from inside his jacket and placed it next to me, then waited while I picked it up and opened it. The bill was outrageous.

"How would you like me to pay?"

"Traveler's checks will do if cash is a problem."

I went to my briefcase, took out the checks, signed them, handed them over, feeling that I somehow owed this.

He had said without preamble or pretext—was this the last time I saw him?—"You know, son, there was a time I couldn't swallow." He nodded in cheerful affirmation. "The food wouldn't go up or down. I just sat there gobbling like a turkey. I was in a right state, I can tell you. You were young at the time. I don't suppose you'd remember."

"No, I don't think so." I moved his breakfast tray from the bed, dwelling on the nastiness of the cold bacon rinds.

"Things weren't so good at home in those days. Living with your grandmother, we were. Going mad, I was, trying to keep your mother happy and her happy too. Couple of strong-willed women there, son. They never did get on. There was all that and you—a brat, you were—and I was working all the hours God gave to save some money so we could move to our own place. Studying as well, I was—your mother wanted me to get on.

"Well, I just stopped being able to swallow. The old doc gave me all sorts of things to take. Didn't do a blind bit of good. I just got thinner and thinner. I'd put a bit of food in my mouth, expecting to swallow it, and it just wouldn't go down. Your mother used to bang me on the back, which only made it worse. Couldn't tell her to stop. Couldn't get a word out." He laughed. He was cheerful.

"It was a bad time, son. I got as thin as a rake. Thinner. I thought I was going to die. And they couldn't find a darn thing wrong with me! But you know what helped me through it?"

I waited, then saw I would have to respond. I shrugged. "Prayer?"

"Well . . . no. Maybe that helped, of course."

Now he looked embarrassed and I understood, with a real shock, that he had given up all that without bothering to announce it.

"No. I just decided that I could only do so much. That I had to limit myself to what I could handle. I decided to settle for my job. Not much of a job, I know—not a job like yours, not important—but a job that has to be done. And I decided I'd do what I could for people, you, Mum, and Gran, but I wouldn't be able to do everything they wanted. I'd just do what was right by them, nothing fancy. I had to limit myself, see? You've got to make your world manageable, cut your coat according to your cloth."

He paused and I waited. Perhaps he had expected something back from me. Eventually I said, "So then you just got better, did you?"

"Oh, yes. I was able to swallow again, and I soon started to put on weight. I was only off work for a week. Last time I was ever off sick."

I waited again, rigidly. All this had made me tense.

He said, as epilogue, "I've tried to do right, son."

I stood, lifted the tray. I still had to give my mother equal time before leaving for my plane. "Well, I'm sure everyone thinks you have, Dad." I paid attention to my tie, made sure it didn't touch the bacon grease.

Later, on the plane, I felt he had burdened me. It did not occur to me that it might have been help, or wisdom, or a clue to him, that he was offering me. It just seemed wrong that he should expect my blessing for his weakness. The cheerfulness with which he told the tale was irritating, as if it were a story of lively roguishness, not of failure. It was wrong that the father should ask the blessing of the son, not the other way around.

I slept, and when I woke, the films had stopped. I was alert and desperate for distraction but it was the dead of night. I wanted to keep myself from my mind and I remembered I had bought a book in Bangladesh months before and had carried it in the bottom of my case ever since. I had only bought it for appearances. The United Nations driver who was loaned to me for my stay had tried to please me by taking me to a market brothel in Dacca. Though I had suspected his intentions, I proclaimed myself shocked when we arrived. And in fact, it was shocking. A line of twenty thin girls in garish clothes and makeup were tied together, and on the command of a whip-bearing fat woman, they forced themselves into brief, lewd animation for prospective clients. It was in the open, in daylight, and the girls looked sorry to be alive.

"Let's go," I insisted firmly to the driver, and I marched off through the maze of market stalls. The bookstall seemed what was necessary to separate myself from low-rent depravity, and to further show my seriousness, I bought something. There were few books in English and the one I chose was old and hardbacked, a faded beige. I thought it might turn out to be worth something, a book found in so odd a place.

The book was *Sailing Alone Around the World,* Joshua Slocum's story of his voyage, published in 1900. I had not heard of it. Now it immediately seized me. It cooled me, soothed me. It was not just that it was a good tale well told; it was a relief I found in Slocum's tone. He had no hesitancy. Certain things had to be done and they would be done. His fellow man was either a good fellow or not, nothing to dwell upon. His views were firm but not overbearing. If a man held different views, well, let him. He did not defer, neither did he claim authority. He was simply a man at ease with his own existence.

Before I realized I was caught up in the book, I had reached page fifty-one, the part where Slocum has set out from Massachusetts and becomes lost in an extended Atlantic fog, where he experiences a terrifying loneliness. He wrote that "a feeling of awe crept over me" and that "my memory worked with startling power." He reported the distress of it: "I heard all the voices of the past laughing, crying, telling what I had heard them tell in many corners of the earth." But then, on the next page, he was able to write: "The acute pain of solitude experienced at first never returned." Just like that. I laughed out loud in my hotel room at the insouciant breadth of it. He'd done with loneliness and would never again experience it.

This was splendid. He went on to accept illness and halluci-
nation with the same matter-of-factness with which he rebuilt
the rigging or sailed through a storm. I sat up on my bed at the
Pearl Continental and felt I was in good company. I was braced:
loneliness was nothing; cowardice, never heard of it; uncer-
tainty, a waste of time. I could hardly recall what it was that had
been so troubling me.

In the morning I went down to breakfast in the hotel restaurant, taking my project notes with me. Neither Yamada nor
Akira was at breakfast, nor had they contacted me the previous
day. In the case of Yamada this was no surprise, since his
exhaustion after the journey from the mountains had been
obvious and he had declared his intention to rest. It was odd
that Akira had not attempted to consult with me, but I attrib-
uted this to our earlier disagreement. I saw no urgency for a
reconciliation; in many ways my job in Peshawar would be
made easier without the need to show a formal deference to
Yamada or to laboriously penetrate Akira's poor understanding of English in order to establish in him the basic principles
of realpolitik.

It was true that I knew very little about the project area or
the target people. Of my two field trips, one had been aborted
because of the snow and the second had been wasted by
devious officials and Yamada's frailty. Although the project was
nominally to improve the lives of the population, I knew it was
unlikely that our total ignorance of them would be a stumbling
block. Much more important was that I should correctly comprehend the unstated interests of the three signatories—the
provincial government, the national government, and the DCA.

My mind was clear that morning, unmuddied by nagging
doubts, unreconciled facts, or personal concerns, and over
cups of coffee I prepared for my meeting with Shareef, expe-
riencing that old heady feeling of being above the world and
on top of it. The first thing to be clear about was where the
power lay, and it was evident to me that the provincial power
lay with Shareef. Certainly I would have to carry the roundup

meeting with the heads of the provincial technical departments, but Shareef would chair that one, and he was a ruthless chairman. The federal government in Islamabad could, of course, always overrule the North-West Frontier provincial government, which would actually receive the money, but as the coordinator of special projects in the province, Shareef would have a close relationship with Islamabad. Special Projects supervised the supposedly economic international projects, which really had more to do with the government's ambiguous relationship with opium production and the security of the border with Afghanistan—interests close to the hearts of the military government and foreign powers. The top people would listen to Shareef, while they would ignore provincial departments concerned with, say, roads or agriculture or education.

Now that I had established in my mind that if I could win Shareef's agreement I could probably carry the provincial and federal governments, it only remained for me to decide what conditions I must insist on and how to present them. To a large extent, as the lender of money, the agency would have the power to determine the nature of the project and to impose conditions on the Pakistani government. Shareef would certainly be in trouble if he failed to win our agreement. But at the same time, he would know my anxiety to avoid a similar failure. And I had to recognize the special conditions here, with the Americans and other agencies eager to pour money and influence into the region as part of their concerns about communism and drugs. If I pressed too hard, the Pakistanis could always find another source of funds.

I wrote down my priorities in a notebook and examined them. There was only one, I decided, that was nonnegotiable. We needed a bigger project. The trouble with our valley was that, with only a quarter of a million people and a primitive economy, it couldn't absorb enough money during a five-year project period. Maybe only fifteen million dollars. It didn't cost much more for headquarters to administer a fifty-million-dollar project than one of fifteen million dollars, and there would be trouble if I returned to Geneva with something so small. My job—never stated—was to push money. I needed at least thirty. I needed another valley.

That's what I needed. How was I to get it? I clarified my bargaining counters. I could offer Shareef the role of project disbursement approval. He'd sign the checks going to the departments and contractors. There were patronage and bribes at stake. Second, I could hint at further personal reward for Shareef, the promise of well-paid and influential international consultancies through the project. I didn't have the authority, but I could hint. And I wouldn't be around when the time came.

I did not realize while I was working over breakfast at the Pearl Continental that I was simultaneously deciding not to return to London for my father's funeral. It was the last few hours I could hope to make connections that would allow me to return in time, and by occupying my mind with project negotiations rather than airline schedules, I was making the final decision by default. My mind when I entered Shareef's office an hour before the scheduled provincial roundup meeting was entirely given over to the manipulation of our conversation toward a successful conclusion, and I believe I carried with me some of the energetic charm I discovered in myself when I faced a challenge of this sort.

Shareef came around his desk and motioned toward the easy chairs and coffee table. "Morning, William. I was so sorry to hear about your father. Have you decided what you want to do?"

This unexpected question, so removed from my immediate preoccupations, made me miss a beat but I managed a brisk response. "I'll go home when the mission's over."

"Are you sure? We can reorganize things."

He had leaned forward with a concerned expression, and I thought I heard reproach. Reproach or sympathy; either one put me at a disadvantage and diverted the agenda. I nearly said that we were different in the West, that unlike people in the third world, we were not slaves to our families. I nearly said that I was sure he would like it if I went, leaving him to negotiate with the incompetent Japanese. Instead of saying either of these, I swallowed and began, mildly, "Well, you know, Shareef, this is a small mission. . . ."

"And perhaps the rest of your team is not so strong?" He gave an understanding smile. He had a wealthy man's face, creaseless without being fat.

I raised my eyebrows in unquotable acknowledgment.

"Of course," he added, "we're delighted you are staying."

I opened my briefcase, and Shareef leaned back. "Well, William, what plans do you have for us?"

"I'll run through the main proposals. There's one major problem, and I'll come back to that a bit later on."

Shareef was very relaxed; attentive without being anxious. I told him how money would go on agriculture, infrastructure, and administration, how it would be divided between the different departments and between the district and the province. I explained the whole smooth fallacy of it: that the improved agriculture would increase the amount of produce sold, and the new roads would help move it away. The loans to farmers would put pressure on the farmers to sell in order to meet their repayments. It would create a modern market. I dwelt on the organization and the path the money would take on its journey from Geneva to the peasants. "Local approval for disbursements would be the responsibility of a coordinating committee appointed by the governor. Of course you'll be the obvious chairman, and we'll recommend that, if you're agreeable. The money would pass through your Special Projects Office and then on to the line departments under your supervision. The deputy commissioner would be your representative in the project area to give the project law-and-order authority."

"Good. It sounds practical. And the problem?"

"The project's too small. We need another project area." I let it sit.

"Too small . . . Yes, I think I agree. What size is it?"

"About fifteen million over five years."

Shareef pressed a buzzer on the underside of the table, and a clerk immediately appeared, was given instructions, and quickly reappeared with a rolled map. We flattened it on the table between us. Shareef mused over it, tracing his thinking with the long, perfect nail of a plump finger. "We've given this piece to USAID. And the area to the west. Opium substitution projects. The Swiss are here. The World Bank have a marketing and communications project for the province, but we've promised them a mountain valley for an area development project too. Probably this one. They finance my office, you know. The British are up here in the northern areas with the Aga Khan Foundation. Danish aid too."

"What about this valley?"

"Well, yes, but frankly, William, I don't advise it. It's an opium valley. Political problems. A lot of guns. The armed police were defeated there."

"Not a good relationship between the government and the target population then."

"Exactly."

"Up here?"

"Mmm. The Germans and the Belgians are both after it. And the Asia Bank. They've already sent a project identification mission. Still . . . Did you visit?"

"We passed through it on the drive down from the mountains."

"So you've seen it."

"It looked promising. What of the target population?"

"Oh, very cooperative. In history they were always ruled by foreigners. A certain slavishness persists."

I thought to respond but checked myself. In my hesitation, Shareef spoke again. "Of course there's always the tunnel through the mountains. That's a good-sized project."

"It would never get past the board."

I let a silence grow for a few seconds. "Do you have anything from the Japanese?"

"Not very much really."

"You might think about that. We'll be Japanese cofinanced. It's one reason it has to be bigger. And if it goes well, they'll want to use your experience in other countries. Consultant. We can write it into the project budget."

"I take your point about the Japanese. We're part of Asia after all. Maybe the Germans can do something in Kashmir instead. You don't want Kashmir, do you?"

"Not this time."

"So how much do you think? For both valleys."

"What's the total population?"

"About three quarters of a million."

"Then around forty million over five years. Fifty if we stretch it to seven. About eighty percent in foreign exchange."

"Good!" He stood up and smiled. "And what's next for you, William? After London, of course."

"Well, you know. Somewhere else."

"I like your life. Does your family live near St. John's Wood? We have a house there."

"No, not very near."

"Well, let's get this roundup meeting over with."

Am I getting it right? Was I so calculating and closed as it now seems? There were people who liked me in those days, or were at least friendly to me. It is possible that with my new rigor I am being too hard on my past self. Shareef seemed to like me, or at least liked doing business with me. There had been women I met on my travels who were warm with me. I kept myself neat and clean and I don't believe I was deliberately cruel. Perhaps others could see in me a self held back, which I could not see in myself. I rarely asked for sympathy. I was told by several, but first by Mireille, that my face, which is roughened by the scars of adolescent acne, also possesses a compensating fineness of line to produce an attractive combination. And what I did, a little horse trading with the futures of people I did not know, was no worse than other men did with only good feelings about their worldly usefulness and the quality of the life their incomes gave their families. They lived to glow with pride at the sons and daughters who went to good colleges and emerged to be something nice in the arts. Nor were my infidelities to Mireille anything more than commonplace in Washington, where most were divorced and adulteries were routinely concealed. The harshness toward myself is suspiciously excessive, perhaps straining too hard to distinguish then from now.

The trouble with the Large White pigs is the cost of them. The little brown pigs cost nothing but the Large Whites are expensive. They first have to be imported from Germany, and then they need custom-built pigsties with cement floors so they can be kept from contamination and will not waste their energy on unproductive activity. Then the local food is not good enough for them and manufactured feed cake must be shipped from Australia to enable them to reach their full potential of six times the weight of the indigenes in half the time with three times the offspring. And they need vaccinations for protection against infections their streetwise Ruatuan cousins can shrug off. These must be imported too, along with the motorcycles for the veterinary assistants who administer the vaccines, who in turn require foreign consultants to train them for their new duties. Then the director of agriculture must have a new car to supervise his veterinary assistants and the Livestock Department a computer to keep track of it all, this requiring the director's nephew to visit Israel for computer training, and because they must buy the pigs and food and vaccines and cement, the farmers need loans, so the Ruatua Agricultural Bank, which does the lending, must also have a foreign loan and foreign advice and a computer and a car and overseas study tours to see how non-Ruatuans do it.

A lot rode on the Large Whites and it was almost visible in the long swayed backs of the sows, the convex obverse of the long rows of teats they needed to feed the crowds of piglets they had to have to justify the expense of them. I can chuckle at that now, now they are all gone, imagining the director, the director's Toyota, the director's nephew, the DCA deskman in Geneva and his boss, the head of Asian Projects, with a Ruatua project in his pocket for the DCA annual review, all weighing down the back of a dumb Large White sow, with her tendency to muff it by teetering off her high-heeled trotters onto her newborn.

At the time, though, it all made sense: a country under-loaned but experienced in pigs. The local pigs were pathetically undeveloped; the Ruatuans raised them without money and, lacking the economic spur of debt, merely languished, as did Ruatua. It made sense—it still does in its way, like an antimatter universe—to spend a thousand dollars to produce something worth two, instead of spending nothing to produce a pig without a price. I wrote the project in a weekend at the hotel next to Ruatua's airport, a clone of a project somewhere else, and everyone was happy. The most I could swell it to was half a million and it went through on the nod in Geneva, too small a sum for the trouble of a meeting.

The trouble with the cost of them is that farmers with Large Whites needed, in the capitalist way, to sell their pigs in order to repay the loans they needed to raise them, but no one on Ruatua had ever bought a pig. Pigs were free. When the hand-picked "progressive" Ruatuans had produced their first batches of Large Whites, these were, in the Ruatuan way, claimed by the community; in the Ruatuan way the new pigs were called upon for village feasts and celebrations. When their owners, spurred by debt, insisted on payment, family was set against family, villages were split, old ways of communal life fell into abeyance, progressives taunted traditionalists, who reproached the progressives, the government—no more than a bunch of neighbors everyone knew—was set against the people, achieving a novel social definition. Crises flared up throughout the island, sometimes with violence, so that even I, with Emo's prodding, was brought out of the self-absorption of my reflective life at Coconut Beach and was obliged to notice.

We ate the last Large White some weeks ago at a beach barbecue. I calculate it has cost me five thousand dollars in gifts at mateii ceremonies—most of my DCA expense money—to undo the five-hundred-thousand-dollar project. Nobody has complained. The officials keep their computers and motorcycles, and by the time repayments to the DCA come due next century, they'll be gone. It is peaceful here again. Sometimes I imagine traveling backward around the world, unraveling everything I've raveled, cleaning myself away, free-ing other remote places from entanglement with international money, but I know my limitations, and Ruatua will have to do.

Unlike Slocum's teasing maidens, Emo, who I can now see walking between the palm-thatched office and the palm-thatched huts, is not a simple island girl. She is over thirty and has two older children, a boy and a girl, in addition to the one who might be mine. She has a desktop computer, which she can, when she chooses, operate perfectly well. She was once a stewardess with Polynesian Airlines, which was how she met the Australian businessman she married. For a time she lived in Sydney. She has shopped in Los Angeles.

Emo walks without hurry in a calf-length lavalava, and I can't help watching every movement from my lounger on the beach. Now she bends from the hips, straight-legged, to rearrange something at the border of the curving sandy path. Perhaps it is to attend one of the succulent plants that grow there, or to rearrange the sticks of frangipani flowers the girls put out, or it might be to fix more securely one of the shells or one of the Foster's beer cans that edge the path. A more simple island girl, one of Emo's nieces, first saw the glittery beauty of the blue and silver Foster's cans and now they are the fashion here. They give me a special pleasure, cautioning me against any fixed view of things.

Now Emo stands straight and looks over at me and waves. I love that. The wave is exaggerated, a slow, sweeping movement with an open palm, as if the distance between us is so great that it requires such largeness. There's a joke in it somewhere, though I'm not sure where. It might be in the yards of empty sand between us, or in the solitude of our afternoons, now that the hotel hardly operates and our only guest, the old Englishman, is careful to keep away. Or it might be that the joke is in my pen and paper, held against the enormous Pacific, my funny effort; everyone here is amused by that.

I return her wave with one of equal size, and I try to think of chores I might help her with. I could help her change the sheets, or I could mend something. I'm just looking for ways to be with her.

Yesterday I came up behind Emo while she was arranging her hair and I surprised myself in her mirror. There are few mirrors here, no shopfronts or picture windows, and without realizing it, I had given up the dozen daily checks we make on how we seem to others that are part of life in modern places. The way I thought I looked and the way I looked had discreetly diverged, so that I was shocked by the man I saw. I knew my hair was longer and that I had a beard, but I still thought of myself as neat. My pockmarked cheeks had a new seared smoothness of deep tan. I looked wild but healthy. Like a madman. When I smiled, the sudden whiteness jumped out from the darkness of my face.

"Emo, look at us. You look so pretty, and I look like a crazy man."

She considered me. "Hmm. I don't think you'll pass for a banker anymore."

"You should have told me. I've been letting you down."

"I've got used to it. I think I prefer it."

I put my face close to hers so that she could see them together in the mirror. She smiled and asked, "How should I arrange the flowers behind my ears today? Married, single, or immediately available?"

"What would you have done if this wild man had been a passenger when you were a stewardess?"

"I'd be very careful not to bend over while he was behind me."

"Did men grab you?"

"Foreign men. After drinks. I had to learn not to be so friendly."

"I'm surprised the girls here aren't frightened of me. Look at me."

"You don't look so bad. Anyway, why should they be frightened? They like you."

"They tap me on the shoulder."

"Of course."

"Why?"

"They like to do that."

"Oh."

Maybe if Dad had lived here, he would have made a Sunday talk of pigs. God is like a small, hairy Ruatuan pig. He doesn't cost anything. You can't put a price on Him. Yet we can't do without Him. He's what holds us together and keeps us from selfishness. If we value Him He will show us the value in ourselves. He will give Himself freely for our sake. He is constantly renewed by our belief in Him.

No, no, it doesn't quite have the right ring to it. There's a hint of sophistry which spoils it. I'm sure, though, that he wouldn't have liked the Large Whites; he would never have been one of the "progressive farmers" they chose for their confident and thrusting ways. No, there is too much imagination in this. I should return to the facts.

● ● ●

After the Peshawar roundup meeting, which went well, I returned to the Pearl Continental and ran a bath. Only when I was lying in it, enclosed by the bathroom's artificial light and the noise of the ventilator fan, did I realize I was tired and that all the denials of the day had been a strain. Still, the exhaustion had a satisfaction. Even if the deal we had made was cynical, with its veil of service to the poor hardly concealing any of its working parts, at least we had moved something on. Within the worldly rules we had done what was necessary to progress, and there was in this a manly pleasure, as if it were my muscles I had used and not my mind. I had put aside pain and choked down its nausea. This was, I decided, how soldiers must feel when they have killed but know that by doing so they have excused others from the need to take a life. And I recalled my father crossing the bright summer meadow in Austria, the only man among the holidaymakers who did not say that he had killed. I could still hear the false assertiveness in his voice as he tried to claim the lowest place among them. Now I found myself striding through the grass and flowers, among the silent group that would not take him, and I remembered again what he had said more than once: "You're not like me, son. You're lucky."

I added more hot water to the bath. It was plumbed to an American standard, so that the faucet was a generous bore, but the tub itself was shallow, more suited to the shower. I fiddled with the taps until I had maximized the water level by balancing an inflow of hot water with the loss through the overflow. I deserved this wasteful indulgence.

Perhaps he had felt like this, lying in his Saturday bath, even if his hot water was scarce and soiled and the bathroom cold in winter. He had always kept the door locked for that hour of privacy, and there was something in this that agitated my mother, so that she invented chores to chide him with when he emerged. But he had been firm about this one thing and never gave in. Lying there in our Tottenham bathroom, which at least had windows, thirty years ago, when he was about my age, preparing his Sunday talk, was he so very different from me when I prepared myself for an awkward negotiation? He must have had the same nervousness, the same casting around for a tone of authentic sincerity. In a way, he too had to build a defendable version of things for each occasion, and like mine, his version only needed to stand for a day, long enough to please a willing audience. Then I lost the fragile coincidence; it would not hold; the memory of his hesitant voice and funny similes would not line itself up with the sound of expert explanations and my grim poetry of economics.

I had loved to go on the milk round with him, but the occasions were few, requiring some domestic crisis that left me in his care. He was a different man out there, livelier and funnier. When Mrs. Truelock or Mrs. Burnage—hardly more than girls, it now struck me, but to me the homely mums of schoolmates—called out to him, "Ben! Coo-ee, Ben!" to stop him from striding off next door before they could ask for an extra pint or a half-dozen eggs, he was never short of words the way he was at home, or haltingly constrained as he was at the church.

"Morning, dear. What's your pleasure."

"Oo, that'd be telling. 'Ave to settle for a pint of red-top, I suppose. Can't be greedy, can we, Ben?"

The exchanges continued loud and open as he ran up and down the short front paths and made the crucial calculations of how far to drive his electric float ahead of his calls for maximum efficiency.

"Can I pay you, Ben? Better do it while I've got it."

"How are you, dear?" He stood on the doorstep and thumbed through his record book, working out how much was owed, temporarily stowing a pencil behind his ear, talking without thought. "Up to no good, I bet."

"Chance would be a fine thing."

"That'll be three and four, dear. Up to Saturday."

He flirted, and the housewives glowed, as if he were a shared treasure. In this daytime neighborhood of women, I never saw him talk to anyone for more than a minute. He dipped into the homes and lives of the working-class wives in the way I later came to dip into poor countries. But they liked him, and he did a good job. He was as charming to the widowed old ladies who lived for his daily calls as he was to the young ones with bold eyes. On the round he seemed a happy man. I heard women invite him in for a cup of tea—"Time for a cuppa, Ben?"—but he had always refused. "Got to get on, luv. Got the nipper with me."

He was lovable those days. I saw him put his arm around housewives he hardly knew—usually not the prettiest—though never around his own wife. At home he was, by comparison, small and silent, eating alone in the kitchenette on his own milkman's schedule, then working in the garden, or in the garden shed, where he mended things, or down on the allotment, or at the scout hut. He slipped away from us as if he wanted to make his excuses before he was asked to leave.

I wondered if it had been his happiness with the women on his round that had kept him in this job all his life, and I wondered about his odd absence: how little I could guess of what was on his mind for all those childhood years.

I reached this far in my thoughts of my father, in the warmth of my Peshawar bath, without once being reminded that the reason for all this was that he had died. Only when I did remember that did I also recall—and this was with the sort of shock that might have resulted from an electrical appliance being dropped into the bathwater—that while I was being a soldier for economic development, the time had passed when I could have taken my last chance to make his funeral.

"I couldn't do what you do, son." His old pale eyes had seemed quite happy with this. Behind his sickbed pillows—it was probably after his second heart attack—he had rigged up a make-do piece of plastic to keep the grease stains from his head off the wallpaper. I resisted this cheerful admission of failure and reassembled for him his old defenses: his need to leave school at thirteen, the Depression, the two world wars—all those enemies of promise—but he only shook his head, not even sad.

"Of course," he continued, seemingly careless of logic, "I had a good few girlfriends in my time." The forty years of married life, working life, were gone, displaced by the time when he was young and free, with enough money in his pocket to play the gay blade in London's West End. I did not encourage him and it did not occur to me that he might have chosen his words for my sake, not his. I might have understood that his words were to let me know he knew the strain of dislocation, or that he had guessed about me and Han but loved me still. Instead it was the burden of an old man's childishness I chose to see.

It could have been that he knew about Han, or that he did not. It might have been that he wished to say that he had also known the bright, bold lure of passion and that at least in this we were alike. Or it might have been a wish in him to throw up a version of my happy philandering to preempt a truth that could be darker.

I knew he missed Mireille. He missed the pleasure of flirting with a pretty woman and the extra spice of embracing one from a class above his bosses. My mother missed her too; she had been a jewel in their lives. Did they know of Han, a younger woman, Chinese, of no identifiable status? When I strained to remember, I could not recall what I had said. Certainly my father had known something, because he had asked, "How's Mireille?" then quickly added, "I don't suppose you see much of her these days." I might have mentioned my Asian statistical assistant waiting for me at the airport; he might have added two and two. I had fancied then that everything about her would be unacceptable to them:

she wore sex close to the surface; she did not honor her mother and her father; she had no time for anyone who was of no use, no sympathy for the weak or mediocre; she was foreign—not cultured-European foreign but Chink-on-the-make foreign; she was not nice. Believing this, wanting to believe this, I had taken pleasure in the break she made for me with everything, my dismissal of the pull on me of my parents' enslaved timidity. And now, in Peshawar, she worked for me again, the vivid turbulence of Han pushing aside the old, pale eyes of Dad.

She had peeled me away from all that attached me to the world. Our places were in planes and hotel rooms, behind the heads of drivers in official cars. I could not remember a single occasion when she cooked. In Bogotá, on our first mission together, she gave me the first version of her history, a winning version, one suitable for bed. She had lived in all sorts of places—Greece, Paris, Hong Kong—had been taken up by powerful men. She hinted at heads of state. "I'm not going to tell you any names. We don't want any unexplained deaths." I listened. Han had been desired, had played the hard, brave game of desire for high stakes. In Las Vegas— one episode of many—she said she had strayed into something that was distinguishable from common prostitution only by its scale and quality. "I spent fifty thousand on clothes in six months." She had stayed until she had been beaten by "some shit from the mob."

On the wide, flat stage of a bed in an American hotel in Bogotá, I ran my hand down the smooth length of Han— mine now—and slipped fingers into her while she talked, accommodating me without missing the rhythm of her words. I looked at her carefully and I could find nothing on her face or body—unless it was the wry, ironic charm of her smile—that showed she was anything more than a smart Asian girl just out of school. Bad behavior, it seemed, had no penalty for the brave. She had my complete attention.

"I know I'm good," she said, turning to take my look. "That's why they all wanted me." I did not hear the pleading.

"I know you're good."

"We haven't even got started."

"We haven't? So show me."

"I'm going to keep you hungry." She took my hand away and replaced it with her own, smiled. "Ever see a girl do this?" She dived down and I intervened to pull her to me; we began again.

I was awoken that night, or one night soon after—near the beginning of us anyway—by the grinding of her teeth. She was asleep but fidgeting, like a dog in dreams, and her face was more troubled than I had ever seen it in wakefulness. I turned on a low light and watched her engagement with the inner struggle. I shook her gently. She stilled, and the grinding stopped. Then she opened her eyes, looking straight ahead as if it did not matter what there was to see. Then she smiled, almost smug.

"You were grinding your teeth."

"Oh, yeah. I forgot to tell you. I do that."

"What were you dreaming about?"

"Telly."

"Telly?"

"Some fat Greek bastard. I did everything for him. His business was on the rocks when he met me. I sorted it out. Then he thought he could give me to his friends, just like that. He made me fuck his fat rich friends. I'm going to find a way to kill him one day. Have him killed. Him and some others." Then Han cried, the tears streaming, and she made no attempt to hide them or brush them away. I held her rigid body, aware even then that this pain was something extra which would hold me, something I wanted her for.

She stopped crying abruptly, saying, "Enough of that," with a briskness that suggested the crying could go on forever, so it might as well end now. Her expression changed and a new fury in it became fixed on me. "Fuck me!" she demanded, while in contradiction she pushed me away with her strong arms, which when I closed on her beat at me, real blows. "Fuck me! Hurt me!" She took back one hand and squeezed her own nipple viciously, showing me the pain on her face. "Get in me, goddamn it." It was as if there was a need in her to force back a surge of inner pain with something external of equal strength. She made pity indistinguishable from cruelty. Mercy would have been obliteration.

When she came, the gurgle she made rattled in her throat and her eyes stayed open, filled with me but not seeing me. I would be the last sight posted on the victim's eyes. Then she relaxed, raised her eyebrows. "Getting better," she said. Then Han kissed me tenderly on the lips, out of either love or sympathy —in either case, a new, rich confusion—then brushed the length of my body with heavy Chinese hair, finally leaving the bed when she reached my feet.

When she returned, immaculate in a white silk robe, she stopped by the bed to look down on me. "Hope you know what you're getting into, Dr. Bender. Other than all my orifices, that is."

"Aren't I already in it?"

"Oh, yes. Just don't forget you're my boss, Dr. Bender."

The next morning, Han had drafted the Colombian aide-mémoire before I woke. The pattern was set; four hours of sleep was all she could ever bear. From then on she took up the slack in my work, wrapping our projects for the third world poor until they were as neat as her. Mireille hardly crossed my mind those days, just a faint impression of good manners, polite kindliness, a single strand of pearls, an unwillingness to remove her nightdress or fully open her legs when making love.

I believe it was the first time—lying in the bath at the Pearl Continental—that I had relived any scene from the months I traveled with Han, though it had been over for a year. Something in my train of thought had invoked it now and held it up like a cross held against a greater terror—perhaps that of sentiment. I had forgotten the continuously running water of the bath and I had forgotten all the world outside the white noise of the fan, but the enclosure suddenly upset me, so that I burst dripping from the bathroom into the carpeted space of my hotel room, where the sun was still forcing afternoon light through the curtains.

. . .

Did he really say Jimmy Riddle for a piddle, for a pee? Was it he who called a mouth a north-and-south before he learned how the posh talked and became quiet? A boat-race face and mince-pie eyes? Are those his lively, pale mince-pies and his funny north-and-south entrancing me while he rubs me down at three—me standing on the bathroom stool—singing "Daisy, Daisy, I've gorn crazy, all fer the love of yew" and "I've got sixpence, merry little sixpence" and "Oh, that daring young man on the flying trapeze . . . ," which he tells me he also was once, down at the gymnasium, a lad amongst lads, one of the best, no coward then, not cowed, before he was cash-and-carried, before he got me mum for his trouble-and-strife, before he had me as a nipper, ten years before Johnny Hitler gave us World War Two, when, even if the Mother Hubbard was bare, he always had a few bob rattling in his pocket to go up West and dance with the girls at the old Palais, long before the apples-and-pears made him queer, made his ticker falter?

Did he really say all this; was he ever so close to the ground? No I don't think so.

Here they tap you on the shoulder. I don't know why. At night as I lie on my back, the baby between us, within the sound of the sea, I can't tell whether I'm swimming or sleeping, or whether the sound I hear is Emo's breathing or the dying of the surf. The old man's coughs come to me across the sand like catches I have to hold.

This book is worse than loneliness. I don't think that even the author could keep his mind on this book. It's about a plot to put Legionnaires' disease into the air-conditioning plants of hotels in the Bahamas—or it may have been Bermuda; it doesn't matter. The criminals want to ruin the economy and take over the country, or the drug trade, or the world, or something. I can't remember which. There's a lot of technical stuff about hotels and boats and air-conditioning plants, but who knows if it's right? The hero is masterful but I bet the author isn't. I'm reading it to escape but I can't find a place to hide in it. I have started to cry out at my father. The three hamburgers from the Little America Café are still sitting on the International Dateline Hotel stationery. Outside, fat Tongan voices fall and rise, singing hymns.

There's a need for explanations. A comment on the two earlier explanations of human civilization.

I can't remember now which side I'm on. It was the structuralists, I think, who said the way we are is because of the way the world is, and the structuralistes, with an extra e, the French ones from the Left Bank, who took the opposing view, that the way the world is is because of the way we are. They have their reasons, and I can't remember now which side I joined. It all depends on the e, I think, and it all depends on the sight of little fish and the movement of the sea. I take pleasure in flirting with the current, being twisted and turned according to its whim.

A need for explanations.

God is like a plug hole, he might have said. I lay there in my bath last night. . . . I thought to myself, God is like a plug hole. . . . I don't know why. You wallow . . . yes, you wallow in dirty water. You know how it is, all the week's grime, all the result of everything you did. Maybe you were not as good as you might have been. . . . Maybe you traveled on the buses; they always make you dirty. So when you lie in your bath, you're lying in the dirt of everything you did. And all the dirt *your family picked up, too, if you're the last to go. Then you pull out the plug and it all drains away—or nearly all of it—and you're ready for another week. It's like that with God, isn't it? We do bad things. We are not as good as we might be. Maybe we're not very kind to someone. Maybe we've told some fibs. And we wallow in it. But He forgives us. He pulls the plug so that it all drains away, and we're left there clean, ready to start afresh. If you see what I mean.*

No more than a speck on the Pacific, dust on a glass of wine neglected for a conversation, Ha'apai is a place to tread softly, a low island which is very quiet, just coral with some sand caught in it. From the light plane which brought us here, I could see how it almost did not make it at all; the light green and dark green of underwater hills and reefs almost did not hunch themselves enough to make Ha'apai. A few thousand people and thousands more palm trees have not noticed that their home is just a shrug, and they have rooted themselves here. It's very quiet on Ha'apai, very flat. As the icecap melts because of something done elsewhere, it will not be noticed that Ha'apai was the first to go. There's nothing to invest in, on Ha'apai, no need, but in memory I hold it to me as a mermaid clasps her child, loving it, looking for a place to lay it down.

We lived under false names. They called my father Ben, though his name was Jack. I was a William when I should have been a Bill. Her Reston women's group makes Mireille Mary for the convenience of their lazy tongues. Han gives herself to Honey and then to Hannah at everyone's convenience. My mother chose Margaret early on because her Mavis was too common— then resisted Peggy. We are pretenders, every one.

We say we are white collar because of his white coat. We are the best of families, and there's only love between us. In the long term, everything is for the best—my work, our ways, our luck.

And Mother says you should never put shoes on the table, especially new ones, because it is unlucky, and if you drop a glove you must not pick it up yourself, and that education is the thing to pin your hopes on—don't be like your father— and that bird shit on your head is fortunate, and that breeding counts and you can always tell a gentleman, and that you must never put up an umbrella in the house, walk under ladders, or spill salt, and that gentlemen know how to govern—not like us—and that if you do spill salt you must throw it over your left shoulder with your right hand, into the eye of the devil, and that a broken mirror is seven years' bad luck and a crow is death, and that you should never pass another on the stairs, and that if you go out you should never return prematurely, but if you do, you must count to twenty and turn around three times and you should never give anything for nothing—not like your father—because others won't, and all the nice girls will be gone by twenty-three, and horseshoes are lucky but crossed knives are evil and a black cat crossing your path is lucky too, except this is disputed among the women and some say it is unlucky.

I keep my eyes on his back in the morning twilight as he makes his way up to the brow of the railway bridge. The morning is cold and wet, the black road shining, and I can hear the hiss of bicycle tires and the angry strain of my breathing. He's already not the man he is at home because he's left me behind on my eighteen-inch wheeler, him on his heavy twenty-six-inch Hercules, when he's always flattered me before by letting me cycle faster. For some reason I have to go to his work with him today. Other men on bikes cut in between us, all capes and caps and sharp knees in the icy rain of six a.m. The factory hooters have gone once, and this early shift is in terror of a second time. I am shocked to find among the dads a fierce energy, a rawness, grim tight lips, ruthlessness. I'm soft, a ten-year-old who, up to now, has considered himself a manly cyclist. Now I'm out of my depth and before I can reach him, he's off again, rain shining on his hatless head. He cries, "Come on!" with something close to terror in his eyes, which I saw again when his first heart attack brought him close to death, a man powerless between two duties, between the equal pulls on him.

Is she laughing at us boys? She says, Miss Khan, that she's had her fun and that peristalsis is like this, it's how food moves along, and she moves among our desks touching this one and that, the only motion among us, telling us that she's watched us boys, the way we've started to look at girls with our eyebrows slanted just so, as if we're tough. She knows what we're up to, she says, she knows it's no more than simple biology that it's the man's job to chase a woman and plant his seed in her and move on, and that it's the woman's job to make him stay. And she says, laughing, moving, touching, catching eyes, that she can tell the ones who will lose the game of biology and get caught, tricked into babies, homes, and immobility, not like the men she likes, those with life in them, men of the world, from here to Pakistan, those with independence, style. And she does laugh at us boys, mesmerized as we are by this perverse foreign version. She says that the world is full of killjoys and little men, and the best of us—her eyes rove—won't listen to them but will keep moving as she has, will have their fun.

I look, though Han does not, at the face of the old woman pressed against the window of our car. She is poor, one of the ones Han wished us to be among while we did this. The woman may be nearly blind, which could be why she's approached so close; I can't tell from the blankness of her eyes. Han is not looking at the woman but is twisted back to look at me. She wears only a blouse, which is undone. She's on my lap and I'm still high up inside her; her hand is still in place *underneath herself. She ignores the old woman, a hand's length away, whose inexpressive eyes sweep back and forth over us. On our side of the glass the temperature is comfortable. On the old woman's side it is more than a hundred degrees. We are in Liberia. Han has twisted back to me, the little wry smile on her face, somehow pleased. I look from the old woman with her flaps of empty breasts pressed up against the door—surely the metal is burning her flesh—to Han's wry smile. Though I can't hear her, she has just said, "That was weird!" in a tone of deep gratification. I am definitely with Han.*

Captain Slocum said he never saw the need to learn to swim, that his purpose was always to be upon the sea, never in it. He said he had never encountered an instance of a life lost at sea that would have been saved by the ability to swim.

Expert explanations:

Target population: Victims.

The long term: Unquantifiable; not our problem.

Social factors: Unquantifiable; not our problem.

It's the problem of being born.
    You try, you try. You want to make progress and, as time passes, move further and further into life, leaving distant and diminished the darkness of the womb, the coziness of home, the familiar cloy. You want this country to turn into that one. You want progress. You want a straight line. You want to be stronger than the current that draws you back in sleep. You want to get bigger and richer. You want to live forever. You want to duck into women on the way, way stations, but not too long or you'll stop being born. So there's another country

---

where you mustn't stay too long or know too well, another woman, but the new country brings you nearer home, not farther away, as often as you leave you must return, and soon there's just a lot of leaving and returning and you can't keep going forever, there's that damn death and there's that heart attack that's going to weaken you, the body that's keeping its accounts, the long-term return, so you do slide back and you can't keep moving the way you used to, you can't stomach it, you haven't got the heart for it, and the new women don't want you so much, and the money goes around too fast for you and you don't get anywhere and you're sucked back into the black hole and that's it.

The light twinkles with the slight disturbance of the water by the breeze. From out in the lagoon the palms could be a sturdy crewcut on the forehead of the beach. I push my mask up and let the snorkel dangle. I have it now, how to keep afloat with just the slightest pawing of my flippered feet. No clouds up there, just one jet on a high curved path between places more important than Ruatua. I like that. Passengers dazed by the hours of uninterrupted blue might accidentally spot the island and at first not believe it. Then they would come to stare at this little eye of white beach and dark palm forest, wondering if it was a desert island, if this might be a neglected tropical paradise that only they had seen and whether they might discover a different life here, one that made them happy. They would not imagine me out near the thin eyeliner of the coral reef, looking back at them. They would never in a thousand years imagine the son of a London milkman suspended here, treading water. They are gone now.

About bicycles, he said the thing was to keep them oiled and greased, that greasy dirt preserved them better than shining chrome. A strong bike would last a man a lifetime, and never mind the weight of it. Three gears were enough for anyone.

*Care should be taken going downhill in the rain. It was better,
and more proper, to dismount and walk a hill than to stand on
the pedals, straining. Favor steadiness over speed. Raleighs
were best, though his was a Hercules.*

A certain slavishness persists.

*They ask questions but offer no answers. They have access to
transport. They decide to build a road or not for no good
reason. They make your enemy a village official and give him
power over you. They have no known homes. They never stay
overnight. They rarely eat and never shit. They fix the price of
wheat, raise taxes, dam a river, redistribute the land, favor one
side or the other in a war, turn up again to organize the
refugees. They lend you money and make you alone. They
don't speak your language, are unable to explain themselves,
refuse to discuss God. They are a weather that cannot be pre-
dicted, a power that cannot be appeased.*

*I miss Akira now and I regret that I allowed him to return to
Tokyo, but his fear was intense, and although his compact
body seemed able to take all kinds of punishment, I felt I
should be kind. I think his terror was that we would arrive at
a place so small that it would be comprehensible with the
naked eye and the confusion would only be in him. Yet his
background was humble, and he was never happier than on
the beach in Ha'apai, hooking the fish who have become my
friends. But now I miss Akira's passion and his love, and although I could never give him the sense he craved, I am happy
that on Ha'apai he once found a woman who was not repelled
by the wild divergence of his eyes.*

After I had dried myself and dressed, I called Yamada. His voice on the hotel phone sounded remote and uncertain.

"The meeting went well," I said.

"Ah, Will. Yes."

"Fifty million over seven years. They've given us another valley. That would mean at least twenty of Japanese cofinance."

There was a moment's silence, as if he had to bring himself back from somewhere very distant. "Twenty. Good, good."

"Yes, I think we've done well. Do you want to meet?"

Another hesitation. "Shall we make it tomorrow?"

"How's your health now, Mr. Yamada?"

"I'm well. Quite well. I think I should stay in my room today. Paperwork. Thank you. I'll see you tomorrow, Will. Thank you." He replaced his phone.

I called Akira, but there was no reply. Only because I was at a loss as to what to do with myself and because the morning had, after all, been a sort of triumph, which demanded recognition, I walked down the corridor to Akira's room and rapped on the door, not expecting a response. His Do Not Disturb sign dangled from the doorknob.

"Akira! It's me. William."

Apparently Akira had double-locked himself inside, since the first sign of his presence was the rattling of the security chain. When everything was finally unfastened, he opened the door a few inches and stared out at me without expression. I searched around for the right greeting, and while I did, the smell of Akira and the room moved through the opening and around me, musty, sweaty, sharpened with the scent of whisky.

There was a wildness in this blankness, so that it seemed the rage of a strong emotion was held in check by the force of an equal and opposite emotion. I felt he was comparing the way I looked with some mental picture of me, like an immigration official checking a dubious passport photo, and I sensed that he was in some sort of heightened mental state, with which I should deal carefully.

This situation was not unfamiliar and I felt myself accept the responsibility for its management. It was almost routine that in the course of a mission one member or another would lose his balance. The shadowy rationale for the work, combined with the distance from home, the cultural confusion, and the inescapable scrutiny of unfamiliar colleagues, regularly produced temporary madness among mission experts, so that the convention had evolved that aberrations would be forgotten on return to headquarters. Once home, the falterers were again allowed to present themselves as confident and capable men.

"Hi, Akira. I just came by to brief you on the meetings I had with the provincial government. Can I come in, or are you busy?" I edged forward and he turned his body enough to let me pass.

Papers covered his bed, the floor, the chairs, and the narrow hotel desk. Reports and volumes of statistics were pressed open and strips of paper with Japanese characters marked other pages. Mixed up with the slewed papers on the bed were pornographic magazines, so that the straight white edge of a sheet of tables dissected a girl's open legs and a flesh-colored segment between scattered pages showed a woman being had by at least two men. I noted two empty whisky bottles in the wastebasket and another half empty on the desk. The TV was running soundlessly and its movement caught my eye. The video film showed a domestic scene in an American house. A man was shouting at a disheveled housewife who screamed back at him. There were plastic children's toys in primary colors on the kitchen floor. When the man's expression softened and he moved toward the woman, the film gave a little jump so that he was immediately moving away, a reminder that this was Pakistan.

I turned from the visual refuge of the screen toward where Akira waited, near the door. "Looks like you've been busy."

He stared at me and I knew that for the last two days, while he had been doing all this, I had been on his mind. I took things gently, and carefully picked up a sheaf of his incongruously neat handwritten tables from the desk chair.

"May I?"

He did not respond, and I sat. I glanced at the top table, a breakdown of Pakistan's agricultural exports for the year 2020.

"Interesting."

Over the next two hours Akira gradually returned to animation. At first he silently handed me successive sheets of tables, waiting for me to scan each one. As he went to the corners of the room to unearth new papers other pornographic magazines were revealed. He showed no embarrassment. I recognized one element in the room's musty odor as semen, and a feeling of claustrophobia grew in me.

In time he began to offer gruff responses to my bland indications of interest and approval: "Backward projection . . . World Bank data . . . not actual dollars; 1980 dollars."

As the tables accumulated, the hugeness of his enterprise dawned on me. He had abandoned his attempt to reconcile the dubious official statistics, which maddened him with their contradictions, but instead of taking my advice to construct a set of plausible figures for our immediate purposes—which would of course themselves be irreconcilable with all other data—he had constructed an entirely new statistical world, in which all the figures were completely harmonious.

His starting point was the year 2020, apparently on the basis that his guesses for that year were more realistic than any data we had available for the present. His argument seemed to be that we still had the opportunity to make his figures for 2020 come true, whereas we knew that all of the current figures we had were false. From this imaginary future he had worked backward to the present day. For each year he had world production of manufactures and commodities broken down by country. For Pakistan there were tables for the production, import, and export of everything from wheat to household appliances, together with the labor and natural resources required for their production. Using annual discount rates based on estimated rates of national growth, he arrived at estimates for current resources and production, which he then subdivided by province and district, so that at the end there was a perfect summary of the present situation of our project valley, fully integrated into space and time. It was madness, but I found myself silently impressed in the face of it. I was unable to explain to him, if he did not instinctively understand, why his false version of the world was madness and the false version I had wanted was simple sense.

I remained sitting, staring at the final page, until he said, "This is what you want." It was not a question.

I nodded, then replied, "We can use this."

Akira's muscular face broke into a smile, and he piled his pages into my arms. "You take them. I sleep." He guided me toward the door.

There had been one occasion when my father offered me a theory of the world, and although I still treasured it deep in me, I had long overlooked the circumstances. Like most of the men I knew as a child, he did not think it his place to have large opinions. Even the oblique lessons of his Sunday-school talks had a shaky defiance about them, as if he expected someone more authoritative to throw open the door at any moment and dash his assertions.

The two of us were playing the board game Circumnavigation on a Christmas Day when I was about eleven, just old enough to want to win on my own account. The board was a map of the world with pathways linking the major ports. It was a game manufactured before I was born, and the trade routes it showed were a celebration of the extent of British colonial power. By throwing the dice, the players set about circumnavigating the world by various routes while avoiding hazards. I had always loved this game, though my father did not, only agreeing to play with me on Christmas Day, and then only one game. While its scale excited me, he found no pleasure in it, preferring the closed and separate world of cards. He played cards well and regretted the lack of a serious opponent, but Circumnavigation caused in him an obscure upset, so that he would throw the game halfway through to give me an unsatisfying victory.

I never saw my father drunk, but on this one occasion he had taken a sherry before Christmas dinner and also wine—a present from a customer—with it, so that by the time we reached our annual game he showed some of the high-spirited jokiness that was usually reserved for the housewives on his round.

"Come on, son. See if I can't get the better of you this time."

By the time we reached Asia, he was ahead of me and for once giving no quarter. He moved from Jakarta to Shanghai.

"Ask me no questions, I'll tell you no lies. I saw a Chinaman doing up his flies."

"Ben!" protested my mother from the easy chair where we thought she was asleep.

Dad winked at me, but quietened, the successfully scolded child.

"OK, son, let's see what you can do."

We did not speak while I moved from Penang to Hong Kong and he threw a two—"Deuce!"—to be caught in a typhoon off Japan, causing him to miss a turn.

After my next turn—a six took me straight to Tokyo—he took the dice and shook it in his fist, for a moment lost in thought. Then, in a low voice, one that kept what he said from his wife, he confided: "I'll tell you something I've noticed, son. Civilization moves around the world this way, from right to left." He paused, then refined the idea. "Well, since the world's round, it's clockwise—looking from the top."

I waited, and he organized his thoughts before continuing. "China here had the first civilization. That's right, isn't it? Did they teach you that at school?"

I was unsure but I conceded this.

"Right. Then there was something in India and then the Greeks, then the Romans in Italy, here. Then us. Now it's the

Americans coming up, isn't it? You see, it always goes this way."

His voice went even quieter. "You know what I reckon? I reckon it'll be the Japanese next." He nodded to confirm himself. "If not in my lifetime, then in yours."

I could not recall another time he offered me so large an understanding of the world, and I never heard him repeat this one. If he continued to contain the ideas that led to it, they were kept safe in him. Perhaps this was not simply fear of rebuff but also because, among our men, the impression of understanding, the holding of theories, outspoken opinions, were considered bad manners, arrogant, incitement to discord, asking for trouble, vanity. Those with power—officials, employers, the upper classes—might turn at any time and carelessly punish us for our presumption.

I looked at the board with eleven-year-old eyes. "So what happens after Japan? Will it go back to China again?"

He averted his eyes as if I had caught him out. "I don't know, son. I suppose it could go round again. That's too far ahead for my poor old brain to think about."

But he was suddenly shifty, and it occurred to me for the first time in Peshawar that what he had shied away from was a secret belief that when it was China's turn again, the world would come to an end.

He threw the dice, but now his gaiety was all spent and he made a foolish decision off the Philippines, so that the game was lost. Still, I carried my father's single big idea away with me, as deeply hidden in me as it was in him. It was probably this, twenty-five years later, that had made it seem a shrewd idea to get involved with Japanese money when others still held back. I had agreed without hesitation, easily embracing the idea of an inevitable Japanese ascendancy which he had planted in me.

In my room I turned again to Slocum for his buoyant sanity, happily at sea. Outside Gibraltar he single-handedly outsailed a boatload of marauding Moors until they were dismasted in a storm. He was modest: luck was on his side. Off Chile a sly Portuguese trader persuaded him to exchange his ship's store of good potatoes for a load of bad ones. He chuckled at his gullibility and sailed on. I was beginning to feel a rift opening up between me and Slocum. His vigor did not sit well with the whiff of nausea and my shifting aches and pains, and I was not sure I was equal to serving as his crew. Off Tierra del Fuego he slept peacefully below, his gun next to him, relying on carpet tacks strewn on the deck to alert him to barefoot savages. His own company continued to satisfy him; the past no longer bothered him.

I went to the window and pulled aside the curtain to look out on the hotel pool, shining in the still-bright sun. The water was blue and undisturbed, the surrounds paved with light, hot stones. A scattering of white people sunbathed on slatted loungers, reading thick paperbacks or American news magazines through dark glasses. They would all be aid workers, mostly Danes, judging by the blond hair and the skimpy swimwear. To one side the guard, with his handlebar mustache and fancy-dress uniform, stood ready to hold open the door or shoot terrorists. I considered reaching for the relief of the new, going down and chatting with the Danes in the common language of development. But then I thought of those steady blue eyes, the careful English, their simple tales of what they did, how useful it was, and how the Pakistanis needed them. I let the curtain fall. Inside the room a sentimental American film had a young athlete bravely facing up to terminal cancer, while a blonde with a porcine face was tearful with love for him.

Somehow, during the two days he spent closed in his room, Yamada had staged a recovery, so that early on the morning of our third day in Peshawar he called me for a breakfast meeting. His voice was vigorous and commanding, and when he joined me in the restaurant his walk was brisk. His hair had been trimmed, and his shoes were shined.

He dropped a pile of reports next to my place setting. "All

yours!" He was cheery. If he had been American, he would have slapped me on the back.

There was something mysterious about the completeness of his regeneration, as if magic were involved or some higher state of being had been artificially achieved. I had the impulse to reach across the table and ferret behind his tie and shirt to discover whether the raw scars on his chest had miraculously disappeared.

"Will, it's good you are still here. I thought you might leave us to go home."

"No."

"You are right. Sometimes one must push aside personal things for something bigger. That is what separates an extraordinary man from an ordinary man. I am pleased you are still with us."

He turned to make a small but definite signal to the waiter, leaving me to consider this—whether the "us" was the North-West Frontier mission or the company of extraordinary men. During the days of Yamada's failing and Akira's craziness, I had come to think of them with me, not me with them, and perhaps it was this understanding that Yamada was now determined to reverse. He told the waiter to put my breakfast on his bill.

"So, you have tied up the loose ends of our project with the provincial man?"

"Shareef?"

"Yes. I talked with the minister in Islamabad. It's all right. It will fit in."

Yamada paused to dig enthusiastically into his scrambled eggs. I had never before seen him do more than play with food before. With his new vigor, I felt my own grip slackening. I considered asking him what it was with which the project must fit, but I counseled myself to silence; appearing ill-informed and requesting explanations were both positions of weakness. I said, "Of course we don't know as much about the target populations as we optimally should. We only drove through the second valley. We don't know who lives there."

"Ah, Will, don't worry. The Pakistanis know their people. It's

their problem. That's the other thing which separates extraordinary men from ordinary men, Will—they can distinguish
what is worth worrying about and what isn't. They don't worry
about little things."

He was lecturing me and at the same time welcoming me as
a junior initiate. There was a slight sarcasm of resentment in
my response, but I don't believe that even Yamada was Western enough to hear it. "So what's the big thing I should be
worrying about now?"

"Ah, you'll see. I've been busy. Did you think I was doing
nothing these last days?" He laughed. "Diplomacy. How would
you like to meet the president, Will?"

"Of Pakistan? Zia?"

"Of course. Why talk to the servants? Do you have a good
suit?"

Yamada was garrulous, not waiting for my replies. He said
that the Japanese Embassy had applied for our mission to be
upgraded from technical to diplomatic. Our project, which
must of course still be presented as aid to the poor of the
North-West Frontier, even more so now, could be made a
pretext for sounding out the basis for longer-term negotiations
on financial and security matters. Yamada, released from prac-
ticality and detail, was like a dying fish that had made it back to
water. He was on his way, flashing his tail. He did not notice
that for my part, I was spinning, dizzy with the abstraction,
shedding the tiny memories of recent days that had so pressed
their importance on me. Circumnavigation in a cluttered
Christmas room was lost; my father's prescience about the
Japanese was eclipsed by the reality. A residual puzzling at the
exact meaning of that expression on Han's face, and a passing
love for a young Mireille lost to joy on a forest path, must be
left behind if I was to join Yamada in his ascent. My father
faded in the face of Yamada's smile to me, his warm approval
of my staying on and his assumption of my company.

At last he paused, read and signed the bill, said, "Shall we?"
and stood to leave. He added as an afterthought, "You're supervising Akira, I hope."

"In a way. We're working together."

"Good. He needs supervision. I'll leave that to you then."

I had pushed aside the remains of a good room-service khorma when there was a knock at my door. The steward had already been in to turn down the bed for the night, and I guessed it would be Akira. He stood in the doorway, composed, his feet together, his head bent in formal deference. There was a clean white shirt and dark trousers, but the large cow-horn buckle on his belt brought back Yamada's judgment: that Akira was an irredeemable rough diamond. I wondered whether, if he had known the English class divisions better, Yamada would have seen through me. I doubted it.

"Akira! Come in!" I was hearty for the time of night; a clear signal of welcome and normality to cross the distance between us. He chose an upright chair, and I chose an easy chair to put myself below him. I waited. I was ready to manage Akira as Yamada had managed me.

"I think I was crazy yesterday."

"Crazy? I didn't notice. You may have been a little over-worked perhaps."

"No. I think I make your work difficult." He was humble.

"No problem. We've already got agreement on the project."

"Agreement? Agreement without figures?" He looked toward my coffee table, where I had set his three hundred tables of harmonious statistics, a complete world. I followed his look.

"Ballpark agreement. We'll need to put some figures in the project document of course."

"I think I will take these." He moved toward the pile like an artist protecting his work from philistines. "I was a little crazy."

"No, no." I had also stood and when he did not stop I put my hand on his arm. "No, really, Akira, we can use them." I was suddenly determined not to let them out of my sight. Han would have used them. They were too good to waste.

"But they are—what you say?—a novel!"

"Well, maybe. But useful."

Something of the old intensity of panic came back to Akira's face, as if a recently established definition of sanity were being snatched from him.

I rushed to edit myself. "Not a novel, Akira. A model. We economists always need models."

"But the project area . . . not like that."

"Maybe. Maybe not. Who knows?"

He held my look, and shadows passed across his face, none staying long enough to make it to an expression. Then he let his head fall and said, "I think I miss my wife. . . ."

I waited and he continued. "The women here . . . everything covered. Even faces. I like Bangkok. . . ." He looked up. "You miss your wife?"

It felt like friendship offered, and I did hesitate. "Well . . . I don't see my wife too often."

I could have said why and mentioned Han; there were several ways to go from there, and I did hover for a moment between a common openness and the concealed hand of management. "Maybe it's just as well they keep their women veiled. It keeps them off our minds." It was friendship rejected, and for the second time Akira took on a troubled look, which seemed briefly to entertain the possibility that the madness might be in me, not him. "We could stop over in Bangkok when we're through," I added, as a feeble parting compromise.

In the night I suffered an agitation that I thought might be fever. It focused first on Akira and then on Yamada. I was afflicted with an anger at them both. With Akira, it was the guileless hope for friendship on his face that charged my memory and sent me reeling from affection toward a selective recollection of the repellent divergence of his eyes, his coarse snoring, the vulgarity of him. For Yamada, it was the contradiction between his helpless sickliness on one day and his patronizing claim of authority on another that infuriated me, his wish to have it both ways. Each seemed to have chosen his behavior to aggravate my distress, as if guided by some privileged knowledge of my inner landscape unknown even to me.

I set myself the task of explaining why it was perfectly reasonable for the son of a Tottenham milkman to find himself, at the time of bereavement, in the North-West Frontier of Pakistan with only the cousin of the Japanese emperor and the graceless son of a Japanese peasant for company.

I worked it back to the Americans at the Bretton Woods conference at the end of World War II. It was not accident that set me here but the conscious intent of visionary men. They reasoned, in the confidence of victory, that colonization had had its day and the way to power and influence in the future world would be through money, not crude control. They set up the World Bank and the International Monetary Fund, and while I was still in my mother's womb, they set the mold. From then on there would always be a profitable role for those who had become detached from their beginnings and were uneasy everywhere, go-betweens to peddle money and pretend the innocence of it. It was a congruence, I reasoned, between the times and me that had, not unreasonably, placed me here. And it was only logical, as the money power moved on—clockwise, looking from the top—that it should now be the Japanese I would find for company. One fine Japanese for vision, one rough one for nuts and bolts, and me, the neutral priest, giving my blessing. There was nothing odd in all this.

The reasoning did not bring me to sleep, but it released me from Yamada and Akira by snagging me in the memory of Han and the magic she had found in the name World Bank. As we had moved from Latin America to Africa, before Asia, the connection between us had deepened, forcing out connection with everything else—Mireille, home, principle—and my head was filled with Han's insomniac nighttime stories. With time they seemed to darken from the chancing vitality of early versions toward the cruelty and disappointment she had found in the powerful men she had enthralled: John the American mogul, the German who didn't wash, and the man who pushed a

slight taste for pain along the road to torture. Put into se-
quence, her grievances began in Indonesia, where her father
had fled from the Chinese revolution. The Indonesians, she
said, hated the Chinese and murdered many of them. She had
battled both Indonesia and her father with a child's blind fury,
which, in the telling, reminded me of the nighttime pummel-
ings she gave me, her invitations to her own defeat. She left for
Hong Kong as soon as she was old enough—"Illegal migrant,
right?"—and began to learn what men liked. She had found a
job with Cathay Pacific Airlines and relived, amid tears at the
unfairness of it, how the pink, slow English girls had been
promoted over clever Han, so she had to leave, but not before
she'd compromised her boss and got a payoff. We went from
tears to smiles with that.

The World Bank story came at the end of them all, like a
dawn. In Las Vegas, where the "shit from the mob" had beaten
her, she remembered the World Bank, just a name on a card
a man had given her in Singapore. During the three-day Amtrak
journey from the West Coast to D.C., while her bruises faded,
she rebuilt a plan for her life, and the refrain that played
against the sound of the track was "World Bank."

She knew nothing about the Bank, but she thought she
knew enough. She told this part as a success story. "I wanted
money, so the word 'bank' seemed just right. I didn't belong in
any country, so 'world' seemed just right too." For three days
she looked out the window through dark glasses, a silk scarf
high around her throat, and worked out how to do it. She still
had the card from the man she met in Singapore—someone
from the Operations Division—and she had a bit of something
on him, which she judged she would not need to use—"If
you've got a gun, you can be generous, right?"—and she made
a plan around that. The plan had worked out; the telling of it
soothed her. In the clarity of the train journey she made realistic assessments: she was smart; she had business savvy; she
had dealt with big money for rich men; she knew five lan-
guages; she had traveled; she had social skills. There was no
doubt she could be useful to the Bank, but without paper

qualifications it would be hard to prove it. She remembered the name of a college in Malaysia that was burned down in anti-Chinese riots and gave herself a degree from there: "M.A., Administration. Could mean anything." Her references, from important men, would be excellent.

She was right; the Bank and Han were well suited. In Nigeria, which we visited after Colombia, I began to trust her with my work. I lay tired in bed while she calculated plausible internal rates of return for plausible projects. She had learned that fifteen percent per annum pleased the bosses—too low for commercial banks, too high for charity—and all our projects worked out this way. It was always possible to reach the figure by changing some assumption about the future—prices, the speed of construction, the popularity of a new miracle grain—and she used this sleight of hand unscrupulously. At the beginning I made a token stand for principle, but it was a shaky thing to pit against the warmth of bed, and it turned out that everyone who counted loved the way we made the money flow. I did point out, early on, still thinking to teach Han, that the calculations she made had real consequences for real people, and the project she topped and tailed before breakfast might mean life or death to some. "Screw the peasants, Bill. Nobody ever looked after me. Do you think you're God? Do the peasants pay us? If we crank this out, we can make the game reserve for the weekend."

Her callousness seemed like life. I tried it on for size and it felt like standing up unaided for the first time. "I want to make love in the jungle," said Han, not looking up. "I want to fuck somewhere with lions next to us." I did not see then, and could still not see in Peshawar, how cruelty was close to compassion for Han, and how notions of "world" and "bank" were for her not only home but also the torturer's instruments of pleasure. "I want to hear them roar," she said. "I want to be shit scared." She looked up, pushed her glasses up on her nose, gave her pretty smile.

We tried the thing with lions, which seems so tiring now, now I'm so much calmer and my lovemaking with Emo is quiet, something we take pleasure in and neglect to talk about. It seems mad now that I should ever have had such extreme hopes for it, though, even as I write this, I recognize the old fascination of a straight line followed for its length with eyes close to the ground.

We did frighten ourselves in the Yankari game reserve, where a lioness with a forepaw severed by a trap hurled herself at our Land-Rover in protection of her cubs. She became suddenly so large and solid, so unlike a nature film, that for the first time, and too late to be useful, we were forced to ask ourselves whether we really knew the windows were stronger than her, and whether our dangerous game might not after all be dangerous. Her mouth against the windshield was larger than our heads, her face was scarred and flawed, and while she rocked and battered us, she roared. I reversed rapidly back down the track and finally she slipped from us as softly as a blanket pulled from a bed, leaving us not to cold but to ourselves. Han had shivered, though the day was hot and she had never reached the stage when she would have removed her clothes and exposed herself to large animals that could not touch her. And we never did make love the way she planned, us safe inside and savagery all around.

It took a week and a flight to another country before she again tested her invulnerability with the old defiance, and I felt something had changed in her so that she was no longer completely confident of success and that a question she had asked of the world had been answered. Looking back, I believe it dated the beginning of a change in her, even though I did not see it then and the occasion in Liberia was still to come.

For the first weeks here, while I stayed close to the beach, I kept pressing Emo to tell me about the secret terrors of Ruatua. Were there not obscure insects that lived in the coconut groves and whose sting would kill you in hours? She thought not. Poisonous spiders among the bananas? The cultivated taro plots cleared among the trees and untidy with weeds were the sort of places where I had learned elsewhere to expect deadly tropical snakes. One would put forward a clumsy hand to pull a root, and there was the quick surprise of a fatal nip, life suddenly gone. Emo said there were no such dangers, but it was some time before I would walk inland with her to collect salad stuffs from her family village.

"The sharks?" I asked.

"The sharks? They don't bother us. They stay outside the reef. Bill, are you looking for something to fight?"

I saw the truth in this, and in response I could only fall back among the pillows of Emo's bed, rendered limp by the absence of anxiety.

"Poor Bill." Emo placed her hand against my forehead and peered amusedly at where my brain should be. "This gives you so much trouble."

On the day I arrived back here and first saw Emo again, she was sitting at her untidy Coconut Beach desk, next to her blank computer screen, with a slight, undefined smile on her face. It might have done for an old friend or a new one. Later she told me she had not been sure whether it was me or someone much like me.

On the morning of that day, I had woken in Tonga, at the International Dateline Hotel. I had woken rested and ravenous and my first act had been to throw away the nibbled remains of the three Little America Café hamburgers and to go to the hotel dining room for a full breakfast. The inability to swallow, and the nausea and pains that preceded it, had vanished with my father. Three hours later I was in the light plane to Ruatua. In eight hours I had landed and found an old taxi to take me across the island to Coconut Beach, where I had found Emo, who—after two years—looked exactly the same and looked amused. I cannot remember consciously deciding that I should go across the island to Coconut Beach rather than, as my Ruatua assignment demanded, go into town to meet officials from the treasury. In my mind, though undoubtedly not in theirs, I was already off the job and had been off the job since the previous night's conclusive conversation with my father on the ceiling of the Dateline Hotel.

"You're Emo, aren't you?"

She inclined her head and met my eyes. "You wouldn't be Bill Bender, by any chance, would you?" There was a twinkle.

"Well, yes. You remember?"

She opened a pink school exercise book that lay on top of the pile of old correspondence. "Let me see . . . Mr.—no—Dr. Bender. I have to check." She picked up a large pair of spectacles and balanced them on her soft Ruatuan nose. Beyond her, on the opposite side of the little office from where I had entered, was a second doorway and even though I was entranced to the point of speechlessness by the sight of Emo, my eyes were drawn past her to this. Framed by the doorway, the world was all sunlight: a few succulent plants with blue-green leaves; a line of planted beer cans glittering blue and silver; pink and yellow flowers twined around the roof posts; but most of all, the pale sand sloping to the sea, the ice-blue sea itself, the distant white line of surf at the coral reef, the deeper blue beyond. I wanted more than anything to move into this picture but feared that I might not be able. Except for Emo, Coconut Beach seemed deserted.

"No," she said. "I can't find Dr. Bender here. Do you have a reservation?"

I shook my head, and she stood and walked around the desk, reminding me that she was almost my height. When she put down the pink exercise book I saw that the page was covered with a child's arithmetic schoolwork—some sums with ticks, some with crosses.

"I have all the customers I can manage, Dr. Bender. I'm sorry."

My mind rushed to believe her and the worst, and I quickly

saw how little reason I had for coming here, and how little justification I had for my sense that it was the place to go. Disappointment quickly covered me like a dark and bitter rain.

"Look at me," she said, and showed me that there was still a twinkle in her eye. "No customers, Dr. Bender, but maybe room for one guest."

I took her hand in a soft, ironic handshake. She glanced down at the exercise book and smiled at her careless deceit. "How many days this time, Dr. Bender? Just overnight? Two nights?"

"I'm not sure. Maybe longer."

"That's good. I've got someone I especially want you to meet."

"Who?"

"You don't know him. His name's 'Inoke."

"Something to do with a project?"

"A project? Yes, I think so. Very long-term."

"I've stopped working, Emo. I just want to hide. I've had enough of projects."

"Oh, 'Inoke's very nice. He won't give you a hard time. But we'll wait until another day. Come on. Come and have a beer."

I hang back now. As I write of Han and remember Mireille, I can only see my blundering ways, the way I grabbed at things and valued nothing, the way I loved the pain in Han instead of her, loved Mireille's sweet gentility. I want to do better with Emo, and the only way I trust is to keep my distance from her. Though I share her bed, I never ask her what she feels. I don't tell her of my confusions and the lonely anguish I sometimes experience as, on damp notepaper, I try to inch out the facts that brought me here so detached. I keep it to myself—a novel experience not to seek relief from distress by spreading its extent—except for the mute companionship of fish. I have come, as is the custom here, to tap Emo on the shoulder when I pass—no words. And I watch. I watch her working and I watch her in sleep. I watch how she is with 'Inoke, who is perhaps more like me than her other children, though it's hard to tell at one. She never pulls 'Inoke to her, never presses and rocks him against her breast as if he were possession and her life depended on it. She touches him gently, slowly, and when she lifts him from this place to that, there is time for respect in it, as if his permission is being sought. The women of her family, the ones who come from the village in the morning to weave the frangipani—for no reason other than the world deserves a decoration, since there are no paying guests now, only me and the old Englishman—these women take 'Inoke in their hands without asking Emo, the ownership of him as impossible here as the ownership of pigs.

I watch all this and keep my distance. Sometimes I let 'Inoke crawl to me, and if he does, I continue to do my odd jobs, or to look at the paper on my knees, so that he can make of me what he will, and if he interferes and pushes my pen in a jagged scribble across the page, I've learned to let him do so. Now I just start again and let it come out differently.

In the villages, too, I hold back. As a mateii I sometimes go to meetings and sometimes I am asked, as an expert, on the advisability of goats or the possibilities for vanilla, or some such innovation. I try to keep my hands off. Usually I tell them I do not know enough to say. I ask what they think and admit it is all too complicated for me. When foreigners arrive to propose a new investment on Ruatua and the villagers want to know the questions they should ask, I suggest they ask the experts about their families, their children—how are they doing in school?—and express interest in their religion and their belief in God or not, what they look for in a woman or a man, how much the experts are paid and whether they find it too little for their needs; ask if they are ever lonely and whether they have recently lost a person whom they loved, whether their health is good. Probably they have never taken my advice on this, but they listen to me kindly.

More than once, in the different villages where I am mateii, the question of pigs has been raised. Some miss the Large White pigs, which they remember as magnificent, and can't believe that nothing wonderful could come from them. It's several months since we ate the last, but they retain a spectral presence. The old cement-floored pig houses, with their corrugated-iron roofs, are still dotted around in disrepair, and the stories I hear now are of pigs as big as small cows and so fertile that Ruatua could feed all of Polynesia. Perhaps, I say to them, you are right. Perhaps Ruatua should try again with Large White pigs, but so far the impulse has gone no further, the idea of the vanished Large Whites perhaps too wonderful to be spoiled by practice.

I do try to tread lightly here, as I try to make light my touch of Emo. But I also think of Han and the harsh hurt she seemed to want and how for her the blunt scrape of economics across the earth was a proper return to the fragile, imploring poor. And I think again of how I was drawn to her and the fearless lines we drew around the world when no one could stop us.

In these last few weeks I have written less, and although my swims in the lagoon have ventured farther, I fancy they have lasted shorter than before. Instead I explore inland, often going with Emo into town in her old Suzuki jeep, or attending village feasts. I have taken up photography. For the first six months my camera remained in the dark of my suitcase. I have never been keen to take photos of the places I have worked— that sentimentality—and I carried the camera only for professional reasons. Sometimes I needed, in the absence of a suitable expert on a mission, to take a picture of a local breed of cattle or sheep, or to record the lie of land that might be irrigated. I rarely photographed people because of its irrelevance and because of the enthusiasm it brought out in them, the requests for copies in return. Only in the case of third world girls did I concede, finding the promise of a print, which I never honored, an easy way to leave. Recently, though, as part of my paying attention to things but keeping my proper distance, I have found the camera useful. I took shots of Emo and 'Inoke in bed together, Emo laughing at me or something I had said. For fairness I took an equal number of her other children, and there was one of me that Emo took of my being hugged by the pile of them. I've taken pictures of the beach, the sea, and the island, looking inland; one of Emo at her desk pretending to run her hotel; one of my peeled, broken beach lounger and its ratty palm-frond shade. It looked proud against the sea, a sort of boat.

Last week, when I had reached the full thirty-six pictures on my film, I went to town with Emo to have it developed and to buy a replacement. A little Kis Photo booth promised the pictures in two hours, and while Emo shopped, I spent the time talking to its Austrian owner. He was unhappy and obsessively anxious about his business. His dream had been to make a little money and to come to Ruatua with his Kis Photo machinery to lead an easy Polynesian life. He had even married a local girl so that he could stay, but it was not working out; Ruatua had too few tourists to turn a profit. About once a month a cruise ship anchored off the island and the passengers were ferried to shore for a few hours. This sudden excess of customers teased and tortured him. He had to turn some away, and there were always disputes about films still trapped in his machine's conveyor when it was time for the ship to leave. If only the ship would stay just one night, his business and his life would be perfect. His letter to the American cruise line suggesting this had not won a properly serious response.

I commiserated and paid his exorbitant price. I slipped the photos in my shirt pocket to share with Emo later. In the evening, after the children were in bed and we were quiet at a table set outside, I eased the bottom photo from its adhesion to the pack and was shaken to see not blue sea, or wide smiles on brown faces, but my father sitting in an armchair. The little living room in Mafeking Road looked comfortable and the armchair could not have been cheap. The window was open and a summer breeze filled out the net curtain. There was a photo of me on the mantelpiece behind him. I was taken aback to see the floor was thickly carpeted, and I had completely forgotten that the cheap and ugly furniture of my childhood had long been replaced. On his knee was a book covered in the plastic typical of the public library and I could read the name of the author, Philip Roth. He was just looking up at me, caught by surprise, his jaw a little slack, but friendliness already in his eyes.

It must have been a couple of years since I took the photo, of which I had no recollection. The shock was in the ordinariness of it and the ways it called the bluff of all I had written of him these last months, that version. Here was a calm retired man, living comfortably enough. Outside, it was sunny and the shrubs were in flower. I noticed the snug central heating system lining the walls, ready for winter. I had only remembered him sick in recent years, yet here he looked relaxed and alert in his chair. He was wearing a tie in spite of the sun.

There was another photo, taken in the back garden. Here both parents stood against a background of flowers, a washing line and a fence. They were about equal size—him a little taller, her a little broader—both with spectacles, well matched. My heart gave a little jump to see what I had asserted I never saw: his arm was around her waist.

The third photo, also in the garden, included me, taller than them both. With my father, I flanked my mother. I was smiling; I really looked quite happy. They looked pleased. I could not remember this picture either and it took me a little while to wonder who might have taken it, and a little while longer to see the shadow of the taker stretched out toward us across the uneven lawn. It was Han's elongated legs, the slight bow of them, the silhouette of her hair's sharp cut, a hint of distorted light around her glasses. I would have staked my life on Han never having visited Mafeking Road.

Emo took the one of my parents from me. "They look nice." She studied it. "You have flowers at your home too?"

"Mmm ... the English like flowers. Nation of gardeners."

"I didn't know that." She seemed pleased. "I wouldn't have guessed that."

Now, where am I? There is still a gap to cross, and I am suspicious that my new repose is only an excuse not to cross it. While at first I found that reverie would not come except in the diffusion of the sea, I find now I can lie here on the lounger and daydream my life of recent history, my notepaper becoming curled but remaining blank. In the scrupulousness of my part-completed record, I can see the way I falter in the face of everything difficult that is to come, the shamefulness and pain of later events. But in spite of this unwillingness in me, I know I must attempt to complete the line between then and now, as the break in the reef connects the ocean of past with the lagoon of present—and this clever, artful image in itself is, I know, yet another way of making distance and pretending that the simple carefulness of task I set myself is separate from me. For a rawer truth I would do well to swim to the breach itself, where the fear would be sharper and the danger real. It calls a challenge to me and scratches at the private pleasure of my life with Emo. All the same, I will try to continue here and go through the things with Han, my father, Akira, and Yamada, and if I can no longer maintain a cool neutrality of tone and steer away from explanation, I might allow myself this, admitting the perspective of time and letting reason reassure me of the impossibility of truth.

In the distance I can see the skinny old Englishman, who keeps himself to himself, combing the beach. He has walked in one direction until his hands and arms are filled with treasures, and now he is walking back, redistributing them along the water's edge. Now he is stopping to watch a knot of Ruatuans under the palms, and now he is waving to them, using both arms and abandoning the last of his bundle. It's good to see the Ruatuans are smiling and waving back; for a moment I was worried that they would mock him and treat him as a nuisance. I confess I have been a little hurt that this lonely old man, after all the only other Englishman on Ruatua, should avoid me as he does. He scuttles and dances away from me and my questions as if I were the devil himself. No matter. I am in Pakistan.

• • •

It was as much loneliness as the demands of work that made me seek out Yamada and Akira the next day. I found them together in Yamada's room, Yamada lying on his stomach while Akira massaged his naked back. Yamada seemed perfectly at ease to be found this way, and without lifting his head, he gave me a smile that was almost seductive. Akira ignored my entrance and kept his eyes on his work.

"Make yourself comfortable, Will. Akira is just finishing me. Loosens phlegm." He smiled again.

I watched them together: the younger man tending his frail superior; the older accepting the touch. Almost the venerable father and the dutiful son. The pale skin of Yamada's back rippled under the pressure of Akira's hands, showing the absence of resisting substance. Without his clothes he was all brittle fragility, yet his composure was unaffected.

"Things move ahead, Will. We go to Islamabad tomorrow. The government has upgraded us from technical to diplomatic, so we will have full diplomatic protocol."

He seemed pleased by this. I nodded, "Good."

I had hardly ever touched my own father, but I recalled that once, when rearranging his pillows, my hand had pressed against his old man's flesh, which was waxy, soft and cold. I had drawn away and had not dwelt on it till now. As an afterthought I inquired back into the warm look Yamada had kept for me, "What does that actually mean in practice?"

"Oh, we'll have a military escort for tomorrow's journey. The government will take care of all our arrangements. Everyone will listen to us better. The president will see us."

I found I did not want to ask what it was that we would make them listen to. A tightening in my intestines warned me off, as if my bowel were the arbiter of authenticity and was becoming impatient. The project I had negotiated was never what it pretended to be, only an agreeable public version, and now it seemed this shadow of a shadow was to be the cover for something new and larger. All this was normal, but the pressure of memory in my mind somehow left less space for it, and the naive emotion Akira brought to falsity rankled me. I turned away from the bait of Yamada's words and kept silent.

Akira finished the massage and handed Yamada his shirt. I also stood to leave. "I'll let you rest, Mr. Yamada."

"Thank you, Will. I have to place some calls."

In the corridor outside, Akira looked at me and said simply, "Come."

I followed him into the elevator and out into the ground-floor lobby. While the doorman waited, holding open the main door, I asked, "Where are we going?" but Akira's face remained closed and determined as he signaled our driver over from the parking lot.

When he spoke again we had left the pretty tree-lined suburbs by the Pearl Continental and were in the noisy clutter of Peshawar city, the only car among the pedestrians and the swarms of blue motorized trishaws, and then he only spoke to say, "Come," once more. This time he led the way through the doorway of an old hotel crowded between other old buildings and pressed upon by a street market. We climbed a wide circular stone stairway and after half a dozen floors we abruptly emerged into the light of the roof. There was a surrounding wall and inside it flowers grew in planters, and tables and chairs were spaciously arranged in the shade of vines and small trees. I adjusted my eyes and saw several high officials among the patrons.

The waiter knew Akira, which surprised me then, though I later became used to the way Akira, for all his lack of social skills, made friends everywhere.

"Beer or Scotch whisky?" asked the waiter.

This was Muslim Pakistan, where alcohol was illegal; I raised my eyebrows at Akira. None of the government officials, I noticed, seemed in the least self-conscious. "Whisky," I said.

"One bottle," said Akira to the waiter, who was unsurprised.

We sat for a moment in silence. Akira looked at his knees. "Well?" I said.

"I did not want you to see it." He still did not turn to me.

"See what?"

"Me with Mr. Yamada. Doing . . ." He kneaded imaginary flesh.

"Massage?"

"Yes."

"Why not?"

"William-san, I hate that man." Now he looked up to see my reaction, seeing astonishment.

"I thought you were colleagues."

"I hate him."

"Why?" I tried to look amused.

"Look at me. I don't sleep. I have ulcer. No woman for six months. You know who I am? I am best agriculturalist in Japan. One of best. I like agriculture. My father is farmer. I like plants." He cupped his stubby hands as if he would nurture a plant right there. "I like to help farmers. Farmers everywhere. Pakistan farmers. I am good. But you see what I do? I massage Mr. Yamada. I cook Mr. Yamada food. I servant! I work for him all the time. I must. In Tokyo I work from six in the morning to midnight. Sometimes I sleep at my office. When I see my wife I only want to sleep. Mr. Yamada only want to do big-shot things while I work. He is from emperor family."

"I know. He told me."

"Rich shits! I'm from poor family. Farmers. No, peasants!"

I considered breaking in to confide to Akira that my background was also modest and that we had a bond in this but I could not quite decide if it was best to present myself that way. Akira, lost in his complaints, looked like an awkward schoolboy.

"I always thought you were friends."

"Because we are both Japanese? Ha! I can't be friend with Mr. Yamada. He is my boss." He smiled grimly, then found a new direction. "He has many women. Beautiful women. Young. One in Manila. One in Jakarta. He gives them apartments and they just wait for him. Maybe once or twice every one, two years I find a prostitute. His girls are only waiting."

"Isn't he getting a bit past it?"

"Ha?"

"Too old."

"For girls?" He looked taken aback. "Maybe too sick. I'm sorry about that. Sure." He paused, then: "My wife, she is not beautiful. She is too fat. But she is very kind. You miss your wife, William-san?"

He had asked this before, and because I had not confided then, and because I turned away from the chance to admit my humble origins, I did respond this time.

"We don't get along these days. She's French. I don't see her often. I don't know whether I miss her or not."

"You travel too much."

"Yes, but it's not only that. I went off with another woman."

"You tell your wife?"

"Yes."

"Why?"

"I don't know. I wanted the other woman."

"More beautiful?"

"Chinese."

"Chinese. You leave your European wife to go with Oriental woman?" Akira sat back in his chair and smiled at me, looking relaxed now. "William-san, I didn't think that. From China?"

"Her father. Grew up in Indonesia. American now." I was conscious of adopting Akira's cadence.

"Her mother?"

"I don't know. She never mentioned her mother."

"You leave her too?"

"No."

I looked down, so that Akira saw a need to cheer me up. "William-san. Sorry." He leaned over and slapped my upper arm. It occurred to me that the Japanese were not supposed to do that. But he looked at ease. Perhaps I was mixing up my cultures.

···

Sometimes, early on, in America, Mireille forgot and ran through the landscape just for the sake of the wind in her face, just for the joy of it.

These fish have begun to annoy me, so unresponsive to friendship and impossible to train. Now I go straight for the harsher push and pull of the cooler, deeper water, ignoring the complicated commuter scenery of coral reef I must pass through.

She said she was a third world country in my life, colonized, kept helpless, occasionally visited, liked for its gentle nature, which could be used. She said she would not let me sow in her the way I did in them and claim the product for myself. Mireille said.

A certain slavishness persists. Peristalsis is like this. There's a pleasure in fascist friends and a need for explanations.
   Of course both positions are wrong; structuralists and structuralistes offer nothing against the dreadful roundness of the world, with their common fallacy that one thing leads to another. I am drawn these days to the colder, more turbulent water near the breach.

When I got into my bath last night it didn't look very full—what with the cost of coal these days and everything, we try to economize on hot water—but after I'd got in, it really came up quite high. Then I thought, it's like that when the Holy Spirit enters you. . . . Oh, God, give me a break. . . .

Bubbles. They're like the pleasures we seek in life. They look attractive but they're soon gone. You can spend your life chasing bubbles. . . . No, he won't pick it up.

In Nigeria they are playing the reels of Apocalypse Now *in the wrong order and no one notices. An American film set in Vietnam. Made in the Philippines. From an African book by a Polish Englishman. Italian director? American? I don't know.*

In Liberia we dance among the Zwedru dwarfs, none of them more than four feet. Han wants to . . .

Taps? Hot and cold. You've got to have a balance, see. You need to know what belongs to God and what belongs to Rome. By Rome of course I mean London—well, anywhere really. I suppose. God is like the hot tap. Or maybe the cold. No.

• • •

There had been an occasion, perhaps ten years earlier—I was still with the World Bank in Washington and it was well before Han—when my plane arrived in London early on a Sunday morning. Later in the day I was due to fly somewhere else but there was enough time to go to Tottenham for a Sunday dinner. I rented a car at Heathrow and called my parents from the motorway service area at Heston, where I took breakfast, read the *Observer,* and readied myself for the dip into an earlier life. My mother answered, and after she had settled from the happy panic of my unexpected arrival, she told me that my father would not be at home; he was bearing witness in the church that morning. "Oh, he will be sorry not to be here. Mind you, he's in such a state over this witness business he can't think about anything else. He's asked me not to go. Says I'll make him nervous, would you believe."

"Look, Mum, don't tell him I'm coming. It will only upset him more. I'm going to the church to listen. But don't tell him, all right?"

I was still young enough then that it pleased me to return to the dowdy red-brick Baptist church where I had been a half-hearted member of my father's scout troop and had listened with embarrassment to his talks in the Sunday-school back room. I was pleased that on this occasion of return I had not rented the smallest car available, and I hoped that after the service, there would be people to recognize me and possibly to speak to me long enough for me to let them know I was between planes for the World Bank.

Although the church was a dowdy building, more like a community hall than a real church, it was always well attended, and there was little danger of my father spotting me from his place on the platform. I recalled, too, this business of bearing witness, when lay church members would haltingly expose the mundane circumstances of their faith. The fear of being asked to explain how I came to believe—the necessity for lies—had haunted me as a child and I wanted to look at it again, confident that I could now face it down.

Of course the church seemed smaller than once it had, but I found a discreet seat on a dusty straight-back chair in a back row of such chairs, behind a group of widows in hats. His wavy hair was now entirely gray, and his face had aged in the way of a certain sort of Englishman, becoming not marked with the intensity of experience but softer and pinker, as if experience had been successfully rebuffed. But there was still something about his strong features that made the widows smile and exchange whispers when he was introduced. He was still a favorite with the housewives.

He started, "I expect those of you who know me know I had a bit of bad luck about a year ago. I lost my job. A bolt from the blue. Now, I asked the question everyone asks when they have a bit of bad luck: Why me? And I couldn't answer. I thought about it. I thought I'd always done a good job. I was a milkman, for those of you who don't know. Nobody had ever complained about my work. I was only a few years off retirement after thirty years with Kendels. Then, suddenly, this. I was upset. I admit it. I was angry. And I wasn't just angry at Kendel's; I was angry at God." He paused and nodded for emphasis, as if his words alone were suspect.

"Well, I have to tell you we had a bit of a difficult time. My wife works—bless her—but money was a bit short. We had to get rid of the car. We didn't eat as well as we did before. Not such good joints of meat as we were used to, and less often."

The congregation hushed; the joints of meat brought the horror home to them. I became uncomfortable. I imagined that the widows might turn and loudly denounce me: "You're his educated son. Look at you with your airs and graces. How could you let this happen to your parents, who were always so good to you? Where were you when all this was going on?" I imagined the widows to be capable of a lynching. I wished he was not doing this, that his judgment of what to reveal and what not to reveal were sounder.

"I started to walk everywhere. I had the time now. And one day it struck me that God was teaching me a lesson. I was walking on a road near here—Tyler's Lane, it was—and I found I was looking at the little wildflowers which had come up between the paving stones and the walls of front gardens. I'd never looked at them before. I'd spent all my life as a milkman running up and down front paths, and I'd never taken the time to appreciate little things like that. When I thought about it, I felt my faith coming back. I'd been vain. I'd been a bit of a big-head. I'd thought all that time that I'd been living a good life, and I'd forgotten that it wasn't for me to say."

I tried to think of my father as vain. The idea was ridiculous. Didn't he know that the world was full of men bursting with baseless self-importance?

"So God had taught me a lesson. He had humbled me."

Humbled him! Was that what a modest, gentle, unemployed man needed? My indignation took in the entire congregation, whose silence I felt to be smug.

"Then He said to me, He said: Look, there's all this. When you walk there are flowers. When you're unemployed you have time to think. When you eat less meat you can understand better the lives of less fortunate people in poor countries, and you realize how lucky you are. My son taught me that. He's a good lad. He spends his life going round the world helping the poor. He says they don't have much meat in Africa and China and places like that.

"So my bad luck turned out to be a blessing in disguise and I knew I'd been wrong to be angry at God. I lost my faith for a little while there. I didn't trust Him. I had to learn all over again how to have faith in Him."

Everyone was silent and I could tell, as my father backed away, that he was upset. His witness had cost him a lot. There was respect in the silence and there was embarrassment, but most of all, I thought I could read in the congregation's immobile heads the prayers of men who did not want to receive a similar blessing and the prayers of women grateful that their men had not had their faith renewed through the gift of unemployment.

I had the impulse to stand up above the bowed congregation while they waited to be moved in prayer—they all seemed undersized—and tell them it was all ridiculous. It wasn't God who made my father unemployed, it was a management buyout provoked by the parent company's loss of American market share, and if he had been smart he'd have seen it coming. And if they were smart they wouldn't buy God as an explanation of all this. Grow up, I wanted to tell them, and him, and by the way, I'm not traveling around the world to help the poor; I work for the World Bank.

It was probably the unashamed privilege of the car journey from Peshawar to Islamabad that conjured up this memory of useless humility. The new diplomatic status Yamada had won for us meant a new set of cars and the deployment of a military policeman at every intersection into town—where we paid our respects to the governor—and out of it again. The task on which the policemen's careers were staked was to detect our approach and ensure that our progress was unimpeded. In a bravado show of faith in military efficiency, our drivers did not slow for any of the crossroads and did not turn their heads left or right by even a degree. On each side of us the anarchy of traffic strained to overflow. Ahead, an open police jeep held six armed men sitting upright, the rifles between their knees swaying like saplings. The jeep's siren was oddly feeble, and its faint rise and fall induced a pleasant sleepiness. Beyond the jeep, four motorcycle outriders gave due warning to pedestrians, trucks, buses, and animals that they would count for nothing in our path, and we did cut through the traffic on the Islamabad road like a boat through water.

I found myself to be the sort of man I had always resented, the VIP in the back of a limousine, reclining and taking no interest in the outside world. I settled into the comfort of daydreams, the world reduced to information in the corner of my eyes: shocked and frightened faces, some with angry words on their lips, gilded buses—more art than transport—brought to a halt in panicky chaos, a glimpse of a motorcycle policeman about to hit a man for his slowness in compliance. There was something sexy about the comfort of the car and its speeding disregard, so that I went from church to the glossy segments of pornography I saw among Akira's tables and I thought of the first time I went with Han and the last and the time between in Liberia, which seemed so compelling now because it had seemed so unremarkable then.

Her Washington apartment was light and crisply clean, the furniture white. I left my briefcase by the door and sat on the couch, with a sudden drain of confidence, a suspicion that I might not be in control. I reached for a coffee-table magazine while she stood above me, ready to go to the kitchen for our drinks.

"Here, check this out," she said, taking the magazine from me and replacing it with one from a rack. I opened it to discover an explicit double-page photo. When I looked up, she raised her eyebrows above the frames of her glasses. "Window-shopping. Tell me if you see anything you like." She left for the kitchen, leaving me caught between a view of her departing business suit and the intimate pinkness of a whore. At the beginning the shock was like the invigoration of cold water; there was a simplicity in it, the way she simply offered everything that is usually played for, or concealed, or not admitted. She stood in front of me, holding a drink in each hand, still neatly dressed, and announced that I could do whatever I liked. Later I remembered there had been an oddly childlike moment from her. She had opened her mouth for me to inspect. "See, all gone. I used to think," she added, "that the more semen I swallowed, the bigger my breasts would grow." She squeezed them in a new consideration. "But I think they are pretty cute the way they are, don't you?" I wondered, in the car, whether this had been just one of the things she'd learned that she knew men liked.

In Liberia, on the mission before China, but after Colombia, Nigeria, Zanzibar, and Mauritius, she said, after we had for hours made a lazy, stroking love without conclusion, "I want to make love among the poor."

"How do you mean?"

"I want them near while you fuck me. I want to watch the poor when I've got your cock up my ass. I want them to watch me."

"We could drive somewhere." I had not questioned the proposal.

"Right," she said, sideways smile and innocent glasses.

I was willing by then to leave everything behind. I imagined I sensed a wholeness coming closer.

We borrowed a four-wheel-drive from a World Bank project and drove north from Monrovia for two hours, took a dirt track, and branched off that onto a footpath that linked a simple forest village with its stream. It was the poorest of villages, with no sign of any artifact of modern industry. The round mud huts were simply thatched; it was a village unchanged for all imaginable time, the sort of place where the children would run in terror from the novelty of white skin. Outside the car the air was laden with heat and humidity; inside we were fresh and air-conditioned. Han undressed, and facing away from me on the front passenger seat, she eased herself down on me, bracing herself against the dash. When the village women filed toward us, heavy earthenware pitchers on their heads, she caught their eyes and squirmed on me, moving, letting them see her open-mouthed pleasure, her hand masturbating herself. The women slowed, and milled in a hushed confusion to see a car so far from the road. Then the boldest took the lead to carry on, and Han held her eyes and squirmed, so the African woman with her perfect posture had to see the inexplicable, shocking fact of a Chinese woman fucking a white man behind the glass of a car parked on a path that was like a back garden to them. Her eyes flung themselves to the indecipherable project logo on the door, and finding nothing but the devil there, she ran. The others followed, hands to their pitchers, water slopping down their backs, pushing each other aside from the narrow footpath into the abrasion of the bush. Only one old woman, perhaps deficient of eyesight and sense, stayed and approached. Her bare breasts were empty, ruined flaps above a ragged wrapper so old its pattern was lost. Dry skin was loose on her bones. When she reached the window, Han quickened her hand to bring herself to climax, holding her blank eyes to the old woman's clouded cataracts only a hand's breadth away through the glass. She came, and without thought, I came too, high up in her. She arched back her neck to kiss me.

"That was weird!" she said hoarsely. "I liked that." She did not turn back to the woman, who remained motionless while we disengaged, and I started the engine to drive away.

This still excited me, but there was enough disgust in me—at either the act or the fool she made of me—for my mind to search out a countervailing image. The one that came was of the white-coated women who served us at Kendel-Peat's canteen on the days Dad took me on his rounds. The women were kindly and looked me in the eye. These were common women, with their figures a bit out of control on the generous side, so the buttons of their coats strained. They were round and loud, as wholesome and wicked as cream, and they joked with my father and teased me. "Are you going to be my boyfriend, then," said one. "Not likely," said another, and pulled my pleased and bewildered ten-year-old self to her. "You're mine, aren't you, darling. You won't get jealous now, will you, Ben?"

In Islamabad Yamada forgot the project. When I went to his room at the Holiday Inn, he did not respond to my inquiries about our meetings with the federal government and the drafting of an aide-mémoire. He sat on the pillows of the queen-sized bed in a lustrous business suit and smiled at me with a conspirator's smile. Akira avoided us both and busied himself clearing up the dishes and the camping stove he had used to prepare Yamada's food.

"Don't worry, Will. Don't worry." Yamada seemed likely to break into laughter. "This is only a small project. Fifty million." He made a deprecating grimace. "We must think bigger, Will. You must rise up. Rise up." He lifted the air with his hand and chuckled. For a moment I expected him to levitate above the Holiday Inn's gold counterpane. "Never mind the roundup meeting, the aide-mémoire. We'll talk to the president. He's a military man—he'll leave the details to others. He'll delegate." Again Yamada laughed, fascinating me with the subtle change in him since Peshawar, where he had seemed briefly in control.

"This is only one country, Will, just Pakistan. How many people? A hundred million? Here's India." He reached out with his left hand, fingers outstretched. "Nearly a billion! Ten times Pakistan. China!" He stretched out his right arm. "More than a billion. Africa! South America!" Yamada placed the continents in the air as God might fix constellations, his jacket rucked by the exertion.

Akira left the room without a glance, his arms full of cooking clutter. Yamada only nodded, as if the departure was exactly right.

"We'll see the president, Will. General . . ."

"Zia."

"Yes, Zia. We'll make a banquet for him. To show who we are. Always do things properly, Will. Think big." Again he stretched himself out to demonstrate the size of the world he was embracing from his hotel bed. It was as if his frailty could only be overcome by a span that required him to be fully extended, as if the stretch and pull of it would support him and hold him in place.

"Listen, Will. You are here. I don't know why it's you, but you are the one here. That's good. Listen. The world . . . I told you about Japan. What I wanted. It's only part. Only part. The world has to change. You must have vision. Forget countries, Will. Forget Japan. Forget the United Kingdom. Nothing stays in place anymore. If we destroy the ozone in Tokyo, you feel it in London. All of Europe became radioactive because of that Russian disaster . . . what was it?"

"Chernobyl."

"Yes, that. If Toyota doesn't like Japan anymore, it can build its cars in England. Or America. Or Mexico. We press a button in Tokyo, and the money moves from New York to London. You see? Will, what are these agreements with countries? Don't waste your time on details. The important thing is that every country borrows. And if they don't borrow, they lend. Each time a country signs a loan agreement, it vanishes a little. Gives itself up. And we have to make them vanish."

Yamada closed and opened his hand to show how a bubble bursts to extinction, then he laughed again, letting himself sprawl on the bed. I watched sweat break out on his forehead.

"Make the countries vanish and there's unity. One world. No wars. World government will come from the unity of money. Then we solve the pollution. Then we can look after people without worrying about competition between countries. Don't worry about people now, Will. Forget people. Forget the poor. We can't help people yet. Not with governments. They have to squeeze their people to compete; they can't help it. Concentrate on the money, spreading the money." He put his hands together as if they contained a world that he would polish with his palms. Then he collapsed, the armature that had extended him was suddenly withdrawn, and when he reopened his eyes, the new smile was wan.

"I'm tired, Will. I'm going to die."

"No. You don't know that."

"Yes. We all die. But I will die soon, I think. I will not see one world. You help me do my work, Will. You come to Tokyo. I'll introduce you. No sons. You're good, Will. You understand, don't you? You hear what I say?"

"Yes, I hear. You're doing me a great honor."

The wan smile spread slowly in gentle acquiescence. And I was caught up in all this, Yamada's words and gestures, a higher form of life, more grand. I wondered if it was greatness that I sensed in him, a man who in approaching death could forget himself to talk of higher things, the idealism of money. I was excited to feel in myself the faint, unreliable stirring of something so old that it was almost forgotten, the idea that things could be comprehended and I might be useful, the old, lost comfort of doing good.

"Good. Good."

"I'll go now. You are tired."

"Yes. Please consider it, Will."

At the end of it I was with Han in a room on the fourteenth floor of the Kunlun Hotel in Beijing. There were trays with the leftovers of room-service meals on the floor. We were naked and I lay across her body, resting semiconscious. Climaxes had come to seem incidental to our lovemaking rather than the point of it, so that we maintained an even stimulation, as necessary as breathing and preferable to everything. Beneath her closed eyes Han's expression seemed to say that once again she had got what she wanted and once again it was the wrong thing. Looking at her, I was pleased with myself.

In Beijing Han had shown little interest in her parents' country, her indifference to the sights and culture even more absolute than usual. She was rude to the fawning staff—one to bow and wave us into the elevator, one waiting on our floor to bow and wave us out—and refused to respond to greetings in Chinese or to speculative looks toward the Chinese woman with the Western man. In the glass-sided elevator that rose up through the high glass atrium of the ground-floor restaurant, she asked, "Could we fuck in this?"

"No."

"Too bad. Maybe I'll just flash my tits. They can't touch us." But there was something formulaic in this.

When she announced later that she was leaving me, she left me breathless.

"What do you mean?"

"I mean goodbye, Dr. Bender."

"Are you serious?"

"I'm serious. I don't know about you."

"I don't understand why you're saying this. Out of nowhere."

"Another person. Another male person."

"Here?"

"Don't be stupid."

I searched around for who it might be. I could not imagine where she could have found the time or energy for another lover.

"Is it André?" I took a guess: our division head, my boss, a step up.

"André? Why do you say that?"

"A step up."

"Right. I'm a gold-digger, right?" She gave a harsh little laugh and looked at me with an expression of disgust.

"Who then?"

"None of your business."

"Tell me!"

She paused and considered this. "All right. It's Jorge."

"Jorge? Do I know him?"

"Sure. He Xeroxes your fucking reports."

There was a Jorge in Washington, a young South American who wore jeans and pushed a cart from office to office, collecting files and papers for copying. I had an idea that he was a political refugee, but I was not sure. I had imagined the job was a sort of charity the Bank gave bright young men to whom they owed a favor. I tried to remember more but only came up with the impression of long hair, politeness, pleasant youthfulness—a lightweight.

I looked at Han. "Not your type, is he?"

"That's what you know. He's kind. He buys me things even though he hasn't got the money. He doesn't just want to fuck me all the time. I'm tired of all this. I mean I know I'm good, but I'm tired of it. I did everything for you, right? Did you ever say you loved me? Could you say that? I don't have to do his work. I couldn't—he's an artist. He wants a home with me. I want a home! And he makes me come!"

Looking down from the fourteenth floor onto the old men

fishing by the new concrete canal, while Han packed her things, I could see no way down to the ground for me. I turned and leaned against the window, watching her, and wondered with a shock, if after all the sum result of those grinding nights of tales and tears had been tenderness and that I was in love.

"So I guess you've got your promotion to professional."

"Right, I've got it. Thanks. You were good for that. That's all I wanted, right?"

She had not broken any promises; I had no hold. At the door, after the porter had taken her cases, she stopped and turned to me with that off-center smile, and I thought she might cry after all. She said, "Bill, I did the internal rate of return. Fifteen percent. It's in the file."

I nodded. This was a sort of intimacy.

She took a step and turned again, and with a knowing corniness, she added, "It's been a trip."

Five days later, when the meetings were over, I faxed a letter of resignation to D.C. I had myself debriefed in the World Bank's Beijing office and picked up a consultancy with a passing U.N. team planning a water-control project in Inner Mongolia, and I took an option on the Indonesian Java-Sumatra Transmigration Project for after that. The Bank said that in the interests of interagency cooperation, I could postpone clearing my desk in Washington. I called the house in Reston and left a message on our answering machine to say that my return would be delayed, dates uncertain. But Mireille was probably in France.

. . .

While we're sailing off Ruatua I talk to Captain Slocum. We laugh together at Oom Paul's earnest geographers who came to Slocum at Durban to explain scientifically why his journey had not occurred.

"These gentlemen were most agitated, and since I was their guest and no match for their expert knowledge, I readily agreed that I might be mistaken to think the world was round. Indeed I might just as well have arrived at the country by sailing across the world as around it. And I reasoned that it was their country and they were entitled to make the rules. Besides"—his eyes twinkled from above the wheel—"it had been an eighteen-day leg from Réunion and I had great hopes for their hospitality. So for a week the world was flat for me too." We laugh; then he's stern. "There's no such tricks to be played with the sea, mind you. Let a man call a rough sea calm and he'll get a firm enough slap for his sophistry."

I laugh again and try to tell him that it's the same for me. We all take money to say things are not as they are when no one can say different and the official version rules. I want him to say that it's all right, that's the way it is, that we're both buccaneers, aren't we, living in the world. But he only says, "Oh, yes? Would you shorten the mains'l sheet, and I'll bring her closer to the wind."

Twelve hours from our home port a gale gets up, so we no longer talk amid the noise of wind in the rigging and the hiss and splash of our progress through the waves. At first he just smiles, the only time he's smiled, greeting the first of the spray to reach the helm, then he's active—"Take the wheel, lad"— clambering to the foredeck to pull down our flying jib, all wily monkey limbs, never missing a handhold or a foothold: hand to the shroud, foot wedged against the forehatch—we're heeling well now—then swinging with the Spray's bounce to grasp the forestay, ankle curled round the samson post for balance, one hand free for the jib. Then a cry, a whoop, as we crash into a trough, drenching him, pulling him from his perch, so he lets his forestay arm unbend to take the strain, never anxious. Then a laugh, a full-bellied laugh, the last of the Yankee tightness gone, a snatch of a song, a roar into the wind.

We're on our smallest jib, with the mains'l reefed right down, but we're sizzling along toward Ruatua. The boat is sound, the captain knows what to do, the gale is music in the rigging. He roars again, hopelessly trying to outdo the weather. He looks at me and roars. I roar back, at first self-conscious, then from the depths of me, letting the wind force its way into my mouth and then expelling it with the whole of my body. The water breaks over us, and until we collapse in satiation, we compete to be the one most given over to the world.

Yamada was early at breakfast, neat but pale, the expansiveness of the previous evening gone and replaced by a tightness in his face and posture.

"We have to do the invitation cards."

"Sorry?"

"The invitation cards. For the banquet." His voice was impatient. "First the invitation cards. Then the banquet. Then everything else."

"Yes. We'll have the cards printed. When do you want the banquet?" I matched his impatience with my calm.

"Three days."

"Tell me what you want to say. I'll organize it."

"No, I'll come with you."

"It's not necessary."

"No. It's got to be right!"

We saw the hotel manager, reserved the banquet room, ordered their best menu, informed him of the eminence of the guests. I protected Yamada from the manager's skepticism, deflected the urgent, panicky requests for details. The question of the president's security, I said, would be fully discussed tomorrow. We took a government car and driver to find a printer.

The invitation cards, Yamada insisted, must be this large, have scalloped edges, be gilded. On one side the invitation would be in English, on the other in Urdu. There would be a single line of Japanese on each. Yamada had written the text on the back of an envelope, which was blackened with dense corrections.

The first printer could not do the scalloped edges, the second could do the edges but could not do the Japanese. Yamada insisted that no compromise was possible; this was for a head of state. He was grim, determined, the grandness of his global vision now compressed to the correctness of a card.

We drove for hours along the bright, straight roads of Islamabad, the capital's construction still modern if no longer new, its trees still too small for shade. We stopped at one printer in a planned arcade of underpatronized shops, at another in a half-completed concrete office block. The last one could do the card, but it would take a week. In my mind I checked off the appointments I was missing for the sake of this: Foreign Affairs at nine, Rural Development at ten, Agriculture, Planning.

In the back seat of the car I kept close to Yamada. More than anything I wanted to protect him from the suspicion that his actions might be foolish or too late, or that the wisdom of his age was not honored. He lit a herbal cigarette, and though the car was air-conditioned and he was sweating, he opened the window to feel the billows of hot air.

I looked at him as he looked out the window. The profile was still fine, the jaunty forelock still dipped toward his eyes. He still held the cigarette with style, an inch or two away from his mouth. He could still be taken for debonair, except for the sweat.

"Mr. Yamada, do you think you should see a doctor?"

He looked at me briefly, then away without comment.

I persisted. "Perhaps you should visit the Japanese Embassy?"

"No. Don't worry. I'm fine. Where are we going now? Another printer?"

"The driver's looking for one."

"Good, good."

But he seemed to forget our purpose as we drove through the Islamabad streets with their un-Asian lack of pedestrians. Again, as if trying to catch an old mood by remembering its words, he praised the girls of Manila, their willingness and skill. The girls in Japan were no longer so nice. And for the golf, too, it was better to fly to the Philippines for a game than to wait in line in Japan. Thai girls could also be worthwhile, he added.

He made no move or comment when we stopped outside another uncompleted concrete building but continued to talk of women, while the driver explained that he needed to go inside and ask directions. The perspiration filmed Yamada's eyes. When a young Pakistani woman in Western dress—a decent middle-class girl—came down the building's steps, he called to her and beckoned her over, so that she first moved toward the polished car in obedience, then was frightened by the incoherence and the feverish face, so that she wheeled away.

"That's a pretty girl," he said, though I doubted he could see more than her outline through the sweat. "Shall we have her, Will? Do you want her?"

Perhaps he no longer knew he was in prudish Muslim Pakistan and had imagined a street girl in Manila or Bangkok. There was a determined vulgarity, as if he was willfully summoning the strongest, crudest force he knew to keep himself alive. I thought there was something touching in it.

The Japanese Embassy took care of him, undertook to organize his evacuation by plane in the company of a medical attendant. I sent telexes to Geneva, and in the urgency of it all I forgot myself and my own persisting pains. When the replies from Geneva included the authorizations for visits to Tonga and Ruatua after I was finished with Pakistan, I put them aside, in the same way as I used to hold the escape cards that would get you out of trouble in the game of Circumnavigation.

I helped Akira pack Yamada's things. I said, "In a way I think he's a great man."

Akira let my comment hang alone in the air while he sorted papers, packing some, throwing others into the wastebasket.

I continued. "I've grown to like him. I hope he recovers. Are you going with him? He's asked me to go to Tokyo."

"Ha! Why?"

"I think he wants to make sure someone continues his work." I could not help hearing the pleading in my own voice.

Akira spluttered a sound of impatient disgust and returned to his fierce packing. "What work?"

"Don't you agree with what he's doing?"

"I do his work. You do his work. I massage him, cook for him." He looked at a sheaf of papers in Yamada's handwritten Japanese, considered them with a brief intensity, went toward the suitcase with them, then decided on the wastebasket. "Now we must do this. He should stay in Tokyo."

"You don't agree with his ideas?"

"He's my boss." His hand wavered between case and basket with another bundle of papers. "You think he'll die, William-san?"

"I don't know. Maybe not yet. I think he feels his work isn't quite finished."

"Then he might want these." He pushed the papers into the suitcase.

"Akira, I can see it's not easy to work for Yamada, but I think he's a special person." It wasn't my phrase, "special person." It was an international phrase, and I was aware of some unease as I spoke it, an attempt to armor a slight and suspect emotion in me. I'd heard the expression in meetings where bureaucrats needed to justify the high fees and loose terms of reference for men of international status but no identifiable skills. Because of their superior intellect or political connections, it was believed that it was useful just to have these people around. "It's important to have people with vision. Not many people can go from big ideas to the little practicalities that make them happen."

Akira paused to look up at me from where he was squatted by the case. "So you want to follow him to Toyko?"

"I want to make sure everything isn't lost if he dies." To me, my voice sounded small, though I think it was as firm as usual.

"You don't go home for your own father and you want to go to Japan for Yamada?" He squashed up his face in an expression of disapproval.

I felt stabbed by this, caught by surprise. I turned toward the window, while my thoughts wheeled as wildly as vultures prevented from landing. Akira stood and said, "William-san, I'm sorry." I managed to ignore him.

"It's a matter of ideas. Of doing something important, useful. Something heroic instead of just living . . . Aren't you going with him?"

"Me? Not the same. I work for his company. His company works for the government. I must go. Except if you ask for me. In Pacific."

"I admire him. I want to help him."

"Do you think there's no one to help him in Tokyo? There are plenty people waiting for him there. Maybe he'll forget you there. His ideas . . . they don't cost him. He was born rich. You know that. Why do you want to help him? His big ideas are only because he likes to run things. He makes people do things. He makes you and me do things. You don't think so? You think he's too sick. You'll see who is praised for our work here."

I had no arguments left for Akira, and later my rebellion against his assertions faded in me. I had caught myself in the absurd act of traveling across the world to help a rich, vain stranger die well. There was a path west for me to England and a path east to Japan; both were impossible to choose. The path to Tonga seemed straight on, the only one that would still take me farther. On the map Tonga was so small a cluster of dots in the Pacific that it hardly seemed a destination at all. Ruatua was a single dot.

Later in the day, as if to bless my decision not to honor Yamada, a telex from Morita, the deskman in Geneva, informed me that Yamada's contract had been terminated. His "special person" status apparently no longer held; someone above Morita had decided Yamada was too sick, too old, or too much of a liability. Since he had not completed the mission, he would not be paid. However lucid Yamada might be in the future, the DCA would no longer hear his ideas. To the DCA, his ideas were no longer serious; his vision was now just raving.

It was odd that even in the face of this evidence of the institutional fickleness, I gained a new sense of energy and purpose from my official appointment as mission leader to replace Yamada. It seems petty now, and I hope I could never again be so easily affected, but at that time it cleared away my uncertainties. I felt I had met Yamada, been patronized, heard him out, and vanquished him. I threw myself into making the concluding arrangements for the mission and handling the paperwork for Yamada's medical evacuation.

It was, I thought at the time, these new responsibilities, not personal feelings, that led me to go to the airport for Yamada's departure. Yet I thought often, and perhaps too eagerly, of the part of my new responsibility that involved informing Yamada of his termination.

I left the logistical details of evacuation to the Japanese Embassy, which had claimed Yamada as a family might claim a murdered body from a despotic government. They had hardly talked to me and Akira refused to become involved. His loyalties had shifted so that he was truculent with the outside world and antagonistic to the other Japanese, while increasingly attentive to me. My chance to see Yamada, and to witness the completed evacuation, was at the airport. He arrived on a wheeled stretcher, which was propelled swiftly through the spaciousness of the VIP lounge. Half a dozen Japanese in suits moved with him, like outriders to a limousine. I hurried toward them and saw that Yamada was conscious, more than conscious: one end of the stretcher was elevated, so that he was semireclining under the red blanket and looked around with lively interest. I saw him make one of the graceful gestures with which he gave orders and I associated it with the waving of royalty at parades.

If Yamada had not himself given the order to stop, I would have been deflected by the embassy men and the stretcher might have made it to the plane without interruption. But he saw me—perhaps he was looking for me—and made his attendants wheel him to me.

"Will, Will. Good! You're here." He was revivified and I

found myself looking to see if he held a cigarette. "I want to talk to you. Will you be in first class?"

"I'm not traveling. I have to complete the mission."

"So you'll follow in a few days?"

"Mr. Yamada, I have to tell you that your relationship with the DCA has been terminated."

His smile hesitated, then rekindled. "So they've made you mission leader. Officially. That's only right. I told them that. But I still want you to come."

"No, I don't think so."

"No?"

"I don't think you'll be needing me."

"No, you should come." He thought, then: "Do you want to go to London first? We can arrange that."

"I'm going to Tonga. Akira's coming with me."

"Tonga? It's tiny, isn't it? What can be there? Not even a million people. Maybe not even a hundred thousand. No, it's not worth it, Will. . . ." He couldn't find his words.

"Then it's Ruatua. Only twenty thousand people, I'm afraid."

"No, Will. It's not good. You must rise up. It's important. You must take responsibility for the world."

I was silent and my intractability seemed to have the effect of removing his elasticity, so that first his smile went and then he leaned back against the stretcher. While a distance was being spun between us, the embassy men moved in, pushing me aside, seeming to imagine that a conversation that was not conducted in Japanese could have no reality. As they began to move the stretcher away, Yamada halted them for a last moment. "Will, they've terminated me completely? Not just this mission?"

"That's my understanding."

"Then you must come, Will. For linkage. Linkage."

I waited for the second it took for the attendants to edge the stretcher into motion again. Then I offered, "Keep in touch," as I had many times before, as everyone did. For a moment I had considered saying "I'll keep in touch," but for the reason no one ever said that—to easily save a lie—I decided against it.

I watched him go. I saw him unsuccessfully try to bend around on the stretcher to hold my eye. I waved, though he could not see it. Then I turned on my heel and discovered I was in high spirits, as if rejecting Yamada's request had been a loyal and virtuous act.

I canceled the banquet for Zia first thing the following morning. I called Shareef, who was in town for our federal roundup meeting.

"Shareef, I want to tie this up with the minimum of fuss. Is there any problem with the meeting with Zia?"

"Maybe a problem if you still want it."

"No, I definitely don't want it."

"Then it's no problem. I'll make your excuses."

"Can we make the roundup apolitical? Something quiet?"

"That's easy. I'll suggest Ijaz of Planning chairs the meeting. He hates long meetings. And he's a relative. He'll dispense with a presentation by you, and if any of the ministries object, he'll tell them they should have done their background reading. Are you going with what we agreed in Peshawar? Fifty over seven years?"

"I don't see why not."

"OK. If you can just prepare a one-page aide-mémoire for signature, that would be helpful. We'll get it through on that basis, and the DCA can fill in the details later."

"That sounds perfect. I have a briefing meeting for a new mission scheduled in Singapore in two days. And I promised Akira a stopover in Bangkok. Can I make it?"

Shareef hesitated for a moment. "Leaving tomorrow? Probably. Ijaz can make the meeting mandatory. That way everyone will want to make it short, to get back to their prior schedules. It might be a good thing. This is Pakistan. We know how to get things done."

"OK. Confirm things to me as soon as you know. And if anyone thinks the loan isn't enough, you can tell them it's just a pilot project. If it goes well, there will be more. OK?" I liked it that this was something I could fix just between Shareef and me.

"Of course. I am sure I will be able to make them understand. And by the way, William, how is your health now?"

It was Shareef's way of reminding me of his local knowledge, the inside track I was exploiting; of course the smooth doctor in Peshawar would have been a relative or classmate. "My health? Perfect. Completely better, thank you."

INTERMISSION

Singapore airport had a restful feel to it: a warm palm to be held in while in transit. The lounge was long, spacious, and glass-walled, organized into a repeating pattern: a seating area followed by a bar area, a café, a shop, a news vendor, a bank, a rest room, a seating area, and so on. Beyond the glass wall, on a level below us, 747s nosed about noiselessly. A staff of cleaners, with darker skins than the Chinese cashiers', fretted with their mops, short of marks to erase.

We were very at ease, the four of us, in easy chairs in a bar area behind potted plants. On the advice of the American we had taken Tiger beers. We had run out of things to say and each of us was waiting for his plane: Akira and I for a Qantas to Sydney, connecting with Air New Zealand to Nuku'alofa, the American from the DCA on his way to Geneva, the Australian to Indonesia. The DCA had coordinated with our new cooperating agency, the Pacific Bank, to organize a briefing on Polynesia from the Australian, who had recently been there for Australian aid. The American, returning from China, would debrief us on Pakistan for the DCA head office in Geneva. I felt that the briefing was an unnecessary complication, since I already knew the Pacific well. It was the sort of intricacy that characteristically fascinated desk officers overexcited by airline schedules and the abstract possibilities of networking.

We had fallen into silence. I noticed that we all wore moccasin-style leather shoes of similar design, though the American's were of a heavier construction. We had exchanged various documents. The Australian had told me what he knew about the economics of Tonga and Ruatua, and by politely questioning him I had proved myself to have the better grip, contacts closer to the center, so that he had retreated from his tedious obligation to inform. The American was an old pro, overweight and short of breath, who had made a few notes on contact politicos in Islamabad and left it at that. Akira had said nothing. Perhaps he was puzzled that he could have spent a night in Bangkok without finding a woman.

There was a slight tension of restraint about the group. We were tired from our assignments and in an airport—between here and there—we could find no enthusiasm for business. We could have asked about each other's lives, families, work, tastes, but we did not want to know; we were weary of facts, and we might never meet again. We could have discussed the news, ideas, opinions, but none of us was unprofessional enough to require the others to think for recreation.

The American, the oldest among us, signaled for four more beers without making inquiries of the rest. The waitress, in some sort of native dress, dipped low to distribute the drinks and left behind her a pretext for breaking the silence.

"Now, she's not Chinese," said the American.

"They've got Malays here as well": the Australian.

"I was thinking Indian, maybe Tamil": the American.

"Could be," deferred the Australian.

"I'd guess Thai": my contribution. "They export a lot of female labor. Them and the Philippines."

"You're right there": the American. "I saw the figures for their remittances. They keep the economy afloat."

We didn't take it further; now it was circling back to work. Akira jiggled his knee. The American looked at his watch. The Australian fished into his briefcase and flicked through a wad of stapled airline tickets.

All at once, as I leaned back to relax, a pain like a knife tore through me high up under the rib cage and waves of heat spread through my chest and arms. I jerked forward with such an abruptness that I heard the thump of my cheekbone on my knee. I heard myself hiss, "Jeezus!" Although I wanted to scream, I remembered even at this bad moment not to, and as soon as the first wave receded I looked around to see if I had caused a commotion. People were walking past, not looking at us. From my knee-level view I could see that Akira's leg had stilled. The Australian's ankles remained crossed, and if anything, he had pressed farther back into his chair. The American waited and watched me appraisingly as I lifted my head to look around.

"You all right, Bill?" He said it in a gruff way that pleaded for the answer Yes.

I nodded. I felt I must be very red.

"Heartburn," opined the American.

"Ulcer!" Akira spoke for the first time, with a bird-spotter's triumph of recognition.

"Constipation, I reckon": the Australian. "When d'you last take a dump, Bill?"

I could not unbend or breathe. I cursed myself for not paying more attention to the lesser pains in Pakistan. The only possible relief seemed to be that the cut of pain should rip open my abdomen and let my entrails escape.

In an expert's voice, the American said, "It's best to avoid beer that's too cold. These trips are hard on the digestion." He said he used to have that problem himself, but he thought he'd got it licked now, ever since he'd found out about this special fiber food he got from a shop in Washington and always took with him on overseas trips now, along with water-purifying tablets and three types of antimalarial prophylactic. "Of course it weighs a ton, but I'm not going to be caught somewhere like Zaire again and have to eat the local food."

"I don't know about you," the Australian said, "but I find international hotels just as dangerous as the villages."

"Oh, deadly places, hotels. Don't know how to handle Western food, most of them."

"It used to be all right. Used to be able to eat all sorts of things when I started out. Now I can hardly stomach anything. You know what I mean?"

"Stress!" Akira gained their attention. "Stress kill." He leaned toward me, pushed my glass of beer nearer to my hand. "William? Can you drink, William?"

I heard concern and I waited for a touch, but instead Akira leaned back like the others, reaching for his shirt buttons. "Ulcer. Half a stomach. Only thirty-eight. Stress!"

The floor beneath my eyes was clean; the unconcerned voices circled above my head so that I wished to swat them like buzzing flies. There was a thought, or nearly a thought, that told me I was getting mine, my just return, but that kept the why or wherefore from me.

"I used to eat food with villagers when I was young. Just to show them I was a man like them": the Australian. "Now I throw up or get the shits."

"I'll give you the name of that shop in Washington. I'll put it on my business card."

It could not be possible that I was dying while they talked like this.

Akira said, "I carry all my food. Boiled rice is good." It registered as a complete thought that Akira must have cooked for himself as well as Yamada. "If I eat the wrong food," he continued, "it come back." His hand arced up from his stomach to his mouth and onward toward the coffee table, tracing the path of the wrong food. "Almost not change. The food almost not change. And the shit—like soup."

With the subject of shit their heads moved forward, their attention no longer disengaged, as if this was the true, rare matter of their lives: something delicate, passionate, long avoided between men, like the sex life of husbands and wives, or the matter of who would actually sign a project's disbursement check.

"Soup. That's it. Bloody soup." The Australian addressed Akira directly for the first time, as if a foreignness had disappeared. "That's bloody it. Nothing for five days, maybe a week, then bang, it doesn't stop. Bloody soup. You're in Laos or some godforsaken place, you've done your round of po-faced officials in Vientiane, and some clown says you've got to see the refugees in god-knows-where. So you bounce around in a four-wheel-drive for six hours, and then it gets you, just when you're at the back of beyond, two hundred miles from a toilet. You have to ask the bloody bureaucrats to stop and you look around for some tree or something to go behind, but you know there are peasants out there, women as well as men, you know, hidden in the fields looking at your bum, and probably some pig will come sniffing around to gobble it up as soon as you're finished, and the stuff is exploding out of you and you're trying not to get it on your strides. And the worst thing is—you know what the worst thing is? It's knowing that there's this carload of grinning officials back there, just loving the idea of a white expert with his pants down, shitting and shaking in the middle of the bloody bush. You know they're laughing and loving it and thinking it's great revenge for your being where you don't belong, though when you get back they wipe the smiles off their faces and ask ever so politely if you're feeling all right, and you know that's only because you've got the money and they want some of it."

The others nodded and shared a moment's quiet. The sharp edge was going from my pain; it was spreading upward, distributing and diluting itself, giving me a headache, a backache, a knot in my throat. Soon I would sit up.

"Internal rate of return," offered the American as a joke, though with a lack of emphasis that suggested it was not the first time he had said it and that he had not been the first to think of it. After a delay, the Australian gave a short laugh, and Akira also smiled. "It's what we get for all this work. Read an article recently about something called irritable bowel syndrome. Supposed to be caused by stress, like our Japanese colleague here says. Have you heard of that?" They looked blank, and the American turned to me. "Now, Bill, I want you to think about this before you answer. When you shit, is it really runny, like, say, tomato soup, or is it more lumpy, more like meat stew? Do you understand what I mean?"

I tried to address the question, but neither category fitted. Instead I said, "I'm OK," and started to uncurl myself.

He ignored this and continued. "Mine used to be soupy before I found this fiber food. Now it's never worse than cow shit. I'm hoping for horse shit." He let go a big laugh, then cut it short.

"I wonder," began the Australian, "why the World Bank, the U.N., the World Health Organization, for crissake, haven't come up with a pill, a prophylactic like the ones for malaria, something that would let us do our job. Sure, they might have to come up with different ones for Latin America and Africa, or maybe one for villages and one for international hotels, but if they want us to do this work . . ."

I was sitting upright now. Akira handed me my beer. I tried to take a sip, couldn't, spluttered. The pain had become a tension, and the tension had lodged in my throat so I could not swallow. "I just gobbled like a turkey," I remembered my father announcing happily. "It wouldn't go up or down." I carefully placed the beer back on the glass tabletop, but it clattered with the shaking of my hand.

The American said, "You're looking better, Bill. A bit pale, that's all."

"I knew a bloke once who couldn't swallow," offered the Australian. "Don't know what happened to him in the end. It was worst when someone mentioned his wife."

"That's my plane boarding." The American snapped his case and pushed himself upright. "Gentlemen, it's been a pleasure. Sorry for your discomfort, Bill." He handed out cards with the name of the Washington shop scribbled on their backs. "I'm glad we had this conversation."

SEA

Of course there was a secret life, his unofficial version. I wouldn't see it then; I ignored the clues to it. For thirty years he had a mistress: Flossie—Flo, Florence—from the Kendel-Peat staff canteen, about whom he could never speak to me. My mother knew well enough, but it suited her to hold a moral advantage and to have a husband out of her hair. She was left free to run the show; she commanded the living room from the largest armchair and engineered the tiny ascendancies of their forty years in Mafeking Road: the installation of a phone, central heating, double glazing for the windows, finally a car. In the end her job paid more than his. When other wives envied her aloud for her dutiful and gentle husband, they wondered at the reserve in her agreement. There seemed to be no justification for her outbreaks of shrewish discontent, so that to the neighbors my father's quiet self-effacement seemed to mark him as a saintly man.

Their regular time was three to five-thirty, two or three times a week—when he was supposedly earning overtime at one and a half times the normal rate—and the occasional Saturday afternoon, when it would have been double time. According to my mother, who had been unaccountably fierce on the subject, Flossie and the other canteen "girls" were "dead common." Flossie lived alone in a council flat. Her husband was in the merchant navy and had stopped coming home between trips. A story went around later that he was in prison. She was a full-breasted dyed blonde, and my only personal memories of her were the warmth of her hugs on the occasions when my father took me to the depot to help him on his rounds. She had kind, sad eyes behind the broad lines of her makeup, and she hugged me as if she wished that I were hers. Even though I was only ten or eleven, I picked up something of her fleshliness; there was a fluidity in her touch, the offering of something, an openness to exchange. She was the sort of woman a man might spend the afternoon lying alongside just for the ease of it.

At her home my father lost the tension behind his quietness and became a boy again, talking common, being naughty. There was a routine. He came in and lay down on her sofa, his cycle clips still on. She chastised him: "Take those cycle clips off, Jack Bender." At work she called him Ben, like everyone, but never in her home—she was the only one. "And those shoes. You're the most unromantic man I've ever met." He smiled and blindly held out his arms to her. "And that jacket," Flo continued. "I'm tired of getting stabbed by your bloody pencils every time I kiss you."

But he would grab her anyway and make her sit next to him, still keeping his eyes closed during this transition between worlds, closing them as the awkward Sunday-school teacher, dutiful employee, husband, father, and opening them as a man loved by a sensual woman, his hand inside her blouse.

"Jack Bender, if you think I'm going to be manhandled by a man in his cycle clips, you've got another think coming. I haven't even made the tea." This was said with pleasure.

He sighed and opened his eyes. She bent to kiss him. "And was there another note from Mrs. Hoskins today? Another special order for double cream?"

"Ah, Mrs. Hoskins. She's a very demanding customer."

"I bet." And she tickled him roughly so his cheeks grew pink. "I bet she can never get enough."

Sufficient years had passed for them to know they were safe.

She knew he'd always come, but the play and innuendo reminded them that it was illicit, sexy, outside the proper rules. She reached down for his fly and he freed her breasts with a practiced scoop. "Jack Bender, aren't you ashamed of yourself? Aren't you tired after a day's work? Have you any idea how silly you look with your cycle clips still on and that thing sticking up?"

He drew her to him. "Flo."

"Yes?"

"I'm dying for a cup of tea."

She shook him so he had to open his eyes and wrestled him to the orange shag carpet, laughing. "You old bugger. Toying with a girl's emotions. Not to mention her tits. I'll give you a cup of tea!" She sat down heavily astride his chest and made a show of pressing his arms into submission. "A cup of tea's all you'll get. Ouch! That's your bloody pencils again."

She put the kettle on and prepared common food: thick deep-fried chips, sausages, shop-bought cream buns to follow. Then, just when it was least convenient, he made love to her, giving her the pleasure of surprise, the knowledge that he wanted her enough to overturn order for her. They rolled on the shag carpet—common too, but perfect for this—her skirt hitched up, the kettle whistling and the chips turning brown, the bony milkman and the fleshy canteen girl, both nearly fifty now.

"Jack Bender!" she said, mock stern, standing up, pulling down her skirt but abandoning the brassiere and knickers, leaving him spent below, smiling. "Jack Bender, I will not be diddled by a man in his cycle clips."

At some point, probably after, while they drank tea and touched and were happy and rueful, he looked the way he might have looked for life, insouciant, cheeky, used, a readiness for animation around the mouth, mischief behind the eyes.

At five it was time to clear the plates and cups, and time for Flossie to pick some trivial argument, or to tense things up with some slight, slighting comment about his wife, just words that said it was not easy for her to let him go, although she knew she must. The clips, jacket, and glasses were back on, and the last she'd see of him until he was at the depot canteen next day, and "Ben" again, would be him swinging his leg over the moving bike, the yellow of his rolled cape bobbing where it hung behind the saddle. Then he was back in our house and the snack of bread and cheddar alone in the kitchenette—always an oddly light evening meal for a workingman—then to the evening's work in the garden, or repairing the house, or resoling our shoes, or mending our bicycles in the shed.

My recognition of my father's secret life grew in me while I traveled with Akira. We stopped over in Sydney, then reached Tonga's main island, Tongatapu, via Auckland. It was after we left Tongatapu and the government offices in the capital of Nuku'alofa for the quieter outlying islands of Vava'u and Ha'apai—scouting for something to invest in—that I was able to give my mind over to it. He had been unable to tell me directly about Flossie; the official version of his life had held too long to be disturbed. Instead, during those last meetings he had hinted at his weaknesses and had drawn my attention to the sexy phone-ins on the radio, to a liberality in his reading. He had wanted to tell me, I now thought, that although he had loved Mireille, he could understand about Han.

Once the affair with Flossie had fallen into place, many things were explained. The seemingly unjustified complaints by my mother made sense, as did the feeling I had always had of his not being fully present in the home, of a life not fully lived. I understood where the lively, warm part of him I had seen on the milk rounds belonged. There was that night that he did not come home and I had needed to win him back for us—the time when he had nearly decided to give up all duty for the sake of Flossie.

I also recognized in the memories of childhood a more recent feeling, the sense that what had been seen and described was partial, false: everything I had agreed not to see in Pakistan, not to understand everywhere. I recognized the tension that comes from keeping willful self-deceit in place too long.

In the quiet of the Tongan islands—Vava'u more quiet than Tongatapu, Ha'apai so low and quiet that the sound of breaking waves seemed a vulgarity—other small confirmations pressed themselves on me. There had been the Saturday afternoons when he had refused to take me to a Spurs game for no good reason. And of course his meager, solitary evening snacks had never made sense. There was the way he had uncharacteristically refused my mother when she demanded that he account for his expenditures. And more substantially, there was his reluctance to offer me any sort of moral guidance, any rules for disposing of an adult life. There was a sort of scrupulousness in this which had kept him from recommending a path that he did not himself follow. It explained the way he restricted his advice to the cleaning of shoes or the suitability of pencils. It explained the vagueness of his Sunday talks, the way they shied away from the assertion of right or wrong in favor of his liquid metaphors for spirit.

In Vava'u I leafed through the records of the local suboffice of the Development Bank, which the DCA had financed. I talked to the farmers and fishermen who had received tiny subloans to grow taro or vanilla on their ragged plots of forest cultivation, or to buy tackle for fishing from their dugouts. The records were clean; they had paid back their loans ahead of schedule. They reported no need for further money, so that I felt the islanders had accepted our loans in the first place only out of politeness, a little show of respect toward the international money that had taken the trouble to seek them out. I looked further and discovered that nearly everyone had bank savings far in excess of loans taken, the consequence of visits by relatives to the factories and farms of Australia and New Zealand. There was little to buy on the island; they did not need more money. I pressed on to discover the unspoken story beneath. I asked about undue pressure from government officials, kickbacks, misuse of funds, demands for excessive repayments. No, they didn't think so. No, the money had not changed anything they did; they took it and gave it back, plus a little. No, food wasn't short. No, disease was not a problem. No, they really couldn't think of anything else they needed. I pushed until I saw my suspicions beginning to soil me in their eyes and sadden them. Then I accepted that what I saw was what there was, and this seemed to match the new clarity with which I visualized my father's life.

Akira tired of my interrogations earlier than I did. Without a word of explanation, or even a look toward me, he wandered away from where we sat with farmers on the floors of their houses. I felt a disapproval in his closed face. Once I found him in a farmer's field, hoeing around the taro, then showing the family something he had found. They gathered round to peer at the pest or seed he had uncovered, and I watched them form a group that did not require language. On another occasion there was a girl's laughter as background to my interviews, which I discovered came from Akira's attempts to fix and test a children's garden swing. He had a common touch; he left me more and more on my own in favor of quietly joining the islanders. I saw he was happier and that there was nothing I could do.

The day after we landed on Ha'apai's sandy airstrip, he vanished before I started work. In the evening the one other guest at the home where we rented rooms—Ha'apai was too small and forgotten for a hotel—offered to help me find him. She was a thin Australian girl with a poor complexion, who said, with a placid vagueness, that she waiting for a boyfriend to catch up with her. Somehow she—Fiona—knew better than I where to look for Akira.

He was on the beach, standing in the surf, suit trousers wet to his thighs, a fishing line stretched into the ocean. I saw a whisky bottle stuck upright in the sand. When he finally noticed us, his face sprang open into an unselfconscious grin, something I had not seen on him before.

"Good fish! Good fish!" He turned back to his line and pulled on it, the muscles in his back bunching. I heard him laughing—also something new—a cackle of glee. I stopped to take in this delighted boy uncovered in him. There was the spray, the carelessness with his clothes, the cackling laugh, the wild divergence of his eyes, the staggering and jerking that went with the playing of his catch. I lost any thought of re-crimination.

"William," he called out over his shoulder. "Here is good fish. I will cook for us tonight. You don't eat these days. You too, Fona."

We walked into the shallow surf to be next to him. While he concentrated on his work I put my arm briefly around his shoulder and heard him grunt with a sort of confirmation.

It was true that I had eaten irregularly since Singapore. In restaurants I was unable to eat at all. Although the pain in my abdomen was entirely gone, I was left with my difficulty in swallowing. I ate biscuits, fruit, and canned beans, slowly and carefully, in my room, making myself take in sufficient calories to continue working. I felt no hunger and there was even satisfaction in the slimming of my waist. I had an unacknowl-edged belief that this losing weight was a positive thing, which, if taken far enough, might even be a solution. I thought of my father suffering the same symptoms, and there was a light-headed joy in this.

When he was a young man, before he became a milkman, he visited Dieppe, taking the long Channel crossing from New-haven. He left his mother, and later his young wife too, for weekends in France, telling them it was part of his messenger's job. On the ferry he would take off his worsted tie and breathe the sea air, no matter how cold. Once he was there, in the room he always chose, in the cheap hotel overlooking the docks, he hung up his baggy sports jacket in the wardrobe and did not take it out again until it was time to leave.

The hotel was a four-story building in an old street of four-story buildings, which showed separate origins in their archi-tecture but which had become so joined with time that the paint peeled across the property lines. From his window on the top floor, he could touch the metal letters of the word

"Hotel," where they were hammered into the plastered wall.

The patronne, a smart, lively woman, knew the young English guest well. "Monsieur Bender!"—pronounced the French way, with an upturned end. She said it as if the name itself were a synonym for mischief. She had a bubbling laugh. He laughed back, wondering with pleasure that he could flirt in this way with a French businesswoman of substance while he could only do it with the factory girls of his class in England.

In the evening—a ritual—he ate outside at a good dockers' restaurant with a view of the water. He drank too much red wine. He stretched out his legs and substituted his packet of Weights cigarettes with the stronger stuff of Gauloises— another ritual. He ate cheaply and well, relishing his own company, the nearness of boats, and the piquancy of the sauces.

Then it was on to a café or bar, a little unsteady now, where as often as not he would end up with one, or even two, of the girls there, the sort of girl with spirit who hovered between the intention to be a prostitute and the intention to have a good time. He pissed generously in a pissoir while holding the smile of an unknown woman two floors above him. He talked politics into the night with rough men who spoke a different language. He drank coffee on the quay at dawn. Once, the expansiveness of his night out led him to sweep Madame la Patronne upstairs with him—"Voulez-vous coucher avec moi?"—an event acknowledged later only in a false primness at the corners of her lips. When he said gallantly that she was the queen of the hotel, she had replied that she was only queen of the plumbing.

That evening Akira took over the bungalow's kitchen from its owner, and we kept him company while he cooked. Fiona had taken some care; she had washed her hair, slipped on a cotton dress, applied lipstick. While we waited for the fish, I tried to make conversation. She had lived in a trailer on a beach near Sydney and worked as a waitress to pay for this trip. She liked it on Ha'apai: nobody came here; it was so cheap; there were beaches—the whole, low island was a beach. I searched for something more, an ambition perhaps. She shrugged and smiled apologetically. "Not really. Just want to take things easy, y'know."

I nodded but could not think of how to carry on. She took it up: "What are you doing then? Are you with Cable and Wireless?"

I explained a little about the business of lending money, how it developed backward economies like this, how someone had to monitor the use to which it was put—the whole smooth rationale.

"I wondered because there were some blokes from Cable and Wireless here last week. They want to give Ha'apai television, I think."

Again I could not think how to continue, but she seemed not to notice. She seemed relaxed, content, and after a while she continued. "Need something like TV here. They haven't got anything." In the new silence our looks turned toward the stove where Akira, his back to us, was doing something noisy with the fish and heat. "Your mate doesn't do much, does he?" She nodded toward him. "Just seems to be enjoying himself."

"He's already finished his work," I found myself explaining.

In a way it was true. During our first day in Tonga he had taken his statistics on global production of copra and bananas and the other local commodities and had broken them down for the Pacific, for Tonga, for each of the Tongan islands. The figures were so small that the old, conventional units of thousands of tons and millions of dollars would no longer do. He had given me the figures with a lack of comment that I took to be ironic. I had received them with a matching lack of comment.

Akira did not seem to mind—or notice—that I only played with his fish and rice. He was lively, in high spirits, and even enervated Fiona straightened in her chair and came close to sparkling from the attention she received and Akira's insistence on her appreciation of his cooking and the fullness of her glass. I was the first to leave for bed, and my departure hardly disturbed them.

In the morning the house was silent and I wondered if insomniac Akira had already left to wander around the island. I was on the sandy path leading from the bungalow, briefcase in hand, on my way to the bank subbranch office, when I heard Akira call out, "William-san!" Again he was smiling broadly. He came close to me before he spoke. "It was great!" he said. "Four times. She want to do more. You don't know how long I wait for this."

I smiled back. "Well, I'm glad you had a good time."

"Usually women don't like me. They don't like my eyes." He used his two index fingers to demonstrate how his eyes were on separate tracks. He continued to grin.

I looked down to his bare feet. Broadly spaced peasant toes separated the sand. Apparently he was not thinking of working today either. I wondered why it was that Akira imagined I would indulge his idleness and that I would find pleasure in his pleasure. No answer came to me but I allowed him to continue to think it, and I set off alone to examine the records of loans.

That evening the three of us sat around in silence—the embracing silence of Ha'apai—until Akira stood up. "Fona?" She looked up from where she was stretched on the couch as if a stranger had taken her by surprise. "Shall we?" he asked. I recognized it as Yamada's diplomatic way of giving orders in English. Fiona looked up at him, shrugged, and made hard work of pushing herself upright.

"You all right here on your own?" she asked of me.

"Sure."

"Right. Well, g'night then."

We left next day, and I was pleased it would be soon enough to save Akira from disappointment. They closed makeshift gates across Ha'apai's only road, interrupting no traffic, so that the light plane that came for us could land.

"Another big night?" I asked while we strapped our seat belts.

"I think she was more tired." After a moment he added, "It

was great," with a smile that resembled, but did not match, the one of the previous morning.

He had a racket going. That's why he never changed his job or made it to the top. For a quarter of a century he'd had an arrangement with the housewives on his round. For twenty-five years, while he was the trusted senior roundsman at the depot—the others who stayed so long were all promoted to other jobs—he regularly delivered fifteen percent more milk than he reported in the books. Since he signed the load sheets for the other milkmen, this was easy to conceal. The stolen fifteen percent went to his housewife friends, the ones who loved him so. They got cheap milk; he pocketed their cash.

He could not change his job without his deceit being discovered by his replacement. In all that time he did not dare to take a day off sick, for the same reason. Of course he had needed to keep the details of his income from his wife. His scrupulous attendance won the approval of Old Man Kendel, who never guessed he was being robbed. He nurtured his reputation for low ambition as an explanation for his low mobility. The money, the double income, paid for the double life with Flossie and for an annual beano with his housewife conspirators. He did a little gambling on the side.

It must have been that, the boldness of his secret life, which finally lost him his job. When the accountants for Kendel-Peat's new, careful owners went through the files, my father's route stood out for the low recorded volume of its deliveries. After twenty-five years his secret daring finally caught up with him, without it ever having been discovered. That he bowed out without protest was not meekness but pragmatism; protest might have led to scrutiny. That I never made my complaint on his behalf had been fortunate, for the best.

Back in the capital of Nuku'alofa on Tongatapu, we took rooms at the International Dateline Hotel, exactly across the world from England. The lobby was full of Japanese men. According to the girl at reception, they were buying the hotel. Akira

skirted them without offering any greeting and headed across
the hotel's courtyard toward his room.

"Ruatua, Akira," I called after him as he went. "Figures for
Ruatua." He did not acknowledge me.

In the evening, Akira came to me. I sat on the edge of the bed
where I had been lying and examined him where he stood.
His legs were planted apart, and his head was bent down so
that the black schoolboy brush of his hair was presented to
me. I could smell whisky. I had been daydreaming and now I
waited for Akira to explain his visit. My eyes moved down to
his hands, which held no tables of figures but were curled
inward with an oddly restrained tension.

"William-san."

"What's up, Akira?"

"You want us to go to Ruatua?"

"There's a DCA livestock project there. I designed it. It needs
a quick supervision."

He struggled with something. "Population twenty thousand,
William. Whole country."

I thought before speaking. "It's a sovereign nation. Independent."

"I can't do tables for this country." He continued to look at
the floor, as if looking at me would draw him into some treach-
erous falsity. "The figures vanish!"

"The figures don't matter too much. It's only a supervision
mission."

"After Ruatua?"

I had begun to consider this. The visit to Ruatua was scheduled to last only three days. Considering this, I had let my eyes
continue north on the DCA's map, from Tonga, past Ruatua, to
the next dot in the ocean. The route followed the international
date line, going neither east nor west. "Tuvanu. I'm sure we
could persuade them to let us look at Tuvanu. It would be
another country for the DCA."

"How big? How many people?"

"I think it's around seven thousand."

Akira's curled hands completed their tendency to fists. "We vanish, William. We vanish from the tables. We go from the map."

He looked up at me and there were tears on his cheeks. "I want to help you, William. We are friends."

I puzzled over this, as if the nature of the contract was entirely strange to me. I kept silent.

"You do not need me."

Was it a question or a statement? Was it bitter or relieved? The statement sounded familiar but I could not place it. I was unable to interpret him. His inflection eluded me. My thoughts, which had been elsewhere when he arrived, were still unready to deal with Akira. I remained silent.

"I like to work with you, William. You are . . ." He took time to come up with the final word, which was only "good."

Was my work good? Was I good to work with, a good boss? Or was I good? Simply good. I could not believe that. Neither could I bring myself to ask.

Akira's eyes swept over my face. He had gathered himself so that the last tears were dried on his cheeks. "I think I miss my wife. Much. I enjoy Fona, but I miss my wife. I think I go home now."

The tears were welling up again behind his eyes, so that I became alarmed. Akira shook, and I thought for a moment that he was going to approach me, perhaps to embrace me or attack me.

"It's all right. You can go home. I can manage." My voice was perfectly calm, even soothing.

Akira's head fell forward again, as if he had initiated a nod from which he was unable to recover. He turned and had made the two paces to the door before I thought to speak again. "Don't worry, Akira. They'll pay you. I'll tell Geneva you finished the mission. Ruatua is a separate mission. Technically."

He stopped, then, still not turning to me, he made the short violent dismissive movement with his arm that was characteristic of him.

It was two days before I again thought of Akira, and then it was only because the girl at the reception desk handed over a file of papers, which she said he had left for me.

There wasn't only Flossie, there were Carol, Betty, Blossom. Once each year he organized an outing for all the housewives in his scam. On one autumn Saturday each year, a day when he told us he would go straight to the church after he had finished with the allotment and would take a change of clothing with him, he would instead take his women to the Palais Bar in the West End. The barman there knew him from twenty years before, when my father was a single man and cut a dash in the dance halls of Piccadilly Circus with his silver-topped walking stick.

The women, homely housewives, swapped their aprons and head scarves for tarts' dresses with diving necklines and no backs, high heels. They blew their milk-money gains on bubbly drinks in long-stemmed glasses, and they would laugh too loudly. My father, in evening dress, held the floor with his jokes so that strangers wondered who he was. Nobody had a better repertoire of old music hall songs for when the evening moved on: "Daisy, Daisy," "My Old Man Said Follow the Van," "That Daring Young Man on the Flying Trapeze." And when some toff thought the common folk were getting too noisy and above themselves, Dad's women and his hangers-on went quiet with happy anticipation of the quick, kind thrusts of his repartee, which would floor the opposition.

Later, just before the women became tearful and sentimental, he took them to the suite he had reserved at the Ritz, where the women would be led to sigh to one another: If only all men were like him.

By nine-thirty he was home, ready to take his seat quietly by the radio in the kitchenette and check his football pools coupon against the day's results.

. . .

Of course none of it was true, my story of Dad. Writing it here makes it seem foolish. I cannot make myself now give to it a tone as convincing as the conviction I felt then. My scrupulous recording is failing here, now that the story depends so little on the facts.

The more I try to order my memory of events, the more I am drawn to the narcolepsy of the sea, which induces in me a disorder of impression that seems more right than this order I have demanded of myself. At the time, I believed the explanation of my father's life to be true, the only one to fit the clues and account for the lacunae in his version. With this new truth, I grew close to him, or so it seemed. It did seem that, after all, I was like him.

So far I have not gone to the break in the coral that they say would draw me away from the lagoon. I have skirted close, so that I could feel the tendency in the current, a wavering, almost a breathing, a suggestion that there could occur an unforewarned greater breath—an exhalation—which would rush the water out and take everything suspended with it. There's a coldness there too, so that I have been scared by the sense of a sinister force at work. In the deeper waters around the break I have seen larger, darker, uglier fish, which no longer seem merely the comic and ill-favored cousins of the bright and lively tropic schools. And even the familiar colorful fish in that place no longer seem a friendly animation of the sun but make me think of treachery, glittering will-o'-the-wisps leading me from safety. And on the bottom, where I cannot sense the current, the seaweed floating up from its secure attachments moves back and forth to prove to me that I have drifted within the pull of something larger, stronger, and deeper than myself.

Emo would, I think, guess nothing of this. Last night she brought the baby out to me here at dusk, and we sat through the sunset, sipping beer. For more than an hour we sat without talking or touching. There's little to do these days; the old Englishman keeps himself to himself, and the beach was entirely quiet except for the lapping of the tamed ocean. I held the baby, and he slept in my arms with a trustfulness I felt to be foolish. I don't think I have anything to offer this child.

In the end it was I who broke the silence, to ask what I had never before asked Emo: "What are you thinking?"

"About Dick. The hotel. Money."

"Has he been in touch?"

"I get letters from him. He always wants me to send him money."

"Shouldn't he send you money? For the kids?"

"I don't know. He's useless. Maybe he thinks that because he's not here the hotel is doing well."

"Does he know about me?"

"I don't think so. You were just a passing guest."

"We were lovers."

"No, we just did it, that's all. We were both drunk, Bill." She turned to smile at me.

It must have been my second visit to Ruatua, my first to Coconut Beach—an attempt to steal a weekend vacation from a stopover project supervision. Two years ago, not long before Han. The evening had been noisy, with a beach barbecue for the holidaymakers, followed by a display of native dancing led by Emo. When it ended she headed straight to me and put her lei around my neck, pulling me upright to dance. Her staff headed for other guests. She had a nervous gaiety about her, which I did not know then was out of character. She laughed loudly at what I said before I had finished saying it. When she headed from the beach toward the hotel office, she gave me a tug in the same direction, then looked over her shoulder fetchingly to see that I was following. She passed straight through the office, which looked ransacked, and into the dirt road beyond. An old white taxi stood there, filled with luggage, and a small man in his fifties wearing shorts and long socks stood by it, apparently entranced by the disorder of the piled bags and the driver's clumsy handiwork with string. His face was a fierce red, and his mouth had the too-firm look of determination that is only found in weak men. Emo hung back in the hotel porch, and after a moment he switched his look from the car to her. She was still in the extravagantly colorful dress and flowers she wore for dancing and was irreproachably lovely. She looked like simplicity, beauty, good nature, health, all that was absent from him. I know now this was no more accidental than was my face appearing, no doubt full of anticipation, behind her shoulder. The man stared at her with an intense alcoholic blankness, which I identified later as the look of someone for whom everything has become internal. When I drew up close behind Emo in the doorway, he shifted this blank attention onto me, so that I felt the shock of strong emotions outside my concerns. Abruptly he broke away and yanked open the taxi door with unnecessary force.

After the car had disappeared, Emo explained, "My Australian husband." She laughed lightly and smiled over her shoulder at me. I moved closer, and recognizing the promise in disorder, I placed the full extent of my right hand on her right buttock.

"No," I said now, "we hadn't done it when he saw me."

"No? I can't remember." She looked away and sighed.

"We did it after. I took you to my hut. It was immediately after."

"I behaved badly that night."

"I'm glad you did. I have this one because you behaved badly." I placed my forehead against 'Inoke's forehead.

"Maybe."

"Maybe he's mine, or maybe because you behaved badly?"

"Maybe, maybe." She laughed again and leaned against me.

"Why did you choose me?"

"Mmm. You were here alone. I was angry at Dick. You looked like a business type. And I knew it was your last night. I thought you'd be no trouble."

"So it was love."

"It was Australia. Australian husband. Australian beer."

She snuggled, and we looked toward the moon on the sea.
"I could have been anyone?"

"Anyone lucky." She thought for a moment, then relented.
"No, you did look kind. I think I thought you would not hurt
me. You weren't a rough type."

Of course none of it was true, though it had seemed so convincing. I am alone, and I am unable to swallow. I am in the International Dateline Hotel. My other symptoms have disappeared, and I am left only with the inability to swallow. It has been three days since I last walked through Nuku'alofa town, five days since Akira left. I do not yet know that I will soon leave Tonga.

Nuku'alofa, the capital of Tonga, on the dinner-plate-flat island of Tongatapu, is a simple affair, a grid of level roads with low buildings and infrequent traffic. There's at least one of everything, but usually only one: a market, a cinema, a travel agency, a bank. Earlier I have been to the bookshop—the Friendly Islands Bookshop—and bought a secondhand thriller by Desmond Bagley, feeling that its genre simplicity might cool my imagination. On the way back I called in at the town's American-style hamburger bar, the Little America Café, and bought three hamburgers. The American owner explained to me at tedious length how difficult it had been for him to find the American-style stools, find a painter for the American-style sign, and obtain hamburger meat of American quality. The smartly dressed Tongan girl at the till—his wife perhaps—placed the three excellent hamburgers in a bag, together with napkins, and rolled the top for easy handling, in the American way.

I still have the hamburgers—though I have given myself every chance to eat them and I believe they are the food to which I would normally feel the least resistance. They are nibbled around the edges, and in the course of three days they have gone from succulent to dry and inert without ever looking dangerous. I have found that whether I chew or don't chew, I am completely unable to swallow. The hamburger becomes caught in my throat. To try and remove the inhibiting effect of self-consciousness and anxiety, I have tried to take them by surprise. I lie on my hotel bed and try to concentrate on Slocum or Bagley. It is not easy; Slocum's robustness is a reproach, and although Bagley's book is about tropical hotels, I can't get interested. I force myself to stare at the pages, and just when I feel I am nearly interested and my mind is nearly elsewhere, I jump up and take a bite of one of the hamburgers. I am pleased to say it has never worked. Now I am just sitting on the floor, leaning against the wall and talking to my father. I sense he can venture close now I am alone and as far from Tottenham as it is possible to be.

I recount to myself the achievement of my aloneness, working backward. I am as gratified by the proof of this as I am by my inability to swallow. Akira has left; I've lost him. I sent Yamada away, evacuated him and took his place. Han ditched me, and I don't expect to see her again. I managed to shake off Mireille some time back. My mother is far across the world. I have no friends here. I am clean and ready to meet my father. It's Sunday. Outside, the Tongans are singing hymns. Nuku'a-lofa has many churches. I run through the clues he gave me to his life.

I have attempted one further outing into Nuku'alofa before settling for my International Dateline Hotel room. I fancied that I would take a stroll along its seafront. I could see the sea from the entrance of the hotel, only separated by a white road surfaced with crushed shells. The road was very bright and hot in the sun. I concentrated on my walking, keeping my spine straight and kicking up my feet when I felt they were dragging unnaturally. Still, three uniformed schoolchildren—two girls and a boy—found something comic in me, and I was obliged to stop by a roadside tree and lean against it nonchalantly. While I was in this pose, trying to marshal myself to continue, the king of Tonga passed by. He was fat, though not particularly old, and was riding a bicycle very slowly. He wore a track suit. Around him half a dozen young men—soldiers, I supposed—jogged in formation, though this was flattery, since the king rode at a walking pace. None of them seemed to notice me, and the incident convinced me that I should not be out in the world but should return to my room as soon as possible.

I sidled back along the edge of the footpath, pressing myself against the trees and fences. I had hoped to make my room without further encounters, but the girl at the reception desk called to me. I remembered the girls from my arrival—trim, pretty, smiling in their orange dresses, flowers in their hair. This girl was no larger than the others but now she towered above the desk, while I could scarcely reach the counter. I remembered a time when I would have swept her away with my self-importance. She said she had a package left for me by my Japanese friend and I reached up to take it without speaking. Then she checked herself and checked her records and told me I had to pay an installment on my bill. I was unable to reply. I pushed a credit card toward her, and she studied it carefully. When I went to sign the slip, my hand began to shake, and the meaning of the signature flashed around my mind: the bill would rush across the world to the credit card company in America, the money to settle my account would be transferred from my Swiss bank, payment would go to the hotel's new owners in Japan. All on the strength of this shaky scrawl. I scribbled my name and, nauseated, quickly turned away, hugging the wall all the way up the steps and along the walkway to my room on the upper floor. I hung out the Do Not Disturb sign and locked the door. I sat here, on the floor at the base of the wall, my knees bent up. I am still here. I am very small.

He said so little, but now as I study him above me against the white ceiling of my room, he opens his mouth to speak. Then he closes it again. He's benign, looking down on me, and he's comforting in his white coat with the *K-P* on the breast pocket, over his old sports jacket with the woolen jumper under that, and a woven tie. His breast pocket is organized with milkman's things: sharp HB pencils, points uppermost, a stubby indelible pencil, in a patent clip. For a time I look for his row of ball-points, before deciding that this must be before the days of ballpoints.

His lower half is a faded presence, but I don't have to insist on it to know there will be gray flannels, a bit baggy at the knees from cycling, and black toe-capped shoes, scrupulously polished. He might be wearing cycle clips, his turn-ups neatly furled above gray worsted socks. Yes, I think he is.

It's the lips that are clearest, full lips, a little loose now, because even in heaven he's at a loss to choose hard words, to crystallize a meaning. So I ask him, "Where do I go from here?" And the lips do begin to move, to ready themselves, but he's still scared of saying the wrong thing. I urge him on. I point out to him that I am like him after all; I've seen his shadow life; what he says is relevant. I point out to him that he's up there now, his knowledge is at last absolute, no longer tainted by any need for the dubious versions of things that help us through the day and make the world go around. And I have come to a place he knows; he has suffered this himself, the point where you can't go on or back, where the food in your throat won't go down or up, where you might die from indecision, where naturalness goes on strike in protest at its lockout by the will. I'm here, as far from home as it is possible to be, beached at the Dateline Hotel, in Nuku'alofa, on Sunday, ready to receive instructions. But he still only wets his lips, and his eyes are pained, or perhaps there's a mist of fear behind them, as if heaven turned out to be like England after all, and he's still in a room surrounded by braver men, men with more education, men with brash confidence who've made a packet, loud men, men of quick violence, men with pungent, unre-flected opinions, men who can put up an argument and de-fend it down the line against contending points of view. Yet I believe him to be wise, and I wait for the wise old man of his last years, when he could no longer be burdened by calls to action, to speak. Instead it's the younger man of fifty, who still wore the cycle clips, who persists above me in a place strangely empty of women. The lips prepare themselves, but the words aren't spoken now. They are: "You're not like me. You're lucky, son." And I swear at him, so that the apprehension in his eyes is justified, and he sadly fades away, leaving me uncomforted, the machinery of the air-conditioning all that is left for sound.

Far from England, far from land, I dive again among the little fishes, all with kissable lips, yellows, reds, electric blues, the occasional grumpy one in brown. Too far really to return against the current. They say, they imagine, I think, that beyond the gap in the coral reef, which I can now see—a church's arch, the eye of a needle, old bowed legs, a promising woman—sharks wait with open mouths, steady against the draining sea.

I can still hear the hollow, mortal sound of breathing, though my own breath is held and I'm going quickly deeper, drawn toward the swaying seaweed fronds and pink anemones, over slow, black, and ugly bottom fish hanging back in their bad temper. I'm making progress now, twisted and turned, against the dreadful roundness of the world, smiling almost, eyes kept on the gap, which is lit by another sun on another sea, the untamed ocean outside the reef. And I do try to resist, but there's no help now. And I'm with old Slocum, going down, surprised, wondering if it wouldn't, after all, have been wiser and more modest to have learned to swim, about to be a loss at sea mysterious to him. And I'm with my father too, lying in his bath, regarding the fractured light above. And with dear Miss Khan, who'd had her fun, and peristalsis must be like this. And with sweet Mireille, whose touch brushed my cheek and whose laughter bubbled with all that was not lost of her. And with Han, who ground her teeth like machinery in the night, like sand against the current, and the hiss-hiss of receding seas, the deep, enormous gulp of the breached lagoon, and poor old Yamada going down, reaching out for lust, and Akira-san, as efficient as a Japanese, the sound we give the sea, whose hook I'd welcome now, explanations heard in shells, explanations of all this.

Until above me, on the other side, I look up to see that what they said is true, twenty, thirty, fifty sharks between me and the

---

light, holding position, most of them no bigger than I am, unconcerned with me, tranquil almost, going about their easy life; until I am, without my consent, vulgarly sucked back into the domesticity of the lagoon, and like a child pushed school-ward by its mother, I am shoved by buoyancy into the sense of air.

• • •

Of course it was not true, his shadow life, and I'll never know
the secrets he might have had, and he'll never talk to me in
cycle clips through the ceiling of a tropical-paradise hotel.
Sometimes I tiptoe in the shallows, considering an eastern
return, sometimes a western.

I fancy that the old Englishman here is one like us, someone
who was raised to expect little of himself, who thought de-
cency was the highest attribute of a civilized man and who
worked diligently all his life without ever fully understanding
the purposes he served. We don't make good fascists, he and
I; we don't really believe we deserve the rewards, and the iron
effort of ascendancy tires us in its contemplation.

The old man's skinny body has the round shoulders and
hollow chest of a man who never, in all his life, called upon
himself to make an imposing entrance. His smile is nervous,
and he seems at his happiest playing the fool with Emo's children and their playmates, who, though they cannot understand
the old man's antics, are happy to lend him their goodwill. But
I can recognize his half-completed actions from memories of
childhood seaside holidays. There, he's drawing hopscotch
squares in the sand and getting it wrong so the lapping fringe
of sea erases most and he makes his little remembered jumps
in the bubbles of surf, to the laughter and pleased smiles of
children more composed than he. Now he holds a stick to his
shins—French cricket—and makes the jerky movements of
batting a ball away, though the children do not have a ball or
understand its absence. He energetically piles loose sand and
stands on top of it—king of the castle—and the children don't
know they are supposed to push him off.

This old man is a very long way from home, and I think he
may be dying. I know little of his situation or his past, because
he has given up speech entirely. When I first approached him
he danced away from me, and I remain the person he most

avoids. He spends his time with the children or with the Ruatuans who sometimes lounge under the palm-thatched beach shelter where we used to hold barbecues for guests. He seems to speak to them, but what he says is gibberish, accompanied by overenergetic gestures and grimaces. They treat him kindly. "You're a funny old man," I heard one say, as if there had been an opening for a funny old man at Coconut Beach and he had happily come along to fill it. I like the way the Ruatuans are unembarrassed by him.

What little I know of him comes from the postcards he sometimes leaves on Emo's desk for her to mail to England. They are usually addressed to people in Reading, Berkshire, and particularly to an Irene, who I take to be a married daughter. There's no hint on these cards of his antics or his gibberish, nor of his hacking cough and insomnia. The last one read:

"The weather is always good here. Lots of sun. Not like poor old Reading! I spend my days on the beach. The South Pacific really is the paradise they say it is. Only more so. I plan to stay on a bit longer while the money lasts. Hope you can manage without me! Love to Bob, Julie, and Gavin."

I have the sense of a man staying away from where he is not wanted while he dies. It's our way that everything is left unsaid. They will never have to say they did not want him, and he will not have to say it to himself.

He's wrong; Ruatua is not quite an island paradise, though it is more paradise than island. The population is falling, as those who go to New Zealand, Australia, and America to improve themselves stay away longer and call their families to join them. They send back cash for their dreams or retirement here, and the ones left behind ship them sacks of taro so the emigrants can eat like Ruatuans while they work in foreign factories. The government lies about its declining population to score more foreign aid.

This island is beautiful. Its population is well fed. Coconuts and bananas are so plentiful that they are free. Diseases are few, and those that do occur are well combated. No poisonous snakes here. But all this exists only by international license and its insularity is only physical. If all the world's Ruatuans were sent home, the land would run out, fighting over territory would erupt, communal harmony would be replaced by a scrambling for advantage, the sunny nature of the islanders would change, and there would be no foreign exchange for the medicines they need or the imported meat they like. Ruatua is too far from anywhere for industry, and without the remittances of migrants it could only sell itself for the gouging exploitation of mines, or sell its isolation for the dumping of industrial wastes or the testing of military devices—all the world's nastiness.

I tell myself this to bring myself back from the simple, phony comfort I've derived from keeping out the foreign pigs, my contribution to Ruatua's exemption from the connected world, that version. And I can't be Gauguin now, or Robert Louis Stevenson, and live away, apart. My permission to stay, renewable every four months, comes due for the third time soon and may not be granted. The government is wary of poor foreigners with their South Seas dreams, wanting to be beach bums, wanting the friendly girls for easy lays, and I have not cultivated the prime minister well enough; he will have realized I am no longer well connected.

The Englishman's old body, which was clearly never that of an athlete, or even a fit man, now looks ruined. His legs are spindly and his ribs protrude, but he never hides himself under more than bathing shorts and an old floppy sun hat, which looks like it was meant for a woman. The Ruatuans, rounded and well shaped, exaggerate his jerky angularity by their contrast. His skin no longer takes the sun; it is too loose and dry; it becomes gray. I have wanted very much to comfort this old man and bring him into the warmth of the little temporary family I have made with Emo, but he has refused this. He is dying alone, and I sense he is gaining some satisfaction from this. His giddiness is a sort of heroic triumph. Now I restrict myself to transmitting warm, silent thoughts of approval to him, telling him he's as fine a man as it's possible to be and that his life has certainly been good. We no longer raise with him the question of his bill. At night, listening to his cough, and during the day, while I swim, I send to him waves of telepathic approval, and in addition to this, I encourage death to close in on him more quickly. I say to death, take him, this is a good place to take him, a good time.

I believe my own time here is also coming to an end, though not, of course, through death. Something is beginning to move me along, giving me a momentum that was lost when I fetched up here at the end of the downhill run from the Himalayas to the sea. It is probable that I will visit again, and last night I sat Emo down with her desktop computer and we went through her options together. I might be able to raise the finance to buy out her husband so she could run Coconut Beach for her own sake. I am almost certain that New Zealand or Australian aid would give her a concessional small-business development loan. I drafted letters for her. We did not talk of 'Inoke, who might or might not be my son. I still puzzle this, but I try not to give it importance.

Recently Emo returned from market with a bundle of telexes and faxes which her sister at the Ruatuan treasury had kept for me over the last eleven months. There were invitations to join missions from several international agencies, though not the DCA. So far I have not responded, and most are out of date, but I notice that I have not thrown these invitations away. Perhaps an offer will one day strike me as sufficiently mixed in its intentions to be given the benefit of my doubt. There was a fax from Shareef in Peshawar, forwarded through Geneva. He greeted me, said the appraisal and loan negotiation for the Valley Development Project had gone smoothly, that I had designed a fine project, and that he looked forward to the chance to work with me internationally. It was strange to think of Shareef just carrying on in his old way, assuming I was going along in mine, when I had been writing about him as if he were dead. I found myself embarrassed.

My mother is still in Tottenham, and it is time I consoled her for the loss of her husband and offered my assistance in the reordering of her life. There is also Mireille and our neglected family home in Reston, which has lost the appeal it once had for me in its uncomplicated newness. I hope to make my peace with Mireille, though I doubt I will again attempt to stay forever in one place with one person. As for Han—I will leave Han alone and wish for her that the routine of ordinary, settled life will soothe her so that she no longer grinds her teeth in sleep. I will try to put aside from me the pull of her dark, seductive invitation to annihilation, just as I no longer linger in the pull of the current close to the break in the reef.

A telex from Tokyo to my old office at the World Bank in Washington regretted to tell me of Mr. Yamada's death. I was invited to a memorial dinner—now long past—in Manila. My request through Geneva for Tokyo's permission to take Akira to Tuvanu, which I must have made before his departure, had been refused. A fax from Morita at the DCA informed me that as a surviving senior partner in Yamada's recently disgraced consulting company, Akira faced fraud and corruption charges brought by the Japanese government. I fear he will attempt to tell the truth and will defend himself poorly.

For myself, I think I will, while there is still time, pad once more across the too-hot sand into the warm water of the shallows and splash out to sea again to swim among the little fishes.

One more piece of mail reached me, this time a handwritten letter sent by surface post from England to D.C. and taking a year to find me. There was no return address on the envelope, no zip code for America, insufficient postage—all the signs of a sender unfamiliar with the international mails. A woman, Nancy I think from the signature, said she thought I wouldn't remember her from Kendels, but she had known my father, had thought the world of him. They had been close in a way. She said it was difficult for her, in the position in which she found herself, when she heard about his death, not having anyone she could talk to, and she hoped I didn't mind, she knew how much he thought of me, only she just wanted to write to someone to say how sad she was, and being my father's son, maybe I wouldn't mind that it was me. She hoped this was all right.